POSTPARTUM

NOLON KING
LAUREN STREET

STERLING & STONE

POSTPARTUM

Chapter One

Alice endured the unyielding screams pouring from the baby monitor on the marble bedside table beside her like water through a busted dam. She was trapped in a cage of her own fatigue with no escape.

Each wail was yet another wave crashing against the shores of her sanity, eroding the sand bit by bit. In the stillness of their room, Ellie's cries seemed to take on a life of their own, becoming a chorus of doubts and fears that motherhood had ushered into her life and soul.

Ellie's crying climbed in pitch, growing into a thundering tsunami that threatened to drown Alice in an ocean of maternal guilt and exhaustion.

The room closed in on her, the eggshell walls absorbing those shrill screams only to hurl them back, amplified and inescapable.

Max lay oblivious in the bed right next to her, or perhaps indifferent, lost in the depths of his precious slumber. He had been irritable and somewhat distant lately, more concerned with legal briefs and client calls than her or Ellie.

The baby monitor belted another unbearable screech, Ellie's crying now so high-pitched that her vocal cords sounded like frayed strings on the verge of snapping. Alice's heart pounded with a tacit indictment for failing her daughter.

Alice clenched the bedsheets until her knuckles turned white, and her breathing felt jagged like shattered glass.

Enough.

She pushed off her silken covers with a sigh, climbed out of bed, and tiptoed to the door, looking back at Max before leaving. A rumbling snore rolled out of his body as he stirred on the bed, apparently falling deeper into his sleep, adding insult to her mounting injury.

She studied his silhouette, the rise and fall of his chest a silent mockery of her unrest. She was ashamed at the angry thought, but she couldn't help wonder if he was only pretending to sleep so he wouldn't have to get up and take care of Ellie. How had the man who once promised to do anything to help her through the night feedings become this distant, unmoving fixture beside her?

But that was just new-parent sleep deprivation talking. Her doctor had told her the resentment was normal, and all the baby books had agreed.

She crept out of the room and took just a few steps down the hallway to the very next room and peeked inside Ellie's room.

The nursery, a realm of soft blues and muted grays, was meant to be a haven, yet now it felt like an alien landscape, where the familiar comfort of the rocking chair and the playful mobile above were overshadowed by the insistent cries that filled the space.

Unlike the rest of their penthouse, the nursery had a minimalist design. Overhead hung a chandelier with geometrically-arranged glass panes that Alice had declared as "perfection" after searching for something similar — if not exactly like it — going on half a year. It sent shards of light in a gentle dance of luminescence around the room during the day, and cast a gorgeous glow onto the white iron crib in the corner on moonlit nights, cushioned by plush pillows that promised plenty of lullabies with Mommy.

Right now the room was awash in those moody blues and grays filtering in through the curtains, casting eerie outlines onto the crib from the night outside. The high-pitched keening of Ellie's cries ripped through the semi-darkness like a sonic knife buried in her back and scraping down her spine.

Shadows stretched long and twisted like dark fingers reaching out for her, a tangible darkness that seemed eager to wrap around her, a manifestation of her spiraling thoughts.

She rushed over to the crib, eager to quell her daughter's crying.

But when she got there and looked down into it, Ellie wasn't there.

Instead of her baby, Alice was staring down at a great horned owl standing on the mattress. Her heart thrummed a frantic rhythm, a silent scream in her chest, as its golden eyes pierced her, a silent witness to her unraveling.

The bird turned to look at her, fixing its golden, predatory eyes on Alice.

Her heart started pounding even harder. Of course the owl couldn't dissect her soul in the darkness, even if that was exactly what it felt like right now.

The bird opened its beak and the sound of a wailing baby pierced the air like a dissonant siren, send an icy cold shudder through Alice, her knees buckling and forcing her to grip the crib to keep from falling. . Another agonized note to fray the edges of her sanity.

She opened her mouth to scream, but nothing came out.

She tried harder, opening her mouth wider, and working to bellow from the depths of her lungs. But her vocal cords seemed sewn shut, that terrified yell swallowed by an oppressive darkness as—

ALICE SUDDENLY STARTLED awake in bed, listening to the sound of a crying baby.

Max nudged her and grumbled something. The sound was a tether to reality, dragging Alice back from the precipice of her own mind where nightmares lurked in every corner, waiting to bleed into her waking world.

Another bad dream?

Jesus, this was getting out of hand.

She pushed off her silken covers with a sigh, climbed out of bed, and tiptoed to the door, feeling the oddest sense of déjà vu as she looked back at Max before leaving. Of course he was snoring.

She opened the door to the nursery. Ellie was crying, but it was hardly the soul scraping scream that Alice and been suffering in her dream.

She rushed over to the crib and looked down, unreasonably scared that she might see an owl or worse and was immediately relieved by the sight of her daughter.

Alice scooped Ellie into her arms and cuddled her on the way to the rocking chair, nestled in the opposite corner from the crib, where she tried and failed to get her infant latched onto her breast. The harder Alice tried, the more Ellie kept crying. Each failed attempt to nurse her was another whispered indictment, a maternal rite she could not fulfill, leaving her feeling like a tapestry fraying at the edges, threads of her confidence unraveling with every sob from Ellie.

Alice kept trying to angle her breast toward the infant's quivering mouth, hoping to transform her baby's crying into the rhythmic sounds of nursing. But Ellie's wails crescendoed as her tiny mouth opened and closed in frantic failed attempts, leaving mom and daughter in a fog of frustration.

Bouncing Ellie gently and rubbing her back as she walked, Alice retreated from the nursery, headed back to her bedroom, a reluctant surrender.

The door creaked open to a haven of understated opulence — onyx walls embossed with arcane motifs provided a rich backdrop to the grand bed. Plush linens were awash in gentle rose hues, seeming to blush in the glow of the bedside lamps that cast an amber cocoon around the room. Even right now with her daughter screaming and barely any light, Alice still took in the tufted headboard with all those intricate carvings staring mutely back at her.

Slender windows flanked the bed, their sheer white curtains playing a tantalizing game of peek-a-boo with the moonlight. She had designed this room for dreams, and yet it had become a theater of nocturnal anxieties for Alice.

Ellie's screaming seemed loud enough to wake the dead. But apparently Max was beyond dead. He continued to lay there, his breathing so measured that it sounded almost mathematical. She hesitated, her hand hovering over his shoulder, the divide between them more than physical — a chasm wrought by unspoken grievances and sleepless nights.

She shook him awake.

"Brugreablmnvergbuy," he said.

"She won't latch."

He stirred, his eyes blinking open reluctantly. "Did you try what the doctor suggested?" He sounded irritated at being woken up more than concerned about his wife and daughter.

Sleep deprivation, she reminded herself. That was why she wanted to slap him. Anyone sounded grumpy when pulled from a deep sleep, herself included.

Not that she remembered what deep sleep was like. She tried to smile at Max. "Of course. She just … she won't."

Max got out of bed and held out his arms.

See? He's willing to help when you ask him, just like he said he would.

Relieved, Alice handed him Ellie, and the moment she was in his arms, their baby stopped crying.

"Prep a bottle," he said. She tried not to be annoyed that it sounded like an order.

Sleep deprivation.

Alice descended the staircase to the kitchen, the sound of her steps softening as she transitioned from hardwood to cool, tiled floors. The kitchen was a gourmet dream ensconced in opulence — a place where form met function with effortless grace. Polished cabinets climbed into the ceiling, gleaming surfaces reflected the understated elegance characterizing the rest of their gorgeously appointed apartment. Underneath a wooden sky, her marble counter gleamed like a frozen lake under the moonlight. Blue and white porcelain china sat poised on display boasting timeless design. The kitchen, like all of the rooms she designed, whether they belonged to her or not, was a masterpiece.

The sink was carved deep into the solid stone, the basin anchored by a chrome faucet statuette to double as abstract sculpture. The indoors flirted with the outdoors through ebony framed windows granting a view of orderly potted topiaries stationed like sentries guarding the yard. Bright green leaves were a lively contrast to all that sterling and stone in the kitchen.

Right now, she would've traded it all for a weekend alone in a cheap hotel room with a pair of earplugs and a bottle of Ambien.

Alice passed the porcelain bowl cradling sun-kissed lemons and opened the refrigerator door to grab the bottle she had pumped last night.

She ran it under warm water, swirling the bottle to heat the milk evenly, before finally wiping it dry with a towel embroidered with a cheerful *Bon Appétit*.

She climbed back up the stairs, bottle in hand. She returned to the bedroom, easing the door open to find Max propped up with his back against the headboard, and Ellie cradled in the crook of his arm. She handed him the bottle, then climbed into bed beside them, leaning against her biggest pillow while guiltily watching him feed their daughter.

There was both relief and a hollow ache within her as Ellie quieted in his arms, a painful reminder of her own apparent inadequacy, the warmth of motherhood eluding her grasp like sand slipping through clenched fingers.

"Everything is going to be okay," Max reassured her.

She nudged up closer against him, grateful for his words. "Thanks for saying that. Because it sure doesn't feel like it right now."

"It's a hard time. This will all get better. I promise."

"How can you promise that?" Alice felt weak for asking.

"You're doing an incredible job. You just need to be kinder to yourself."

"That didn't answer my question."

"I can promise because I've never let you down before, and I'm not about to start now." Max kissed Alice on her forehead.

Ellie's contented gulps landed like a balm on her frazzled nerves, but a creeping thought took root in her mind.

"Do you think it's possible that …" She couldn't say it. Didn't even want to finish the thought.

"What?" He put his arm around her. "You can tell me. No judgment."

"What if she doesn't like me?" Alice blurted.

"Don't be silly." He actually rolled his eyes, but only to make her feel better. "Ellie is an infant. It's not about liking or disliking. She's getting used to the world, to us. And we're getting used to her."

"I know, but it seems like she's getting used to you a lot faster than she's getting used to me."

"Why don't you take a shower?" Max gave her a warm smile. "I promise it will make you feel better."

"You're making a lot of promises tonight." But Alice was already getting out of bed.

"Better than breaking them."

"That's for sure." Alice laughed. "Thanks for making me feel better."

"That's just the start." He grinned at her. "Wait until you're done with that shower."

Chapter Two

ALICE STEPPED into the shower and turned the water on full heat.

Steam filled the air, furling around her, slowly fogging up the glass and mercifully obstructing her own reflection. A pulsating shower head unleashed a torrent of cascading water that felt like luxurious on her scalp, even if it failed to wash away her insecurity. The water's embrace was a cruel reminder, droplets tracing the contours of a silhouette she barely recognized, each one a whisper of the identity she feared was slipping away.

Alice felt estranged from her own body, a vessel that seemed to be failing in its newfound maternal role while also feeling like a strange echo of what it used to be.

Steam enveloped her like a shroud, the warmth nothing like the numbness spreading from her core. Her reflection, now obscured by the fogged glass, seemed like a distant memory of someone she once knew. The shower was less about cleansing and more about trying to feel something, anything, that resembled the woman she'd been before motherhood changed everything.

Ten minutes was less than she wanted, but still twice as long as she needed. Then she was grabbing a towel from the golden rack and drying off. Her skin seemed different now; not just softer, but strangely unfamiliar as she wrapped it in a plush robe and cinched the belt at her waist to make the robe more like armor.

Alice might feel shitty when it came to her body, but this beautiful bathroom still filled her with pride. She had designed the space as a sanctuary, an oasis for her to unwind. Emerald-hued tiles stretched from the floor to the ceiling. Their glossy finish caught the ambient light and created a tranquil yet decadent aura. The fixtures were all kissed by gold, their lustrous gleam looking opulent against a soothing green. The floor was a playful mosaic of hexagonal tiles in muted shades, and the pristine porcelain pedestal sink stood on gilded legs.

But since Ellie had been born, her sanctuary had become a symbol of a peace she'd lost, and feared she would never regain.

Max was gone from the bedroom, so she went straight to the kitchen. He wasn't in there either, but Alice found herself glad to have another few moments alone.

But then he entered, looking as exhausted as he sounded. "I put her down."

"Thank you for helping me."

"Of course. Just promise that you'll eat something and then get back to sleep."

"What about you?" Alice asked.

"I'm going to take a quick shower, grab some coffee, and get to the office early."

"It's not even five in the morning, though."

"Exactly. The office we'll be empty. I'll be working on the Laurentian deposition all day, so I'm already going to be coming home late, no matter what. This means I won't be *as* late, and it's not like I can go back to sleep now."

"I'm sorry."

"Don't be sorry, Alice. Just eat something and get some rest."

"I promise."

"And get outside for a walk today."

"I will."

"I mean it. You'll feel a lot better if you get some fresh air."

"I know." Alice nodded. "You're right."

Max kissed her on the head again, then disappeared from the kitchen.

She stood in front of the open fridge, its light spilling out as she scanned the shelves in search of something that would be easy to eat yet filling, not really wanting to eat anything so much as feeling honor bound to do so after promising Max.

She grabbed a carton of Greek yogurt and a ripe banana. She methodically peeled it, sliced her banana into a bowl, and dolloped a generous serving of yogurt on top.

Then she dipped her spoon into the yogurt, feeding herself while looking outside at the sun just starting to kiss the sky, blushing in soft shades of rose and gold, as if the day itself was waking up and stretching its limbs in the early morning light.

She rinsed her bowl and left it in the sink, then went back upstairs to the nursery.

She felt compelled to check in on Ellie. Of course her baby was still breathing, but ever since giving birth, she couldn't stop worrying that she was failing Ellie, failing as a mother.

She looked down into the crib and saw that her worst fears had been realized.

Ellie wasn't breathing, and Alice was already starting to feel hysterical.

A cold fist of dread clenched her heart as she stared down at her daughter's still form, her mind unraveling into a symphony of panic and disbelief.

Until Ellie stretched with a yawn before falling still again.

And Alice felt instantly calm, silly for yet another paranoia-fueled overreaction.

She left the nursery, hearing the shower shutting off as she went back downstairs, her thoughts oscillating between relief over Ellie and the continual tug of her own anxieties.

She paused in the entryway, still elegant, but also the simplest space in their entire penthouse. Alice stood in front of a classic bench made of cherry wood stood against the wall in front of an antique mirror. But she ignored her reflection there, same as she had ignored it in the bathroom, looking instead at the brand-new stroller parked next to the bench. Crisp-looking fabric and still-shiny wheels were untouched by the elements. The thought of taking Ellie out of the house made her head spin with anxiety, even though she hungered for the normalcy of her old life: heading out for a coffee, going for a walk in the park, meeting friends to go shopping on a Saturday when Max had to work. She hadn't gone to a movie theater in ages. How long before that became possible again?

The question hung before her, a threadbare lifeline amidst the tempest of her thoughts, an invitation to step beyond the confines of her gilded cage.

Max was right. She should go outside and get some fresh air.

Alice heard a soft clatter and muffled voices from the hallway.

She peered through the peephole. The hallway was

empty but the noises persisted. She opened the door and peeked to the right, just as the elevator dinged at the end of the corridor and its doors slid open to a pair of large men maneuvering stacks of boxes onto the floor.

Someone was moving into the penthouse next door. That apartment had been vacant ever since Mrs. Cohen's untimely death eight months ago — a tragic tumble down the stairs that had sent the entire building in a state of mourning and shock. Life's relentless march echoed in the rhythm of the movers' footsteps. It sounded harsh compared to the stillness that death had left in its wake next door.

Alice felt a mingling of curiosity and melancholy at the thought of new life filling a space marked by loss, watching the movers efficiently unload their cargo with motions so methodical that they almost seemed rehearsed.

One of the movers glanced her way and caught her looking. She offered him a tight smile and discreetly retreated, pulling the door closed behind her just as another one of Ellie's piercing screams sliced through the air to hit her like a physical blow. Each cry was a siren call, a primal alarm beckoning her with an urgency that bordered on pain.

She raced back upstairs to find Ellie in the nursery, red-faced and wailing. She reached into the crib and carefully lifted her up, cradling the baby close to her chest.

Alice swaddled Ellie in a plush blanket, the fabric positively silly with planets, moons, and stars. She moved toward the balcony as she heard the front door slam downstairs. She opened the sliding glass door and stepped out onto the terrace. Yet another haven of serenity designed by her. Plush seating in muted tones, a wooden trellis overhead, interwoven with delicate tendrils of ivy that made for dappled shadows on the ground.

Sounds from below — the faint chatter of pedestrians on the move amid distant honking of horns — were far removed from the soft rustle of leaves in her meticulously potted plants or the gentle caress of an early morning breeze.

Ellie's body relaxed against her, screams quieting, as Alice stepped up onto a bench, then up against the railing of a brick balustrade, looking over the edge surrounding the balcony, so she could stare down at all of the traffic and pedestrians down below.

Vertigo flooded her system as she looked down at the miniature world below. Traffic crawled like mechanized ants while humans moved in a herd along the sidewalks.

Her grip tightened on Ellie, her baby blissfully unaware of their precarious perch.

The city's discordant orchestra rose up to meet her, amplifying her internal turmoil to an unbearable crescendo. She needed to step down from the balustrade. The world below pulled at her with the gravity of a thousand unspoken fears, a mesmerizing dance of chaos at the edge of oblivion.

But Alice felt too compelled to stay where she was and stare down into the abyss, her heart pounding like a frantic drumroll, each thud echoing whispered taunts from her inner demons.

Her breathing turned shallow, each inhalation laced with the crisp morning air. Time almost felt suspended, the universe holding its collective breath in the face of Alice's unthinkable contemplation.

A rogue gust of wind tousled her hair and sent a shiver down her spine, reminding her of the danger, begging her to reconsider this irreversible step.

Ellie cooed softly, the innocuous sound reverberating

through her like a shockwave, almost jolting Alice back from the edge of her pitch black thoughts.

But it wasn't enough.

So Alice stepped over the edge and—

SHE BLINKED, standing in the foyer and staring at her stroller without a clue as to how much time might have possibly passed. The only thing Alice knew for sure was that Ellie's screams were like nails getting hammered into her skull.

She rushed to the kitchen and grabbed a bottle from the fridge, warmed it up fast, then ran to the nursery.

Tried and failed to feed her daughter.

Her daughter who seemed to hate her more each day.

Feeling even more worthless than usual, she considered going out onto the balcony and taking the leap for real this time.

Chapter Three

ALICE MUST HAVE BEEN in some sort of wonderland deep in the recesses of her own mind when Max finally dragged her out of it, his voice slicing into her thoughts through the urgency of Ellie's razor sharp screams.

His sharp call pierced the veil of her reverie.

"Alice! Where are you?"

She opened her eyes to find herself in the bathtub, skin pruned and chilled, enveloped by water that had turned lukewarm a long time ago, thoughts floating on the surface of her consciousness like flotsam on a turbulent sea.

Meanwhile, her daughter screamed like she was being murdered in her crib.

Max rushed into the bathroom, his eyes widening at the sight of her lying listless in the tub. "How long have you been in here?"

"I don't know," Alice admitted.

His gaze sharpened as he studied her. "Did you go out for a walk today? Get some fresh air like you promised?"

"Of course I did." Alice was probably lying, but hell if she could remember anything about her day.

"You're not telling me the truth." He didn't even pretend that it was a question.

"I can't remember."

Their eyes locked.

Then Max turned around and walked out of the bathroom.

She climbed out of the bathtub, her movements sluggish as if to prove her embarrassment. Something was seriously wrong, and she could see it in the way Max had looked at her. She wrapped a towel around her torso and pulled the plug, watching the water spiral down the drain and knowing just how it felt.

Ellie suddenly stopped screaming, and Alice felt a surge of gratitude for Max, while at the same time resenting that he could quiet their daughter instantly when she seemed to have the opposite effect on the infant.

She dried herself in a hurry, then donned her robe for the second time that day and went downstairs, chasing the fragrance of frying garlic and roasting herbs to the kitchen. Max was at the counter, a blur of muscle memory as he cooked. His rhythmic chopping against the backdrop of sizzling sounded like a symphony of normalcy compared to her dissonant thoughts.

"Have you fed Ellie?" Alice asked, hating her own wavering voice.

Max paused, his knife hovering above a red bell pepper. After a long sigh, he said, "No, Alice. I haven't."

"Why are you doing that?"

"Doing what?"

"Looking at me that way. And using my name. You only do that when I'm in trouble for something."

"You're never 'in trouble,' Alice. I'm not your boss."

"You do scold me sometimes."

"I'm sorry. I'm not trying to scold you."

"It's fine." But Alice wasn't sure if she meant that as she walked to the fridge for a bottle of pre-pumped breast milk.

She filled a bowl full of warm water and dropped the bottle into it. "I'm sorry. I lost track of time."

His eyes met hers and the exhausted concern she saw in them filled her with guilt. He wasn't angry, he was disappointed, and that was always worse.

"I don't want your apologies," he said. "I want you to do better."

Her hands trembled as she tested the milk's temperature against her wrist. "I'm doing the best I can. The birth wasn't easy for me, physically or emotionally. You know that."

"I understand. That's why I suggested you see a professional." His voice softened, but his eyes held their searching intensity. "I can't help you if you won't let me, or fill in the gaps you're letting widen around you ... and us."

She felt a frisson of unease skitter up her spine as Max mentioned therapy, a suggestion that dredged up memories she'd rather keep buried. She gripped the bottle tighter.

"I don't want to see a therapist." Then, in case it wasn't clear: "And you know why."

"I understand that you had a bad experience in the past. But that was *one* therapist, Alice. They're not all the same."

"Do they all keep asking questions until I start crying?"

"Of course not," he said.

"That wasn't a serious question!"

"My question *was* serious."

"I never actually heard a question. Just you telling me that I need therapy. *Again.*"

"I guess that's because we're having this conversation *again.* I think we can agree that the situation is getting worse instead of better, and that at this point it would be irresponsible to not do something about it."

Alice looked at Max, but his eyes had already lost their wells of patience from earlier, and now looked clouded with the sediment of swallowed grievances. His gaze pinned her like a butterfly specimen to a display board, turning her into a child with not just her hand in the cookie jar, but crumbs on her lips and an alibi crumbling to pieces.

"I promise to do better. But I don't need a therapist."

There was either something in her voice or her eyes, or perhaps even both, but Max finally blinked and dropped it.

"Have you eaten today?"

Alice remembered bananas and yogurt, but had no idea what time it was and no memory of anything between standing in the entryway and waking up in the bathtub. But there was a good chance that her stomach was empty, especially considering the way the aromas were making it growl, and it she would be better safe than sorry admitting defeat instead of claiming a victory that he could easily refute.

"No." She shook her head.

"Great." He turned from the stove and smiled. "Get dressed and I'll take you to dinner."

She blinked, wary of the sudden shift in both the conversation and his mood. "But you're cooking?"

"I was cooking. Now I'm taking you to dinner." He turned off the stove and put a lid on his pan. "I can finish that later. I think you need to get out of here."

Hesitation wrapped its cold fingers around her words, a dance of fear and desire, as Alice grappled with the idea of stepping outside the fortress of her domestic confines. "I don't think that's a good idea."

"Why not?"

"What if something happens to Ellie while we're outside?"

"Nothing will happen to her."

"How do you know that? You can't *know* that, Max."

"We aren't taking her with us to dinner. We're going out, just the two of us. You've been wanting Thai lately, so we're going to get a table for two at Curry Up."

"Then who is going to watch Ellie?"

"Ellie will be fine on her own."

Alice blinked twice. She could feel the disbelief that must be flooding her eyes. "You're crazy if you think I'm leaving our daughter alone."

His jaw hardened, and it looked like he was chewing through an entire meal of things he wanted to say. But then he took what felt to Alice like a performative breath and said, "Fine. We won't go out."

"You don't have to cook. We can order in."

"I'm fine cooking if we can't go out."

"I think I want Thai."

"Are you trying to pick a fight with me right now?" he asked.

"Of course not."

"Then what is your problem with my cooking? If you don't want to go out—"

"It's not that I don't want to go out, Max. It's that I'm not leaving Ellie alone, and I don't even know what to think about you suggesting that!"

Now Max was glaring at her like she was the unreasonable one for not wanting to leave an infant alone for a couple of hours. And the guilty voice in her head accused: *You already did that once today.*

Alice took a breath, because she really didn't want to fight, then said, "I'm sorry for making you feel like you couldn't cook. Of course I would love for you to make dinner. But you mentioned Curry Up and that made me think about their basil fried rice, and of course I wanted some once I started thinking about it. *I'm sorry*."

"I told you to stop apologizing." He gave her a smile. "Let's order Curry Up. I want some basil fried rice too. That sounds great."

He'd seemed so angry just a moment before, it was hard to believe his sudden enthusiasm. But she would rather believe it was genuine than fight. "Are you sure?"

"Positive." He nodded. "I'll order it."

"Can we get egg rolls too?"

"Of course we can get egg rolls."

"And Nam Tok?" Alice asked.

"All of that and more. You want dumplings, we'll get dumplings."

"Green curry." She smiled.

"Only if we Curry Up!" Max took out his phone and she laughed.

Even without remembering much of the day, she felt sure that was her first time laughing since waking up.

The mood became much breezier after that, and Max even offered to feed Ellie until dinner arrived. He was still bottle feeding their daughter when the house intercom buzzed like a nest full of bees and the doorman's gruff voice brayed into their apartment.

"I have a delivery for you guys. The Thai place was dropping off, so I said that I'd take it up." Rory was a great guy, and infinitely nicer than his hitman for the mob's voice made him sound.

"Come on up!" Alice told him, then announced that their food was on its way to Max. But after several minutes passed and Rory still hadn't knocked, she impatiently opened the door and looked out into the hallway, just as a well-dressed woman approached Alice while holding two large bags from Curry Up.

She met the woman's eyes while taking in her polished appearance — a tailored charcoal suit that accentuated her lean figure, minimal makeup highlighting her angular features, and dark hair pulled back into a sleek, low ponytail.

"Good evening." She smiled, extending one of the bags toward Alice. "I'm Flora Keys. I'm moving into 902. I happened to be coming up as the doorman was delivering your food, so I thought I'd bring it with me. You must be Alice?"

"Yes, I am." She took the bags. "Thank you. That was very kind of you."

"You must be Max's wife."

"Oh, you know Max?"

"Not personally." Flora shook her head. "We just happened to share the elevator this morning on his way into work. Early riser, your husband. He mentioned that his wife was an interior designer. I was actually hoping to get your opinion on a few things in my new place, if you have the time?"

Alice's pulse beat harder with the realization of how little she wanted to be having this exchange right now. She had taken the year off after Ellie's birth, intentionally stepping away from her career. Part of that time off of work meant not talking about interior design at all, which Max damn well knew, despite pretending like he didn't by pressuring her to return before she was ready.

Sleep deprivation, she reminded herself. Max was worried about her, he'd probably thought it was a great excuse for her to get to know the new neighbor, maybe make a friend. He just didn't understand how hard it was for her right now.

"I'm taking some time off right now. Maybe another time." Alice forced a smile, suddenly aware of her towel dried hair and robe in front of this well coiffed woman.

"Whenever you're ready," Flora said.

Alice gave her an uncertain nod, then hugged the bags of food like a shield and slipped back inside her penthouse apartment.

Chapter Four

ALICE FINISHED SETTING all of the food out for her and
Max, then handed over his chopsticks before ripping hers
out of the packaging and separating them with a satisfying
snap.

She dug into the green curry first, feeling the warmth
spreading from her belly to the tips of her toes. It had been
a long day, apparently, and the comfort food felt like a
consolation prize for her paranoia and the sour aftermath
of their almost-fight. If Ellie would just sleep for a couple
hours, they could have a decent evening together. She
could prove to Max that she was fine, that she didn't need
therapy.

"So you met our new neighbor?" Alice said between
bites.

"Mmm." Max nodded, stuffing his face.

"Me too." He tore a spring roll in two with his mouth
and swallowed it in only three bites. "Lily something."

"Flora."

"Right. Flora. We barely talked. It was just in the
elevator."

"But that ride was long enough for you to tell her that I was an interior decorator?"

"I'm proud of you, Alice. I tell everyone that you're an interior decorator."

She probably shouldn't say it, but she couldn't help herself. "You remember that I'm taking time off, right?"

"You're great at what you do." Max stopped chewing to interrupt her, but his mouth was still full of food. "And you should seriously consider getting back into it."

"We agreed that I would take a year off for Ellie. Why do we have to keep having this conversation?"

Her plea hung in the air, a threadbare cloak of frustration, woven with the fabric of promises they had both made now fraying at the edges. She shouldn't have said it. But she did.

Max sighed. "We agreed on that before ... Never mind."

"No." She shook her head. "Don't do that. Finish what you started. We agreed on that before what?"

"Nothing."

"It's something, Max."

"I just thought that going back to work would take your mind off of Ellie."

"Why would I want to take my mind off of our daughter? Isn't that the point of taking some time away from work? So that I can be fully present?"

"Of course." He even smiled, but Alice sensed something off in his concession. "I'm sorry. Can we go back to talking about how delicious this dinner is?"

She smiled back at him, but the mood had curdled into something they were both clearly dying to escape.

"I'll clean up if you have paperwork to look over from the Laurentian deposition," Alice offered before Max had finished swallowing his last bite.

"That would be great." His entire body seemed to exhale. "I brought piles of it home with me."

Just a few seconds into stacking the empty takeout containers, Alice startled at the sharp wail erupting from the baby monitor to cut through her moment alone like a scalpel.

"I've got it," she muttered to herself.

Alice moved to the knife drawer.

It glided open with a whisper, her hand trembling as it gripped the nearest hilt in her sweating palms.

Then she headed upstairs to the nursery. Ellie's cries kept getting louder and louder as she approached, slicing through her psyche, sharper than the blade in her hand.

Ellie's door was ajar, a looming barrier between reason and an unthinkable act.

Alice stared down at her daughter.

Why are you so loud?

Why can't you ever be quiet?

And how can you cry when your mouth isn't even open?

It was if Ellie's screams were seeping out of her pores.

She stood there, knife in hand, staring at Ellie's crib as if waiting for some divine signal, her thoughts a vortex of despair and confusion.

But then the wailing ceased, just as abruptly as it had started.

Ellie's eyes fluttered open and met her mother's gaze for a fleeting moment before closing again. Silence enveloped the room. Sound seemed almost sacrilegious.

Max touched her arm and Alice recoiled, turning around while swinging the knife in an instinctual arc, blade glinting as Max staggered back and a thin line of blood appeared on his forearm.

His eyes widened in a cocktail of shock and anger.

"Jesus, Alice! What the hell—"

"I didn't — You startled me!" A hoarse whisper, laden with regret and a darker emotion she had yet to identify."

"Why the fuck are you walking around with a butcher knife?"

"I don't know, Max ... I was doing dishes. Could you please not swear at me?"

"Got it." He nodded sarcastically while holding his arm. "You can cut me with a machete, but I should keep the four letter words to myself."

"It's not a machete."

"That's your defense?" Max cried out as he stopped holding his gushing wound to pluck the blade from her hand.

Then he staggered toward the bathroom, a few drops of blood sluicing between his fingers to fall on her beautiful floor.

Alice followed him in and left the door open behind them. There were no words as she dressed his wound, tearing open a sterile packet of gauze with trembling fingers and a lump in her throat. She pressed the bandage to his arm, her touch clinical and tentative as she secured it with a final pull.

He marched out of the bathroom without saying thank you, though it was hard for Alice to blame him. The cut wasn't deep, but it was deep enough, and all her fault.

The worst part was that she wasn't sure she could explain what had happened. It had all felt like a surreal dream where someone else was making decisions for her with a twisted logic she couldn't make sense of now.

Could sleep deprivation do that?

She stayed in the bathroom alone with her breathing for a few minutes before finally heading downstairs and meeting him back in the kitchen where she could hear him rummaging around.

But by the time she got there, he was ready to go.

"What were you looking for?" Alice asked him.

"Nothing."

"Maybe I can help you find it. I know where everything is."

"I'm going to bed." Max started to leave the kitchen.

"Wait!"

He turned back around and looked at Alice expectantly.

"You're mad at me," she said.

He sighed. "What is it that you want me to say right now?"

Alice had no idea, but she hated the way he was looking at her.

"Say that you understand."

"Of course I understand. I think I've more than proven that." He sighed again. "I'm making you an appointment with Dr. Williams tomorrow and—"

"NO!" Alice shrieked, and hated exactly how shrill she sounded. Like she was the baby, not Ellie. She took a calming breath before making a more reasonable argument. "I don't like him."

"You don't have to like your therapist if he's helping you."

"I'm not sure he can help me if I don't like him." She shook her head because that wasn't exactly right. "I mean, he makes me feel like a failure."

"Well, you need to speak to somebody."

"Maybe you're right …"

"About this?" He finally looked at her with compassion. "There's no doubt about it. So either you find a therapist you're happy with, or I'm making you an appointment with Dr. Williams."

"Okay." Alice didn't know what else to say.

"Good night." Another kiss on the forehead.

Then she was alone in the kitchen.

Alice went over to the knife drawer on instinct, not because she wanted a knife this time, but because she wanted to see if she was right about the rummaging around she'd heard before coming into the kitchen.

And sure enough, the knife drawer was empty. Max had taken all of the sharp objects and hidden them somewhere. A chill rippled through her as she stared into an empty drawer that, in its own way, screamed louder than Ellie.

She needed sleep, but had to ignore the siren call knowing that her slumber would only bring on nightmares about hurting herself or Ellie. Best to stay awake.

Alice stepped into the living room, her eyes sweeping over the familiarity of yet another favorite space. Drenched in shades of the sea and the moonlit night, this more than any other room in the penthouse was her curated haven. A canvas where every hue and texture had been chosen with care. Bookshelves stood tall like sentinels. Plush blue sofas beckoned her to sink in and lose hours in the rapturous arms of a magical book. She laid down on the sofa and closed her eyes.

A gentle breeze wafted in from the open French doors, teasing the edges of gossamer drapes billowing like specters, inviting the scent of rain and the distant hum of the city inside.

She leaned forward toward the coffee table and grabbed her AirPods.

She listened to her music loud enough that her eardrums were starting to throb.

Alice couldn't hear the rain when it came, still lying wide awake and unsettled on the sofa as the first drop began to fall outside. She got up and closed the doors just moments before the sky opened up and it started pouring.

The rain seemed to crescendo, as if mimicking the fear that thrummed deep in her bones.

Chapter Five

ALICE WAS JOLTED into the early morning by yet another round of Ellie's piercing wails, hacking through the fog of sleep and straight into her bones. Each scream still reverberated throughout her entire body, incessant repetition had dulled their edge — like a well-worn blade cutting into a hunk of meat.

Worn down and hollowed out, Alice felt herself incapable of soothing Ellie, let alone the cacophony of inner turmoil that mirrored her daughter's distress. She rolled over with a weary resolve and nudged Max on his arm.

But he lay there inert, a lifeless mass either sunk in the depths of his own slumber or obstinately feigning it, leaving Alice alone to face the agony of their infant screaming.

"*Max!*" she whisper-shouted, then repeated his name in a normal volume when he didn't answer. "Max!"

"What is it?" he snapped, his voice sounding much too alert for Alice to have only just woken him.

"I need you to go and get Ellie for—"

"No," he said before she even finished.

"Please, Max. I'm *so* exhausted."

"I'm sorry that you're tired, but if you want to help Ellie, then you can go and do it yourself." He rolled over and grumbled under his breath. "This is *your* responsibility."

Alice mustered the strength to get out of bed, and for a moment she was naive enough to believe that Max was finally coming to her rescue as he tossed the covers off of his body and swung his feet onto the floor.

"Thank you–" Alice started.

"No, thank *you*. I appreciate you getting me up early. I have a shit ton to do on the brief today. Now I have a nice start." He stomped into the bathroom and slammed the door behind him.

His departure was a silent accusation, each step a punctuation mark in their dialogue of discontent, leaving Alice with the echo of their fractured conversation.

Ellie screamed louder.

Alice got out of bed and went next door to the nursery, rushing to her crib and leaving the door ajar behind her. She looked down at her daughter, but there were no cries because Ellie was now asleep with pleasant little gurgles bubbling up from her throat.

Alice blinked several times, but there was still no sound in the room, almost like she was suddenly under water.

Until she heard the buzzing of a fly circling several times in descent before finally landing on Ellie's face. A grotesque melody, and surprisingly loud. A dissonant vibration in the room's unsettling silence.

Alice brushed the insect away, but another immediately came to take its place, and then another one, and another one, and another one after that as pregnant nests of flies emerged from the room's darkened corners, buzzing with that insectile dirge as the flies clung to her eyelashes, lingered on her cherubic lips, and nestled in the folds of her baby blanket.

A single fly crawled out of Ellie's slightly open mouth, and then hundreds were spilling forth from her parted lips as they buzzed.

Alice screamed again — a pure shriek of fright as she tried to blink the terror away.

"What are you doing?" Max asked.

She looked to see her husband standing in the doorway with a towel wrapped around his waist, still wet from the shower, looking harried as he studied her.

Alice turned away from him and glanced down into the crib again to see Ellie still fast asleep, and the flies that were never there in the first place now all gone.

Was it possible to have nightmares when you were awake?

Did sleep deprivation do that, or was it a sign of something worse?

"Nothing." She spun back around to face her husband, not wanting him to see how unnerved she felt. "I was just checking on Ellie."

"Great," he nodded, obviously annoyed with her. "Then could you please get the door? I would really like to finish my shower. Thanks."

Max didn't linger for her response, abruptly spinning on his heels and retreating back to the bathroom with an air of dismissal.

The door? She hadn't heard—

The intercom buzzed loudly, sounding suspiciously like the flies from her waking nightmare moments ago.

She meandered toward the intercom, weighted down by fear for her unraveling sanity.

Alice pressed the button as a shudder of absurdity

washed over her, for having let the sound of their buzzing intercom usher her into such a horrifying hallucination.

It was already obvious that she had never been more starved for the solace of sleep, but now …

"This is Alice," she said into the intercom.

"Hey there, Alice," Rory replied from his side of the line. "I have someone down here who says they need to drop off a brief for Max. Do you know if he's expecting anyone?"

"He's swamped at work right now. I'm sure he'll be happy to get whatever it is. Go ahead and send them up."

"You got it." Rory hung up, and Alice went to the bathroom.

She opened the door and knocked on the wall as she called out to him. "Your paperwork is here."

"What?" Max yelled back at her, just loud enough to be heard above the water.

"Your brief! The one you were expecting. Rory just called from the lobby and said someone is here to—"

"I wasn't expecting any paperwork." He turned off the water and stepped out of the shower, grabbing the towel to dry himself off again. "Did Rory give you a name?"

"Sorry, I didn't ask. I just figured you would want whatever it was."

"Of course I want it," he said as Alice heard a knock on the front door. He sounded even more irritated with her than before. "I'll get it."

He stomped out of the bathroom to answer the door, still dressed in only his towel.

Alice stayed out of sight, listening to a hushed conversation that she couldn't really hear either side of. Max spoke in an irritated whisper, and she felt a flutter of uncomfortable joy knowing that he was annoyed at someone else.

The front door closed and she hurried back to the bedroom, waiting on the bed and looking up at Max as he entered the room, holding a file and seeming even more agitated than he had before leaving the bathroom to get the door.

"Is everything okay?" Alice asked.

"Just more work garbage," grumbled Max.

"The Laurentian deposition?"

"Of course." A defeated sigh. "The case isn't going nearly as well as I thought it would be."

"I'm sorry to hear that," Alice said, just as Ellie started screaming again.

She ignored it, watching Max as he dressed for work while managing to completely ignore his wailing daughter. The cries died down on their own, but then the screaming started up again right as he was preparing to leave.

"Can you help me with Ellie for just a few minutes before you go?" Alice asked.

"No." He shook his head. "I wouldn't have time to deal with this shit even if extra crap hadn't just been hand delivered to my apartment."

"You shouldn't talk about your daughter like that!" Alice felt infuriated.

"Our daughter whose screams you're ignoring right now?"

"You were ready to leave her alone while we went out for dinner."

The accusation was a mistake, but she didn't care. She didn't care if she was mad because she was sleep-deprived. Not after he'd called Ellie *shit.*

Max refused to so much as look at her once while brushing his teeth, not even in the mirror, maintaining his silence until he was standing in front of the door about to leave.

"I recommend that you call a friend or take a walk today. Do *something*, Alice. Anything but sulking around the apartment all day. Find a therapist, so I don't have to call Dr. Williams."

He didn't wait for her to answer, slamming the door behind him. Ironically, Ellie quieted, as if even the sound of her father leaving was more soothing than anything Alice could do.

Alice wanted to start sobbing now that she was alone, even more than she had when Max was eyeing her with irritation or disgust. She couldn't quite tell the difference these days.

She stepped out onto her balcony, then onto the cushion and up onto the brick balustrade again. She peered over the edge as Max was leaving their building.

She saw a woman waiting for him on the street. A statuesque blonde, if that wasn't just more of her imagination acting up on her.

Max and the woman locked eyes in a verbal dance of obvious displeasure. Words that Alice could not hear were punctuated by animated gestures on both sides and pedestrians steered clear of their battleground.

Her gaze drifted from Max and the woman arguing below her to the yawning abyss beyond the balustrade. Her toes tingled at the precipice as if flirting with gravity's pull, wrestling with the temptation of becoming a plummeting phantom.

She imagined her foot slipping on the moisture-slicked edge and sending her toppling over into a heart-stopping descent that ended abruptly with the crunch of metal and shattered glass as she landed atop the taxi now idling in front of her husband and the mysterious woman.

That would sure surprise the hell out of him.

Then Max would never be able to leave Ellie alone again.

But then Ellie started screaming, her anguished cries rolling out from the nursery and onto the balcony, dragging Alice down from the balustrade and back inside, where the waking nightmares waited.

Chapter Six

ALICE WAS GOING out of her goddamn mind.

That had been true for a while now, but after getting stuck in a vortex of relentless introspection, she found herself circling back to Max's unsettling assertion. His words invaded her thoughts like unwelcome houseguests, lodging themselves in the crannies of her mind, a territory already sown with seeds of doubt and self-loathing that kept on sprouting. The invasion was silent yet chaotic, each syllable a relentless echo.

He had spotlighted her complicity: her self-imposed isolation, the withdrawal from friends, the refusal to step outside and face the light of day. Alice had been burying herself inside and refusing to face reality. Max had called her out on it, and now she was sitting with that truth.

And sitting with the truth felt like perching on the edge of an abyss.

Maybe this mothering thing wouldn't be so fucking hard if she actually did go outside or made an effort to spend some time with a friend.

So Alice went to the bedroom and picked up her phone from the nightstand.

She made herself comfortable amid her many plush pillows and started scrolling through hundreds of unread texts and an embarrassing number of unread emails still languishing in her inbox.

There had been plenty of people reaching out to her in the eight weeks since Ellie had been born (friends, not family), and here she was ignoring all of them while moping in her fancy penthouse and feeling sorry for herself.

Her fingers hovered over her contacts for more than a minute, but all Alice could do in that time was stare. Even after scrolling while working not to hyperventilate, it was impossible to decide which one of her friends she most wanted to reach out to after breaking a silence that had clearly lingered for far too long. The weight of the decision pressed down on her, a burden of potentiality, each contact name a door to a path she feared she might have already closed.

Alice had narrowed it down to two or three or maybe ten choices when she heard a knock on the door. It was subtle enough at first that she ignored it, but the second time sounded like a wallop on the wood. It got her scrambling out of bed and rushing to answer the door.

Weird, because Rory hadn't called her to let her know that anyone was coming up, and Alice couldn't remember when a visitor had managed to slip by him even once since she and Max had moved into the building.

She looked through the peephole and saw that it was Flora, her new neighbor from next door, standing in the hallway and looking somehow awkward yet poised while waiting for the door to open.

"Hi there!" Flora gave her a friendly wave once they

were standing face to face. "I hate to interrupt you, but do you happen to have any light bulbs?"

"Light bulbs?" Alice repeated, even though she had no trouble understanding what Flora had said. She couldn't help resenting the neighbor's interruption, even though it had saved her from the panicky indecision that had been threatening to trigger a panic attack.

Flora smiled apologetically. "I wasn't planning to go out today, but my bathroom light went out. The electric in my place is still kind of shit, and will be until I can get an electrician out here, so I'm having a hard time seeing anything in there."

"Of course. I'll go and get some. Be right back."

Her words were automatic, a programmed courtesy, while her mind raced with the intrusion of normalcy into the fortress of her solitude.

Alice didn't know whether to close the door or leave it open. A small part of her even wanted to invite Flora inside, but the much larger part of Alice didn't want her solace interrupted right now. It was hard enough choosing which of her good friends she should reach out to first. The thought of having to make small talk — or worse, be vulnerable — with a stranger right now was giving her the chills.

She turned away from the door and walked down the hallway to the storage closet filled with ephemeral refugees from her early adult life: old board games, winter coats she would never wear again, and stacks of labeled boxes.

Most of the apartment had custom lighting, with bulbs that needed to be specially ordered, but Alice was sure she had a box of standard lightbulbs somewhere in this closet. She scanned the shelves until her gaze landed on a four-pack.

She grabbed the box and returned to the door.

"Sorry that took so long," Alice said, raising the light bulbs in her hand like a prize as she approached Flora.

"I thought that was fast."

"Here's a four pack." Alice handed her the box. "You'll probably find a few more bulbs burned out."

"Thank you! Now I won't have to interrupt you another three times."

"You weren't interrupting me at all," Alice lied.

"I'm glad to hear it." Flora smiled again and turned to go. But then she reeled back around to look at Alice after only a single step. "Would you like to come over for a cup of coffee? I don't know anyone in New York yet and am already feeling lonelier than I want to. And we are going to be neighbors, after all …"

Flora stopped talking when Alice didn't answer.

Her discomfort was surely clear on her face.

"I'm sorry," Flora started again. "I didn't mean to overstep. My mother has been telling me that I'm much too forward for my own good, going on my entire life now."

"I'm just having one of those days." Alice offered her neighbor a tired smile.

"I have them all the time." Flora laughed.

"I would love to come over for a cup of coffee," Alice said." I just need to feed my daughter first, if you don't mind."

"Of course I don't mind! Take your time and come on over whenever. I'll leave my front door open and get started on the coffee."

"Thanks again."

Flora nodded, then turned around and started back toward her apartment.

Alice closed the door and went to collect Ellie, laying

quietly in the crib, appearing almost unnaturally still with her small eyelids half-closed in a weary daze.

She carefully scooped Ellie into her arms, grateful for the momentary reprieve from her fussing, and headed to Flora's apartment, feeling a mix of nervousness and relief.

Alice knocked on the slightly-open front door, then entered the neighboring penthouse, making her way into what she assumed was the living room, where Flora was waiting.

"Flora, meet Ellie." Alice nodded down at her drowsy daughter.

She looked at the ornate tray sitting on the center of a table otherwise cluttered with unpacked boxes and a scatter of tools. A French press full of freshly-brewed coffee was flanked by an assortment of cookies: delicate pastel macarons, chocolate chip cookies with visible gooeyness, and intricately-iced sugar cookies that looked too pretty to eat.

"It is an absolute pleasure to meet you, Ellie."

Was there something strange about the way Flora had said that, or just another helping of her unrelenting paranoia?

"Those cookies look delicious."

"They're from Butter Me Up."

"Where is that?" Alice asked.

"Right across the street! You haven't been?"

"It must have just opened."

"That's what the sign says. The place smells like Christmas morning, but with more sugar. I took one whiff and I needed a box of cookies. That place gives my favorite bakery back home a run for its money, though my bakery has a much better name."

"What is it called?"

"Bake Me Up Before You Go-Go." Flora laughed.

"That is fun." Alice gave her a smile. "Where did you move from?"

"Boston. I'm surprised you couldn't tell by the accent. I lived there my entire life, but I've always wanted to live in New York, and I finally decided that I wasn't getting any younger, so I bit the bullet and made the move."

"Why did you want to get out of Boston?"

"Because the city is like if an Ivy League school and a dive bar had a baby, then raised it on Dunkin' Donuts and rebellion. The city is historical and hysterical, with streets so twisted and gnarly that Paul Revere designed them drunk."

"Did Paul Revere really design the streets?"

"Of course not. And don't get me wrong, I do love the place, but there comes a time when you've tipped back one too many Sam Adams while arguing about the Red Sox in a crowded pub, and start to feel like you're going in circles. New York is like an open book with endless chapters. And darling, I'm ready to scribble all over its pages."

"I'm glad to have a neighbor again." Alice was surprised to realize that she actually meant it. "This apartment was empty for months, and the last tenant had lived here for over 40 years, so you can only imagine how much the two of us had in common."

Flora smiled. "I can imagine that." Then she frowned. "I heard that she died rather tragically, but none of the details, and I didn't want to pry, but ..."

Flora obviously felt more comfortable prying now, so Alice simply said, "She fell down the stairs."

"Oh, how awful!" Flora covered her mouth.

"Yes, and it was even worse than that." Alice leaned forward and whispered, even though it was only the two of them in the apartment. "No one ever uses the stairs in this building, especially not all the way up here, so she had been gone for days before anyone found her."

Dead for days was the right way to say it, but for some reason that felt like too much.

Flora's only response was to lean forward and grab a cookie, nibbling the end of it through a long moment of silence before breaking the quiet again. "So Max told me that you're a world-famous interior decorator."

"I thought he just told you I was a decorator."

"Your husband is very proud of you. It was only an elevator ride, and he still managed to let me know that you've been in Architectural Digest six different times."

"It's actually seven," Alice corrected her, then felt like an asshole for doing so. "I've just been taking some time off because of Ellie."

She glanced around the living room full of meticulously chosen elements — velvet upholstery in emerald and sapphire tones, baroque-patterned rugs, and gleaming brass accents amid moving boxes stacked in the corners.

"It doesn't look like you need my help at all. The place looks like it's coming along beautifully."

"The living room is fine. It's my dining room I'm worried about — that's where I really need some help."

"I'm happy to give it a look, since I'm here anyway."

"I would love that!" Flora looked like she wanted to clap as she finished the rest of her cookie and led Alice into the other room. "I need this area to look a lot more welcoming, because this is where I'll be seeing my patients."

"Patients?" Alice repeated. "What kind of patients?"

"I'm a psychiatrist."

Alice raised an eyebrow. "That's fascinating."

Flora grinned. "Yes, even psychiatrists need psychiatrists, you know."

Alice surveyed the dining room, her designer's eye cataloging possibilities a beat before they left her mouth. "Given the dual functionality of the space, I recommend getting in some folding screens or partitions. Bamboo or latticed screens would bring texture to the room, and they could be easily moved around to create different layouts. You could have one side of the screen treated with sound-proofing material, which would give your patients a sense of confidentiality. If you wanted a more modern aesthetic, frosted glass partitions on rollers could work — they can catch and distribute natural light while still maintaining that sense of privacy."

Alice turned back to find Flora smiling. "What do you think?"

"I think you're amazing, and feel like I should pay you, or at least trade," Flora said. "I don't suppose you're looking for a therapy session?"

The joke hung in the air, but Alice wasn't laughing. Instead, she said, "Are you serious?"

"Do you want me to be serious?"

"Yes." Alice found herself nodding. "I really think I do."

"Well then, absolutely!" Flora seemed delighted. "How does Monday work for you?"

Chapter Seven

MAX CAME HOME from work with a much improved mood that was obvious from the moment he entered the apartment.

"I brought takeout," he declared, triumphantly raising two bags from Curry Up, one in each hand. "I figured we should try that basil fried rice again, plus all the other stuff, but without my rotten mood. What do you say?"

Max gave her a smile, and she felt relieved by how easy it was to smile back at him.

"That sounds wonderful," she said.

"Is Ellie sleeping?"

"Yes." Today had been like a miracle — Ellie had dozed all through the visit with Flora and then some, giving Alice time to relax on the balcony with a book and a cup of tea. And when she did wake up again, the infant had stopped screaming as soon as Alice touched the bottle's nipple to her lips. Then she'd napped quietly in Alice's arms for a few minutes, as if she was finally accepting her mother.

Alice had wondered if maybe she should give up trying to breastfeed altogether and stick with the bottle.

"I think maybe I'm getting the hang of this mother-hood thing," she added.

"Great." Max didn't seem surprised to hear that she was down, even though this wasn't her usual rest time. "I'm starving."

He tore into the takeout bags like a kid opening gifts on Christmas morning, popping the lids off of the containers and releasing fragrant plumes of steam into the air.

"Did you not get to eat at all today?" Alice started to make herself a plate.

"I ate half a sandwich without chewing." He stopped to look at her. "I'm sorry again about this morning. I was being a real jerk, and it wasn't your fault. The stress is a bit out of control at work right now; it's driving me out of my mind. I already feel like I'm nearing a breaking point, and the interrupted sleep wasn't helping."

His apology hung between them, a delicate olive branch extended across the chasm that the day's earlier anger had carved into their union.

"I'm sorry about that," Alice said.

"It's history." Max dismissed it with a wave of her hand. "Fortunately, my paralegal might have found the right angle for this case, and that means life should be getting a little easier for me, and therefore both of us, starting tomorrow morning."

"That sounds great! I'm so happy to hear that."

"How was your day?" Max asked her as he started digging into his dinner. "You seem a lot better than when I left this morning. Did you go outside or call a friend?"

He looked so hopeful, and Alice was delighted that she could give him the good news. "I met our new neighbor."

"Didn't you already meet her?"

"Yes, but today I went over to her place and we had coffee. Plus cookies. Three of them."

"Three cookies, all the same kind, or three different kinds of cookies?"

"Chocolate chip, some iced thingy, and macaroons."

"Sounds like your day was even better than mine. How are you still hungry?"

"I ate the cookies early this morning. And I think they might have even brought my appetite back."

"That's great," Max nodded again. "I'm glad to hear that."

"Did you know that Flora is a therapist?" Alice asked. "A psychiatrist, actually."

"Nope." Max shook his head and stuffed an egg roll into his mouth, then spoke as he chewed. "How would I know that?"

"I made an appointment to see her, so you won't be needing to call Dr. Williams."

"That's great." Max swallowed his spring roll and grinned from ear to ear. "Are you happy about it?"

"I guess so," Alice said, holding her smile.

Not just then, but all through the rest of their dinner.

But in truth, Alice wasn't sure how she felt about it. Something was pressing down on her mind for sure, because even after her chamomile tea and nighttime rituals, including all of her breathing exercises, Alice still kept tossing and turning.

Then Ellie started to scream, right as she was finally drifting to sleep, after three or four hours of trying.

"Max," she said while shaking him awake, "I need you to get Ellie for me. *Please.* I haven't gone to sleep yet."

She put the pillow over her head and turned her back to him. But Max merely grumbled in reply as Ellie screamed louder.

"Max. Please!"

But he still refused to get out of bed.

And when Alice could no longer take the fistfuls of the nails that were being driven into the back of her skull, she finally snapped at him. "Can you please help me? I've been getting Ellie every night, so—"

"Fine!" Max almost roared at her. "If you want to do this, let's do this. *Right now.*" He got out of bed and grabbed her by the arm. "But you're coming with me."

Max marched her next door into the nursery and over to Ellie's crib, then he reached inside and snatched her out like she was a rag doll instead of an infant.

"You need to be gentle with her!" Ellie exclaimed.

Max only ignored her as he dragged mother and daughter into the kitchen.

"*Here.*" He shoved Ellie into Alice's hands as their baby continued to scream.

Then he walked over to a cupboard and pulled out a box with a red stain, where it looked like someone had smashed a cherry against the side. He set the box on the counter, opened the lid, then reached over and snatched Ellie roughly from Alice.

"What are you doing?" she screamed.

Max continued to ignore her as he dropped Ellie unceremoniously inside the box and then taped it closed. In this moment of grotesque absurdity, their kitchen transformed into a theater of the macabre, with each of his movements now a pantomime of her darkest fears.

"Now, it's time we get rid of her," Max declared, tucking the box under his arm and walking over to the garbage chute.

Alice screamed her lungs raw as she ran over to Max and started pummeling her fists on the back of his shoulders before snatching the box away from him, terrified that the jostling could be hurting Ellie, but unable to pry it from his grasp without jerking it.

She clutched the box in her arms like Gollum with his Precious and ran over to the corner of the kitchen, ripping the tape from the box and scooping a still-screaming Ellie out of it.

Alice expected Max to try and wrestle their daughter back out of her arms, but looking around, she didn't even see her husband in the room.

Alice was standing all alone in the kitchen.

She gathered herself then went and checked the living room.

But there wasn't any trace of him there either, and the entire apartment was midnight silent, Ellie fast asleep in her arms. She had no idea what time it was. This whole situation was so completely disorienting.

Was it possible that she'd been sleepwalking through a nightmare, getting Ellie from her crib and bringing her to the kitchen without waking up?

Could sleep deprivation do *that?*

She held Ellie tight as she went back to her room, peeking inside to see Max fast asleep in bed, his chest rising and falling as if he had been deep in an uninterrupted slumber for hours now.

The air seemed to congeal around Alice as she stood there, her gaze fastening onto Max as if he was a cipher she was trying to decode. Her thoughts careened between two terrifying possibilities: had she hallucinated an unfathomable betrayal by the man she loved, or was he capable of such cruelty?

She forced her eyes away from him, her glance drifting down to the bundle held tightly against her chest. That innocence was a balm, if only for a fleeting moment.

She went back to the kitchen, where the box with the red stain and the tape lay out on the counter.

That suggested an even more horrifying possibility — that she was the one who'd put her infant daughter in a box and taped it up, intending to toss Ellie down the garbage chute.

Her heart almost stopped as she imagined waking up *after* the box had slid down the chute, landing atop all the other garbage in a huge pile who-knew-where. Assuming Ellie even survived the fall, how would Alice get her back? The thought of waking the building superintendent up in the middle of the night and begging him to let her search the trash pile for her baby was sickening. He'd report her to child services immediately, and they'd take Ellie away from her. And they'd be right to, because what kind of mother threw their baby down a trash chute?

And if child services didn't take Ellie, Max would. How could he do otherwise?

With a steadying breath, Alice walked to the garbage chute and dropped the empty box down its abyss. The sound it made as it tumbled away was unnervingly final.

The tape went next, tumbling down the chute after the box.

Alice startled as Ellie started screaming, as if she'd just realized how close she'd come to dying.

Alice took a baby bottle from the fridge and held it under the tap, letting warm water gush over the plastic until it was at a comforting temperature for Ellie. Her movements were automatic, her mind a carousel of disbelief and dread.

She wasn't conscious of a change in the room's atmosphere, didn't hear footsteps or the soft exhale of a breath. Yet a sixth sense prickled at her nape and turned her abruptly to look over and see Max standing in the doorway, blinking against the sudden intrusion of light.

Her grip tightened involuntarily around Ellie, drawing the infant closer to her body.

"Is everything okay?" Max's voice was tinged with a genuine worry that stoked the flames of her confusion. "I woke up, noticed you weren't beside me, and got concerned."

"I couldn't sleep," Alice explained, not wanting to admit what had really happened.

It felt like she was holding her breath as Max approached her.

He leaned down to plant a soft kiss on Ellie's forehead before pressing another to Alice's cheek.

"I'll join you in a bit," she promised.

"Take your time," Max assured her, his lips briefly meeting her cheek again before he retreated to their bedroom.

Alice moved into the dim comfort of the living room, still holding Ellie close as she sank into the plush armchair with the bottle poised at her infant's lips. The baby cooed softly as she drank, her eyelids growing heavy until they surrendered to sleep.

Alice transferred her gently back to the crib, her eyes lingering on the tiny, peaceful face that knew nothing of the shadows stretching across her mother's heart.

She settled into a rocking chair beside the crib, the rhythmic creaking filling the room as she moved back and forth, back and forth, determined to stay awake and make sure she would not suffer any nightmares.

But even as Alice made this pact with herself, she couldn't shake the unsettling thought that sometimes the most haunting nightmares were the ones that struck in her waking life. The thought clung to her like the chill of an unseen presence.

Chapter Eight

Alice woke up in the rocking chair, still in the nursery.

She blinked slowly as she adjusted to the morning light, and guessed it was around eight in the morning, probably around time for Max to be leaving, which explained the noises she could hear coming from down in the entryway as he scooted the stroller from one side over to the other. He liked to do that every couple of days, probably because he figured that Alice would be more likely to go outside if she saw the stroller in a different place.

She stood from the rocking chair and peeked down into the crib, glad to see that Ellie was still sleeping. Then she rushed out of the nursery and over to the entryway, hoping to get Max before he slipped out of the apartment.

"Hey." He turned around after opening the door. "I wasn't sure if I should leave you or not, but you looked so peaceful in the rocking chair, I didn't want to disturb you."

Alice offered him an awkward smile, unsure about too many things. "Did you sleep okay last night?"

He shrugged. "Not great, but better than the last two nights."

"Did you wake up at all?"

"Only when I saw you, right before you said you would be to bed in a few minutes, then fell asleep in the rocking chair." Max narrowed his eyes at her, like he was taking it personally that she'd broken her promise.

"So you didn't wake up before then, not even once?"

"I don't think so." He appeared to ponder the question. "Not that I can remember."

She probably shouldn't ask, but… "Do you ever dream about hurting Ellie?"

"No! Of course not! Why are you asking me so many questions and why would you ask that last one specifically? Am I supposed to not feel insulted right now?"

"I'm sorry." She shook her head. "I had a bad nightmare about you and Ellie."

"Aren't all nightmares bad by definition?"

His question hung in the air as he stared at her like she was an idiot.

"It really scared me, Max."

He glanced at the open door then turned back to Alice. "Would you like to talk about it?"

"No." She shook her head. "I know you need to get to work."

"Today is your session with Flora, right?" He asked like he didn't quite believe that she intended to go.

She pushed back her irritation and tried to smile. "Nine o'clock."

"I'm glad to hear it." He kissed her on the cheek. "It's going to be a great session. I've gotta go, okay?"

"I know." She watched him walk down the hallway toward the elevator.

He gave her another wave as the elevator doors dinged closed.

Alice retreated back into her apartment, annoyed that

he hadn't taken her seriously, dismissing her nightmare as another triviality. But why wouldn't he? She hadn't told him about the sleepwalking, or that she'd found the box and the tape on the counter, as if she might have done the things she'd been dreaming about.

And she couldn't tell him without making him think that she was getting worse, not better.

But she felt like she might be slowly going insane.

She went into the kitchen and peered down the garbage chute. But the dark void revealed nothing.

She thought about the empty box with a smashed cherry stain. She should never have gotten rid of it. It was proof that something had happened, even if she wasn't exactly sure what.

Assuming there really was a box. Maybe she'd dreamed that too.

Then another thought struck her: how much should she tell Flora?

If she did tell Flora everything, would Flora be obligated to report it?

She went back into the bedroom and got dressed without taking a shower, or even wanting one, wondering if she should eat even though she had no appetite.

Alice made her way to the living room, where she thumbed through an older issue of Prestige Interior, scanning the pages without really looking at anything.

She studied ornaments on her mantlepiece, somehow dissatisfied but unable to pinpoint why. She stared for a while before realizing that it was finally time to collect Ellie from the nursery, but she stood frozen in front of the crib too, staring down at her peacefully sleeping daughter. Still, even though it was well past her usual waking time.

Ellie seemed unusually lethargic as Alice dressed her,

barely shifting or making any of her typical coos as Ellie cradled her on the way to Flora's.

She used her free hand to knock on the door. Three solid raps as Alice considered turning around and escaping back into her own apartment.

Then the door swung open and Flora was standing there with a smile, her expression like a lighthouse in the murky waters of Alice's morning, warming the cold uncertainty that had settled in her bones.

"Come in."

Alice entered the apartment, which was already in better shape than it had looked the last time she was there. She followed Flora into the dining room turned client area, already knowing where to go.

"Where should I sit?" Alice glanced from a couch to a chair. The couch looked more inviting while the chair appeared more formal, its straight lines and stiff cushions giving an air of composure compared to the plush sanctuary that threatened to swallow her in its comfort.

"Whichever one is the most comfortable for you, dear."

Alice decided that she'd be more likely to let down her guard before she'd determined that she could trust Flora with the whole truth.

So Alice chose the chair, which was more comfortable than she expected, but not dangerously so. Her shoulders were knotted and her grip on the armrest white-knuckled. And of course, the moment she managed to relax even a little, Ellie started crying again.

"I'm so sorry about that. I don't know what's wrong with her, or with me, but she's *always* crying."

"It sounds like we have a lot to talk about," Flora gave her a gentle smile.

Alice looked at the hardwood floor, and couldn't help but think that it needed refinishing.

"You don't need to apologize for a crying infant and there is nothing wrong with either one of you. Now, may I please help?" Flora opened her arms in offering and Alice handed Ellie over to her.

The infant fell instantly quiet as Flora bounced up and down with her.

"Are you as good of a therapist as you are a baby whisperer?" Alice asked.

"Why don't we find out?" Flora gave her another smile. "Tell me about your family."

"What do you want to know?"

"Start anywhere you'd like."

"Well, I'm estranged from my parents."

Flora nodded. "And why is that?"

"They didn't approve of my marriage to Max," Alice explained.

"Was there a specific reason for that?"

"My parents are rich, like really rich, generational wealth rich. That's why I could always decorate like I do. I was always around it. It's like I had my own '10,000 hours' in the world of design from a young age. I was basically born with a paintbrush in one hand and a fabric swatch in the other."

"So your parents didn't approve of Max because he wasn't wealthy?"

"Not exactly." Alice tried to clarify. "There's a big difference between not being rich and being poor, according to my family. Max grew up poor, and my parents are of the strong belief that people who grew up poor will do anything to be rich."

"And you don't believe that?"

"No." Alice shook her head. "That has not been my experience."

"Was there anything specific between your parents and Max that gave them a bad impression of him?"

She shook her head again. "It was just them being terrible and judgmental, assuming that he wanted my money. I thought they would eventually come around, but they never did. Honestly, they seemed almost happy to cut me off, and indifferent to letting me go."

"And that still hurts you?"

"Not really. They always liked my brother and sister better, anyway."

"You're sure that doesn't hurt you?" Flora narrowed her eyes at Alice.

"Of course it hurts me," she admitted. "But I'm an adult. I've moved on."

Flora stared at her skeptically for a moment, then asked, "What does Max do for a living now?"

"He's a lawyer."

"And you're a world-famous interior decorator?" Flora smiled.

Alice found herself smiling back.

"I knew you could do it!" Flora declared before letting the moment settle into a reset of their conversation. "Let's move to the present for a moment. I want to hear about what's been giving you pain recently."

Alice exhaled, thinking of a hundred ways she could answer that question. "Ellie was a difficult birth. She was breech and her heart rate dropped…"

"I can imagine that was traumatic."

"She almost died." Alice left it there.

But there was so much more that she wanted to say.

She was sitting here in the chair across from what was supposed to be her new therapist, so why was she keeping the truth about Samuel to herself?

Besides the obvious reason that she couldn't bring herself to say the words out loud, even if she was forced to think about them.

"What has life been like since Ellie was born?"

Flora's question hit her like a slap.

Alice started to cry, her sniffles becoming sobs as Flora patiently waited for the wave to subside before handing her a box of tissues. The tears were a torrent, a dam breaking within her, each sob washing away fragments of the facade she had held together for so long to reveal the rawness beneath.

"I'm sorry for all the tears."

"Please stop apologizing." Flora waited a beat then added, "It is quite possible that you have postpartum depression. Has anyone talked to you about that?"

Alice shook her head.

"I had a stillbirth and found it extremely difficult to recover." Flora's confession was a key turning in the lock of Alice's isolation. "I kept having nightmares, thinking that there was something I had done to cause it. I stopped eating, I withdrew from life in general, and I even thought about killing myself. *Several times*. It was the hardest time of my life, especially because my husband left me at the same time."

"Asshole," Alice said.

Flora laughed. "Such an asshole."

"Thank you for telling me that," Alice said. "I'm not happy to hear that you went through the pain, but I'm happy to hear that someone else went through something similar because—"

"It makes you feel less alone," Flora finished for her.

"Yes, that." Alice offered her a brittle smile. "What are the symptoms of postpartum depression?"

"Do you want the long answer or the short one?"

"The long one I guess? Is that better?"

"You tell me." Flora shifted in her seat. "So, you're crying — a lot, like, maybe all the time, and not just your run-of-the-mill Hallmark movie tears, but a constant faucet of 'why-is-the-world-so-gray' waterworks. And you're so down in the dumps that you're practically part of the land-fill of existential despair. All those things that used to give you those warm, fuzzy vibes — *POOF*, they're gone, replaced by what feels like cardboard cutouts of what you used to enjoy. Speaking of replacements, how's that appetite of yours? Are you scarfing down anything in sight like you're at a never-ending buffet, or treating food like it's your mortal enemy? Tossing and turning at night and going through some kind of Shakespearean 'to sleep or not to sleep' crisis, or conked out so much that you're practi-cally hibernating?"

"My appetite is almost nonexistent most of the time," Alice said. "And between the nightmares and Ellie's crying, I barely sleep at all."

"The dreams can really mess you up. Make you ques-tion reality. Your energy is gone and you're dragging your-self around with chains around your ankle. Of course all that guilt doesn't help. That endless loop of *should haves*. Difficulty concentrating, making decisions, or remem-bering things, increased irritability or anger, anxiety, rest-lessness, or agitation, social withdrawal or isolation, and thoughts of self-harm, suicide, or harming the baby in the most severe cases. Is any of this sounding familiar?

Alice blinked but managed to hold her tears. "Sounds like I am a severe case."

"Look, I get it. You're falling apart and everyone's like, 'But why? Motherhood is magical!' Trust me, if you find yourself sobbing in the shower or doubting reality, you're not alone. It's as if we're expected to be these superhuman beings that can do it all, look great, and not complain, right? There's this invisible yardstick and some days you can't even find it, let alone measure up. Has Max been supportive of you?"

"Oh, yes. Definitely." Alice gave her a vehement nod.

"I feel like there might be something you're not saying. Would you care to elaborate?"

Alice sighed, grateful for this place to make her confession. "I have the most terrible nightmares about Max."

Instead of shock, Flora laughed. "I remember those. I dreamed about killing my husband all the time. Of course, I did find out he was having an affair, so I'm sure that played into it a bit. Or a lot. Would it be weird to interrupt this therapy session and go grab a plate full of cookies?"

"It would be weirder if you didn't, now that you've offered."

Flora grinned and went to get the cookies, and before the appointment was over, she made another offer that Alice couldn't refuse, this one for samples of an antidepressant that Flora claimed had been working well for other mothers going through similar trauma as her, and was perfectly safe for nursing babies.

"Would you like to try it?" Flora asked.

"Absolutely."

"Great. I'd like to see you again on Friday just to check in and make sure the pills are working. And if they are, I'll write you a full prescription."

She felt a momentary lift in her spirits, both while leaving Flora's apartment and stepping back into her own. But the emotion was short lived.

The second they were back inside, Ellie started screaming again.

Chapter Nine

Once Ellie was quiet again, Alice wasted little time before considering one of Flora's pills.

The idea initially unsettled her, causing Alice to hesitate just long enough to feel the discomfort and recognize the emotion for what it was. To quell her emerging hunger — she felt awakened by the sugar in her cookies — she prepared a simple meal. Turkey and avocado on whole-grain bread, lightly toasted and a swipe of Dijon.

She looked down at the pill, a diminutive triangle of sea foam green. It struck her that the color was probably chosen for its calming effect, a bitter irony given that the intended recipient of such medication was often caught in the throes of emotional turmoil, trapped on a relentless seesaw between numbness and sensory overload.

Her hesitancy stemmed from a knot of conflicting feelings: the gnawing desperation for relief, the fear of unknown side effects, and the unsettling notion that ingesting it was an admission of a reality she wasn't yet ready to face. The act of reaching for the pill was a dance with surrender, each rationalization a step closer to a threshold she had been reluctant to cross, acknowledging a battle she no longer had the strength to fight alone.

But Alice's hesitance was unwarranted, because not too long after swallowing that tiny little triangle, her day got instantly better. The betterment was a slow bloom, an unfurling of the tight knot of dread within her chest, replaced by an unfamiliar lightness that seemed to lift the haze from the very air she breathed.

Even better, Ellie seemed to be picking on her better mood and responding in kind. The baby had been low energy all day but now she seemed happy just being in the same room with Mommy, and even sleeping for longer than she used to.

Even when she finally woke up after long and unbroken hours lying still in her crib, Ellie took the bottle without so much as a grunt of resistance.

Was it possible that Alice's own depression had been the cause of Ellie's constant crying?

After the bottle was finished, Ellie went right back down for another nap, giving Alice a moment to tidy up a house that didn't need cleaning because she was always there to keep it spotless even through (or even especially during) her most rotten moods.

Cleaning was almost meditative for Alice. The rhythmic swoosh of the mop across the hardwood floors, the spritz of organic cleansers, and the immediate tangible results, both cleaner surfaces and a clearer mind.

As she scrubbed the kitchen top to bottom, meticulously wiping down the stainless steel appliances and disinfecting countertops that were already perfectly clean, Alice found her gaze purposefully skirting the garbage chute — the one place she avoided touching or even looking at.

When there was nothing else to clean short of getting

on her hands and knees with a toothbrush to the grout, she texted Max, *I'm cooking dinner.*

Exciting, he texted back. *What are you making?*

It's a surprise.

She set about making dinner, fettuccine Alfredo, because why not? Max loved the dish, even though Alice usually avoided the calories. But comfort food sounded perfect tonight, so she filled a pot with water, adding a pinch of salt before setting it on the stove to boil. Minced fresh garlic and melted butter in a separate pan, slowly stirring in heavy cream. She cooked the fettuccine to al dente perfection, drained and tossed it in the creamy sauce, and finished the dish with a generous grating of Parmesan.

The table was set meticulously, including a couple of flickering candles.

When Max came home and saw the table, he gave her a smile that warmed her like a quilt. He sat down and dug in. Soon they were laughing.

"How is the deposition going?" Alice asked.

He exhaled with a gust, as if he had been waiting for her to ask. "I don't even know where to start. Everything about the Laurentian account feels like putting together a legal jigsaw puzzle. Evidentiary standards are shifting like quicksand — I swear, half the time I feel like a contortionist trying to navigate hearsay exceptions while establishing a chain of custody for those documents. We went through what felt like a merry-go-round of objections — leading the witness, relevance, you name it. It was like playing chess with someone who keeps constantly changing the rules."

Max dramatically threw his hands in the air. "No! Rooks only move diagonally right now! And no, absolutely not, under no circumstances have they ever moved in a straight line. Cherry on top? The 'fruit of the poisonous tree' argument they tried and failed to make stick. Like we didn't already go down that rabbit hole in discovery."

"Sounds complicated."

Max nodded as he hurried to swallow. "If we don't get those emails admitted into evidence, it could torpedo our case. But to do that, we'll need to leap through about seven different legal hoops."

"At least there aren't eight." She smiled.

"Douglas invited us to his house for dinner on Friday."

Instant panic turned the pasta into lead in her stomach. "This Friday?"

"Yes," he gave her a patient smile. "This Friday. Doesn't that sound great?"

"I assume you already accepted, so it doesn't sound like I'm really getting a choice." She knew she sounded petulant, but she couldn't help it. The idea of bringing Ellie to a stranger's house for dinner — and being judged on how she was mothering her fussy child, because Ellie would no doubt scream half the evening — made her want to cry.

Apparently the antidepressants could only fix so much. Or maybe she hadn't been on them long enough to handle all of her anxiety.

"Do you not want to go?" Max asked her.

"Did you already accept the invitation?" Alice asked back.

"The partner asks us to dinner, we go to dinner. Of course I accepted the invitation."

"I'm glad the climb is on."

"It's not just that, Alice. We both know that it would be good for us to get out and go do something social." *For once,* he didn't add.

"Dinner sounds nice," Alice pasted on a smile, trying to sound like she meant it. "What are we going to do about Ellie?"

"We can leave her at home."

"But we don't have a babysitter."

"We don't need a babysitter. Ellie will be fine."

"You must be joking with me right now." Alice couldn't believe he was suggesting this *again*, after the fight they'd had last time. "Except that you don't sound like you're joking at all. It sounds like you actually think it's a good idea for us to leave our eight-week-old infant all by herself in this house!"

By the end of her sentence, Alice was practically screaming.

"Please, you need to keep it down—"

"You need to tell me what the hell you are thinking!" Alice was just as loud but still not quite screaming.

"I'm thinking that we need to get out of this apartment—"

"I get that part! I have *no problem* understanding that part since you've been harping on it over and over and over."

"The moment you start listening to me is the moment I stop!"

"I'm always listening to you! I have no other choice but to hear everything you—"

"Maybe if you left the house, you would have the luxury of hearing other people for a change, instead of your boring old husband who exists to support you, no matter how crazy shit gets around this place."

"What's that supposed to mean?" Alice snapped, barely containing her fury, because she knew exactly what he meant. And she wanted him to say it out loud.

"If we could have the conversation, I'd tell you."

"You're being evasive and ugly."

"One of those is true." He nodded. "I would tell you which one, but then you'll just start crying that I can't get it right and that I don't know how to anticipate your needs, and it won't matter which one I choose."

"You don't have to be an asshole, Max. I said I would love to go to dinner. I'm just not going to go without a babysitter."

His silence was heavy with things unsaid after that. A curtain closing on their conversation, like the end of an uncomfortable act.

Only the sounds of their heavy breathing and the clinking of silverware punctuated the space between them like staccato notes in an unfinished symphony.

Alice's fury turned suddenly to regret. Max was being unreasonable about the sitter, but she had flown completely off the handle. Something she'd been doing a lot lately, telling herself that it was just sleep deprivation. But now that she knew it was postpartum depression, she wondered how many other fights they'd had that could've been prevented if she'd stuck to her position calmly instead of screaming at him?

It wasn't like Max could stop her from hiring a sitter, although she had no idea how she'd find one on such short notice.

She decided that she'd solve that problem tomorrow.

"Thank you for dinner." Max stood from the table, even though his plate still had plenty of food on it, and the man had an appetite like a lumberjack after a double shift.

"Where are you going? I made dessert."

"I'll have my dessert tomorrow. It's been a long day, and tomorrow promises to be an even longer one, so I'm going to bed."

"I'll join you in bed," Alice suggested, her voice tinged with a desperate hope to redeem the fractured evening, which had splintered in myriad ways she couldn't quite understand, but somehow all felt like her fault.

"You do whatever you want," Max said and started toward the bedroom.

Alice tidied the kitchen with a mechanical efficiency, her movements dictated more by muscle memory than conscious thought. Once the last dish was placed in the rack to dry, she wandered into the bedroom, her ears catching the sound of water shutting off from the en suite bathroom.

Max emerged, donned only in his boxers, damp hair clinging to his forehead. He acknowledged her with a perfunctory nod before slipping between the cool sheets and turning away from her.

She felt like she should apologize, but she couldn't quite bring herself to do it. Not when he was making such a big deal of giving her the cold shoulder.

So she stripped and stepped into the shower. Hot water sluiced over her, but did little to wash away the residue of tension. She stood there longer than necessary, caught in the gridlock of her thoughts.

By the time she returned to the bedroom, Max seemed to be deep in slumber — or a convincing imitation of it. Alice couldn't tell, and maybe that was the worst part.

She eased into bed beside him with a sigh.

Alice willed herself to surrender, but sleep was elusive for hours. It was still too early. She should have stayed up, and would have if she'd known that things would end up this way, with Max going to bed angry and now snoring right next to her.

She was finally dozing when she heard the sound of a scream — a lance of sound, tearing through the fabric of the night, a visceral cry that pulled her from the brink of sleep into the sharp claws of terror.

Not Ellie. A woman's scream.

Alice bolted from the bed, her feet barely touching the

floor as she lunged for the door. But then her eyes darted to the window and she saw it was wide open. A fleeting sense of relief washed over her — someone must have screamed from outside.

She shut the window and killed the distant hum of street noise. But as the ambient sounds faded, there seemed to be even more aural space for the followup scream that sounded even more blood curdling than the one Alice had heard just moments before.

Creeping out of the bedroom and into the dimly lit hallway, she strained to hear anything that might give her a clue. Silence was her only answer.

After making her way to the nursery, she found Ellie sleeping peacefully in her crib, blissfully unaware of any disturbance.

But then a new sound filled her ears: a slow, grating drag, as if something — or someone — were being pulled across the floor.

Her pulse quickened as she followed the unnerving noise, her path leading her toward the living room.

She entered to a scene she could never unsee: Max dragging a strange woman across the room. She had a thick cord wrapped around her discolored neck, and her eyes looked just as dead as the rest of her.

Chapter Ten

ALICE WASN'T sure if the sound that escaped her was a barely-audible whimper or a figment of her overwrought imagination. Yet something — perhaps a shuffle of her foot or an unintentional murmur — caused Max to abruptly halt and reel his gaze around toward her. In the electric silence that followed, every instinct screamed that the life she knew was fracturing before her eyes, each second stretching into an eternity of dread.

Their eyes locked in a charged standoff, time freezing before reality snapped back with the ferocity of a ruptured dam.

Her thoughts exploded in a flash of primal urgency: *run or die.*

Alice whirled around and sprinted out of the living room.

She sucked in courage as if it were the air she breathed, exhaling fear like carbon dioxide from inside her, each heartbeat a drumbeat propelling her forward, every breath a mantra of survival as the nightmare of her reality chased her heels.

The jarring thud of the lifeless woman's body colliding with her otherwise-pristine living room floor was eclipsed by the staccato patter of Max in hot pursuit.

Alice darted into the nursery, slamming the door behind her with a force that reverberated through the room.

Swiftly crossing to the rocking chair, she gripped its armrests and yanked it across the floor, wedging it under the door handle with frenzied strength.

A split second after she barricaded the door, Max slammed into the other side of it, trying to force it open but meeting her resistance. The door became a bulwark between life and an abyss, his hammering fists the harbingers of a threat that had once pledged to protect and cherish her.

He pounded against the solid wood in rising fury, his shouts ricocheting through the tense air. "Open this door, Alice!"

His voice, usually soothing, was an open wound of desperation and rage.

"YOU DON'T KNOW WHAT YOU JUST SAW!"

Maybe. But maybe Alice was married to a liar. If this was another one of her nightmares, then so be it. She would wake up and it would be over. But right now, she was clinging to a life that Max would take away from her, if only to bury his crime.

And yet, doubt percolated through her thoughts. What *had* she actually seen?

The abrupt cessation of his pounding caused a swell of panic to rise sharply in her chest. The deadening silence that followed was more terrifying than his shouts or deafening thumps against the door could ever be.

What was he doing? Had he left? She rose from her perch near the chair, bracing herself in case he suddenly burst through the door. But her ears picked up the muffled sound of footsteps padding toward the fire door that led to the hallway outside the penthouse.

She darted across the nursery to secure it, fingers fumbling over the lock in haste.

She heard his steps stall on the other side of that steel-reinforced barricade and a sigh of relief whistled past her lips.

But her reprieve was fleeting. The rocking chair was a makeshift solution compared to the fortification of that fire door. So without wasting another second, Alice sprinted back into the bedroom and over to the nightstand where she snatched her phone without so much as glancing at the screen.

The bedroom was a dead end, and lingering was a luxury she couldn't afford.

She dashed back to the nursery, fueled by adrenaline as the rapid thumping of Max's footsteps echoed behind her. She wrestled the rocking chair back into its barricading position against the door, then went to scoop Ellie out of her crib, swaddling her in a blanket and then into her arms in a single fluid motion.

Then she hurried through the fire door. Once on the other side, her breaths came out in sharp cries, escalating in volume as she bolted down the corridor toward Flora's apartment.

"Flora, open up! It's Alice! Open the door — MAX IS AFTER ME!"

Her fist collided with the door in a drumbeat of desperate urgency. Max would be rounding the corner into the hallway any second, and if he was bent on erasing all witnesses to his murder, neither she nor Flora would stand a chance.

Alice grasped the doorknob expecting resistance, and was stunned to find it swinging open.

She slipped inside, locking it behind her with a reflexive snap as Flora emerged from her bedroom, her eyes widening in a cocktail of disbelief and alarm.

"Max just killed someone!" The words tumbled from her lips, heavy with the gravity of their meaning, each syllable a plea for Flora to believe her. "You need to call the police — NOW!"

"Dear," Flora said in an insulting possible tone that made Alice want to leap across the room and throttle the woman. "Did you take the medication that I gave you?"

"Max killed someone!" Alice's roar was tinged with an imploring ferocity. "Call the police, Flora. NOW!"

But it was Max's relentless pounding onf Flora's front door as Max tried to beat his way inside that triggered something in Flora. She darted back into her bedroom, presumably to get her phone. Or maybe a gun.

Alice hugged Ellie closer to her chest, her heartbeat a drum line of anxiety as Flora came back out, already on the phone with 911.

Max's voice filtered through the door, a melodic veneer barely masking his threat. "Open this door, Alice! We can talk this through."

Flora finished her call, but kept 911 on the line as she pressed her body against the door beside Alice.

"Do you think he'll break in?" Alice whispered in a dread-soaked voice.

Flora's eyes met her eyes with a defiant spark. "You'd know better about the strength of this door than I would, dear. But even if he manages to get inside, only over my dead body is that asshole getting anywhere near you."

Chapter Eleven

A HIGH-PITCHED SIREN sliced through the air, its distant wail growing increasingly more defined. The banging stopped and Max went silent, leaving behind a deceptive calm.

Tension in the room seemed to loosen a fraction, like a clenched fist finally uncurling. Flora cast a knowing glance at Alice before stepping out onto her balcony. Leaning over the iron railing, her eyes narrowed as she scanned the scene below.

Moments passed like hours, each one weighted with a gnawing uncertainty, until Flora straightened up and looked back at Alice with a nod. "They're here."

She followed Flora reluctantly into the hall. Her grip on Ellie tightened, as if she could shield her infant from the unknown simply by holding her closer.

The elevator hummed, then dinged upon arrival.

Two officers stepped out of the elevator in unison, their eyes scanning the scene before settling on Flora and Alice. The first man was slightly taller with a rugged face, his hair a blend of charcoal and snow. His partner carried the gleam of relative inexperience.

"We received a call about a disturbance here," said the elder officer: *Brody*, according to his name plate. "Was it either of you two who reported it?"

"Yes, officer. I'm the one who called. This is my neighbor, Alice. She woke me up, pounding on my door in a terrible state, and—"

"Can you explain what happened, ma'am?" Brody cut her off.

"I'm trying." A terse smile. "Alice was screaming that her husband has killed someone."

"Killed someone?" the kid (Lemmon) repeated "Do you know who the victim might be, ma'am?"

"I — I don't know who she was."

"But we heard him, officer," Flora interjected. "He was banging on my door, shouting, trying to get in."

"Do you know where he is now?"

"He was right outside my door until the sirens started." Flora nodded at Alice's apartment. "I assume he's in his place now, if he hasn't fled."

The officers traded a glance, then they started toward the door.

"Stay here," Lemmon said. "We'll check it out."

The officers crossed the hallway and knocked on the door.

Moments that felt like lifetimes passed until the door swung open to Max standing there, looking both baffled and surprised.

The officers faced Max, authority against domesticity.

"Sir, we received a call that there's been a possible homicide here," Brody said. "Is anyone else in the apartment with you?"

Max looked past the officers to his wife standing in the hallway. "What are you doing out there, Alice?"

"You know what I'm—" she started to yell, before Lemmon reeled around and silenced her with a vigilant shake of his head.

"Is anyone else in the apartment with you, sir?" Brody repeated his question.

Max nodded at Alice. "Not if she's out there. Definitely not."

"Would you mind if we came in and took a look around?"

"By all means." He stepped back and opened his door all the way.

Alice started toward it, but Max slipped inside behind the officers, then closed it before she got there.

Flora put a hand on her arm. "It's fine. They would have told you to stay out here anyway."

Alice paced, clutching Ellie so tightly to her chest that the infant let out a tiny mewl of discomfort. Alice relaxed her grip as time continued to crawl, until the officers both finally reemerged with unreadable expressions.

"Ma'am, could you please show us exactly where it is you saw this body?" Brody sounded detached. Almost bored.

Alice froze at the thought of returning to that nightmarish scene.

"I'll go with you." Flora put a hand on her arm again. "And both of these officers will be with us. Everything will be fine."

Alice looked from Flora to the officers and back before offering everyone a cautious nod. Then she reluctantly entered her own apartment, eyes darting over to Max, standing there unrestrained instead of arrested for murder like he should have been.

Their eyes met and she expected to see the fire of accusation, but instead she saw the embers of something much softer. Exhaustion or sorrow. Like the world had abruptly shaken him awake from a deeply troubled sleep. Under other circumstances Alice might have found his expression heartbreaking. Right now, it infuriated her.

"Ma'am," Brody prompted her.

She gestured shakily toward the living room, her eyes widening as they swept across the space to see that the horror she had left behind was nowhere to be found. The room was vacant, scrubbed clean of the unthinkable ordeal she had witnessed. Not a surprise really, since the cops clearly didn't believe her. But how had he cleaned up so goddamned fast?

The cops were apparently wondering the same thing, trading a glance before turning back to look at Alice expectantly. The room filled with a coiling tension.

She squeezed Ellie tighter.

"Ma'am." Lemmon that time.

"She was right there." Alice pointed to an empty spot on the floor. "I swear."

Brody's eyebrows lifted incrementally, his skepticism muffled by professional restraint. "We've conducted a thorough search of your apartment. There is no body here, no signs of a struggle, or any kind of disturbance that we can—"

"I saw her! Right there, on the floor. Blood was—"

"Officers, I'm at a loss for her claims," Max interjected, his voice as smooth as polished stone. "Feel free to give the apartment another search if you'd like."

Brody exchanged a glance with Lemmon, conferring through the unspoken language of shared shifts and responsibilities.

"We'd like to take another look, if that's alright," Brody said.

Max gestured at the entire apartment. "The place is yours."

The officers moved with well-practiced efficiency. They checked under furniture, opened closets, peered under beds, their eyes scouring every inch of the living area.

Max slid open the glass door and invited them out onto the balcony.

They swept their gazes across the space. Brody leaned over the railing and looked down at the street below. Lemmon tapped the floor with his foot as if expecting to discover some hidden compartment, or maybe he was performing for Alice, who watched the scene from her living room sofa while sitting next to Flora and clutching her daughter tight.

Brody turned back toward Alice and Flora, his eyes meeting Alice's in a gaze that felt designed to sift her soul for fragments of truth. "Ma'am, I need to ask you some very important questions, and I would appreciate it if you could answer as candidly as possible."

Lemmon gestured to Max. "Would you mind stepping outside with me, sir?"

"Sure," Max said, his voice still disconcertingly calm.

"You claimed you saw your husband dragging a body, is that correct?" Brody asked once the door closed behind Lemmon and Max.

"Yes, officer. A woman's body."

"And did you know this woman?"

Alice shook her head. "I've never seen her before."

"And what exactly was your husband doing with the body?"

"He was — he was pulling her by the arms. Like he

was trying to move her somewhere." Her voice faltered. "Toward the kitchen. I didn't see more; I ran."

"Did you get a good look at her? Anything that could help identify her?"

Alice shook her head. "It was dark, but she had long, blonde hair and was wearing a white top with a blue skirt."

"And you think your husband killed this woman?"

"Of course I do."

"But you didn't see him do it, is that correct?" Brody asked.

"We were the only ones in the house."

"And what was he doing with this body?"

"I already told you." Now she was gritting her teeth. "He was dragging her toward the kitchen."

"Would you mind showing me?"

Alice took him to the kitchen, but of course there was no body.

"He could have put it down the trash chute, like he tried to do with the baby."

"I'm sorry?" Brody looked at her like either the situation was nuttier than he had previously realized, or she was. "Can you please repeat that?"

"My husband tried to put our baby down the trash chute."

"That baby?" Brody nodded at her.

"Yes." She nodded, clutching Ellie even tighter.

Brody probably didn't believe her. He studied Alice for another long moment before he opened the chute and peered inside. "Seems a little small for a body."

"Maybe he took it outside when I went next door."

"You mean in the hallway?" Brody didn't wait for an answer. "Why don't we check."

But of course there was no body out there either. Same

for the stairwell or the hallway on the floor below them, and the floor under that.

"And how did you get involved in all of this?" Brody asked Flora, once he and Alice were back in her living room.

"Like I told you already, Alice woke me up because she told me what she had seen. I believed her enough to call you."

"We're wasting time," Alice cut in. "Can we please go down to the basement, and check the garbage bin under the chute?"

"Fine," Brody replied in a tone suggesting that he was humoring her. "Let's check the basement."

He followed Alice and Flora into the elevator, a squeaky beast that groaned under the weight of its load. Alice clutched Ellie even tighter, the infant's face nuzzled against her mother's chest, blissfully ignorant of the surrounding drama. And surprisingly quiet.

The elevator doors opened to reveal a dimly lit basement, cluttered with old furniture and abandoned memories. They all moved toward the giant garbage bin beneath the chute. Alice couldn't start digging through it because she was holding Ellie, and Brody had a look on his face that clearly said, *You've gotta be fucking kidding me.*

"Jesus Christ." Flora huffed on her way to the garbage and started sifting through it. Until Brody begrudgingly nudged her aside.

"Officially speaking, I should be doing that." He looked into the bin. "If a body came down, surely it would be on top, not buried at the bottom."

"Someone needs to dig," Alice insisted.

Brody grumbled under his breath, then donned a pair of gloves and started digging through the garbage. The riot of odors hit her nose as he reached into the bin. A sour stench of rotting vegetables mingling with …

His gloves gripped the edges of torn plastic bags, spilling out shredded newspaper, a used diaper, and the discarded carcasses of old take-out. A cornucopia of crumpled cans and the skeletal remains of a broken chair. But no body.

When the elevator's grating screech announced their return, Alice half-expected Lemmon and Max to be gone. But they were both there, Max still disconcertingly placid, and Lemmon regarding her with a newfound wariness.

Flora broke the silence, taking Alice's hand as if to silently reassure her.

"Are you sure this wasn't one of your nightmares?" Max made it sound like a perfectly reasonable question.

"No," Alice replied with a fractional pause.

"Nightmares?" Brody repeated.

Lemmon nodded at Max and explained. "He says she's been grappling with postpartum depression. Sleepless nights, nightmares — the works."

Silence filled the hallway, but it was the kind that fell between the final tick of a bomb and its boom.

Then Max said, "Ever since Ellie died, Alice hasn't been herself."

His words fell like a guillotine, severing the last threads of her composure, a macabre revelation that turned her blood to ice and the world on its axis.

Her stomach twisted into a snarl of ice-cold apprehension.

She looked down at Ellie, then back up at Max.

"What did you say?"

Chapter Twelve

ALICE STOOD in the narrow hallway with her back pressed to the wall, as if the faded wallpaper could anchor her to reality. Max leaned against the opposite wall, arms folded, eyes dimmed with a sorrow that seemed so much older than the moment.

"I said that ever since Ellie died, you've been having nightmares."

"What are you talking about, Max?" She looked down again at Ellie, swaddled in her arms. "You're talking about Samuel, and he died over two years ago."

Max pushed off the wall and took a cautious step toward Alice, his eyes meeting hers in a collision of manufactured grief.

"Yes, Samuel died …" His voice was so gentle. "But so did Ellie."

"No!" Alice shook her head violently back and forth. "That's not true! I'm holding our baby right now!"

A sickening silence filled the air in the second after Alice finished screaming her claim, like the hallway swallowed all sound beyond that of her own ragged breathing.

That he would dare to say Ellie was dead, when she was right here in front of him, was staggering.

Brody raised a hand to silence the escalating dispute. "What's this about dead babies?"

"Our son Samuel was stillborn. Ellie, our daughter, died shortly after she was born," Max explained with a performative sorrow that seemed to claw at the walls of the narrow hallway.

"You're lying!" Alice's shout was a fortress of denial, a vehement rebuke to the siege of his words. "Anyone can see that I'm holding her right now!"

Brody and Lemmon traded a look, visibly disoriented by her vehement claim.

"After Samuel, Alice tried to take her own life," Max continued with his lips pressed together. "She started spiraling out of control again when we lost Ellie. Melinda, our grief counselor, recommended one of those lifelike newborn dolls to help her cope. She said it would be thera-peutic. We talked it out and agreed that to try–"

"HOW DARE YOU?" Alice thundered, lurching toward Max until Lemmon stepped in between them.

Brody raised his hands again and spoke in a cautious voice. "May we see Ellie?"

Alice hesitantly pulled the blanket away from her daughter.

Then everyone was staring at the exposed face of eerily-lifelike skin, plastic but mimicking the peachy hue of an infant, with finely painted details like faint eyebrows and wisps of hair.

"That is …"

"Incredibly realistic," Brody finished for his partner.

"This isn't Ellie! WHERE'S MY BABY?" Her voice climbed into a desperate pitch.

Max took a slow step toward her, reaching out to touch her hand. "Ellie is—"

Alice recoiled as if his knuckles were molten.

She bolted away from Max and the cops, rushing back into the apartment and not stopping until she burst into the nursery.

But there were paint cans and brushes strewn about the floor instead of a crib. The wall was half-painted in the blue of a midwinter sky as if abandoned midway through a major renovation. Exposed electrical outlets had exposed wires, as if awaiting for fixtures that never arrived. A stack of boxes lay stacked against an empty wall.

She bolted out of the room and out of the apartment, then into Flora's living room, looking everywhere for Ellie — surely this was where she left her.

"Ellie! Ellie! ELLIE!" Alice shrieked.

Nothing. No sighs or gurgles or screams.

Her lungs felt like they were contracting as she sprinted back into her own apartment and made a beeline for the kitchen.

"Of course I have a fucking baby!" Alice was practically growling as she wrenched open the refrigerator door. She rummaged through the shelves but couldn't find even one of her many prepared bottles of milk. "No, no, no…"

She slammed the fridge door and yanked open the freezer. But all she found were bags of frozen vegetables and ice trays.

She sprinted to the entryway, where the officers, Flora, and Max were all standing idle, obviously waiting for her insanity to wind down. But now she could prove it. He'd forgotten something.

Alice pointed at the stroller in accusation. "Why would we have a stroller if we didn't have a baby?"

But the stroller stood as a silent witness, its unused wheels and pristine condition an indictment of the narrative she had built, a physical counterargument to her certainty.

"It's never been used, Alice." His tone was soft, and still the words were like shards of glass. "The tags are still on it."

Her gaze darted to the price tag still dangling from the handlebar.

"I haven't had the chance to take her for a walk!" But a strain of sudden self doubt had quivered into her voice.

"That's because she's not here, Alice."

"STOP SAYING THAT." Her face felt hot, veins throbbing at her temples as she turned to Flora. "You've seen her, Flora. Tell them."

She looked pained, brows furrowed as glanced at Max, then at Alice before speaking. "Sure, you brought 'Ellie' over, but honey, it was always the doll."

Alice felt a hot rush to her face, her heart pounding halfway out of her chest. "You're lying!" she yelled, spittle flying. "Why would you lie like this?"

"Alright, everyone. Let's try to keep this civil." Brody had moved from confused empathy to mounting concern.

Max looked ashen but resolved as he quietly moved to a cabinet beside the living room bookshelf, then reached inside and pulled out a neatly folded piece of paper, displaying to for everyone in the room so they could see the gold embossed seal.

He handed the document over to Alice. "It's Ellie's death certificate."

The paper felt like a tombstone in her hands, each word an epitaph for the life she'd once known, an unbearable truth written in the ink of finality.

The floor crumbled beneath her, sending Alice into a bottomless abyss of disorienting spirals. She'd changed

Ellie's diaper a few hours ago. Bottle fed her not long after that. But Max had taken her and hidden her away somewhere, so that he could subject her to this insane charade — and for what? To discredit her, so no one would believe her about the woman he'd murdered?

She dropped the document and dashed into the kitchen, throwing open the drawer full of knives. She seized one, now that they were back in the drawer (had Max really ever removed them?), her fingers trembling around the handle as she stormed back toward Max. "Where is Ellie? WHERE IS MY BABY?"

Lemmon was a lightning strike stepping in between them, his taser drawn, as Brody flanked from the other side, the pair of officers lunging forward in a ballet of precision. Their tasers clicked but remained unused, a last-resort buzzing in the air.

Lemmon swiftly twisted the knife from her unsteady grip, his own hands remarkably steady as Brody moved in tandem to secure Alice's arms behind her back.

Flora's raw scream added a ghastly chorus to the horrible orchestra.

Max's gaze flickered between Alice and the now-secured knife on the kitchen island.

The snap of handcuffs locking around her wrists resounded like a death knell as Lemmon recited her Miranda rights in a voice that was professionally detached and tragically resigned.

And just like that, her hands and reality were both irrevocably bound.

Chapter Thirteen

ALICE GLARED AT MAX, eyes spitting fire as her lips twisted into a snarl of utter disbelief. "You're supposed to be on my side! You're supposed to be family! YOU'RE HER FATHER!"

The agony in her voice felt like a cleaver, cutting through the elevator's claustrophobia. The sterile light from overhead seemed to cast their faces in eerie silhouettes. Her handcuffs clinked in jarring harmony with her husband's nervously shifting feet as he stood beside Alice, cradling her coat.

"*Please*," she implored him. "You have to take me to Ellie, Max. You have to tell me where she is. You can't do this to me. It's too cruel."

She could feel the officers exchanging glances, their disbelief coating the air, making it thick and suffocating. Her skin crawled beneath the heat of such obvious judgment.

"We're going to get you some help." Max only infuriated her further, his voice soft like a whisper and heavy as a sledgehammer.

"Help? You call this help? You're trying to erase our Ellie from existence!"

The elevator doors slid open to the opulent lobby. Late-night shadows stretched their long fingers across the marbled floor. The night doorman was sitting behind a walnut paneled desk, glancing up from his crossword puzzle at the handcuffed woman, police officers, and Max, cradling her coat like a relic.

His eyes widened in alarm, the pen slipping from his fingers to clatter onto the desk as they passed.

"SAMUEL DIED — NOT ELLIE!" Alice roared as they led her outside.

Brody turned to Max once they were standing in front of the building. "Maybe it's best if you don't come. We're taking her to Mt. Sinai."

Max reluctantly relinquished his grip on her coat and handed it to the officers. Then he took a step toward Alice, his face a mosaic of sorrow and regret, opening his mouth as if to say goodbye.

But she spat in his face, turning his goodbye into a strangled gasp.

The car ride to Mt. Sinai was a cacophony of her screams, a torrent of sound that seemed to vibrate through her entire being. Every cell in her body resisted the ride back to a place she couldn't stand the thought of ever seeing again.

"I don't want to go back there!" Alice continued to wail, her voice hoarse but unbroken, until she could only rasp and think the same thing on repeat.

I don't want to go back, I don't want to go back, I don't want to go back …

• • •

ALICE SITS *on the examination table in a sterile OBGYN examination room with her legs dangling over the edge. Her body feels almost as cold and lifeless as the room itself.*

Max stands beside her, his eyes constantly shifting between her and the floor. He's wearing a wrinkled button-up shirt and jeans, looking both out-of-place and uncomfortably at home in this setting.

Alice is a swirl of emotions: hope, fear, and a vulnerability that she can't seem to shake. Her knuckles are white where she clenches the table, eyes flickering between her husband and the door.

Dr. Kapoor enters the room, her face professional but tinged with an empathetic warmth that stops just short of her eyes. Mid-40s, with her pure black hair pulled back into a tight bun. Surely she dyes it, Alice thinks The extra dark hair makes her white coat seem that much whiter, amplifying her aura of clinical efficiency.

"How are we doing?" Kapoor sees the look on her face and adds, "Tell me what's on your mind."

"I haven't felt the baby move in two days," Alice confesses in a quivering voice.

Kapoor's eyes are empathetic, but Max cuts in before she can respond.

"Maybe it's just your imagination. You've always been a bit anxious." His voice is tinged with hope as he tries to reassure her, but that does nothing to quell her disquiet.

"Let's see what we can find." Kapoor gives Alice a smile, then wheels herself over to the ultrasound machine.

She squeezes the cold gel onto Alice's abdomen, spreading it evenly with her hand. Then she picks up the wand and starts the ultrasound, her eyes narrowing as she scrutinizes the screen.

Tension in the room gathers around Alice like a suffocating fog.

Each second that ticks by feels longer than the last, each moment stretching into an unbearable eternity. Kapoor's expression decays into something more serious, each line and furrow on her face deepening as she moves the wand across Alice's belly.

And then, with a finality that chills the room, she puts the wand down and switches off the machine.

The silence that follows is both empty and full, devoid of sound but bursting with unspoken despair.

Alice knows before a word is said that this devastating news might very well destroy her from the inside out.

ALICE LAY IN A BED, her eyes tracing the sterile white ceiling like it might promise an escape route. The chaos of the adult psychiatric ward unfolded around her, a cacophony of disjointed voices amid the metallic clanging of doors, an unsettling arrangement of sounds that rattled the already-frayed nerves inside her as each one of her awful thought spiraling into the next to find something even worse.

This place felt like a maze with no exit.

The psychiatric nurses moved with clinical detachment, faces an indistinguishable blur behind layers of professional composure. A woman muttered incessantly to herself in the bed next to Alice.

The memories wouldn't stop coming.

MAX WHEELS ALICE OUT *of the hospital, the sterile atmosphere clinging to them like an unwelcome shroud.*

She should be cradling a baby in her arms, swaddled in hospital linens, but her arms hang limp, her lap empty. Her face is stricken, a canvas painted in shades of unbearable loss.

The taxi ride home is suffused with a silence so thick, it's almost a physical presence between them.

They pass Rory, the doorman, who wears an expression of profound sadness; Max has obviously already shared the devastating news.

The elevator emits an anguished squeal as it carries them up.

Max tentatively reaches for her arm as they step out into the hall-way, but she jerks away, an electric charge of grief separating them.

She makes her way to the nursery with the heaviest steps of her life until she opens the door. A sanctuary painted in light blue, a crib standing in quiet anticipation, all of it now the most unbearable of sights.

Her legs give way, and she collapses.

Her sobs are like thunderclaps in the painfully-still room.

And then Max is there, no words or attempts at consolation. Only tears as he cries alongside her, two souls adrift in an ocean of sorrow, clinging to each other as if they could somehow sob their way back to the life they'd just lost.

ALICE SAT in a chair in an examination room, her fingers tightly gripping the edges as her entire being filled with the most witheringly terrible sense of déjà vu.

At least the wait wasn't long before a doctor entered. He was middle-aged with graying hair, and his expression said he would rather be anywhere other than here. Alice felt a knot of anxiety tighten in her stomach when he barely looked at her. Her knuckles whitened on the armrests.

"How are you doing today, Alice?" He set his clipboard on the counter next to the examination chair. "I'm Dr. Rufus."

"Is that your first name or your last name?"

"It's my first name." His smile looked tired as he repeated his question. "How are you doing today, Alice?"

"Fine." The word was a shard of glass on her tongue.

"It appears that you're not fine." He nodded at her chart. "I see that you've lost two babies."

A knot of anguish coiled into the pit of her stomach.

Alice didn't want to talk about the ghost that haunted her womb, or the lie that Max was trying to shove down her throat.

"I want to know where my Ellie is. What did Max do with her?"

"Is this the Max you think killed a woman?"

Alice didn't answer him; his tone made it clear that he thought she was crazy.

"Your husband told me about some of your nightmares recently."

Alice held her silence.

"Your baby turning into an owl." Still nothing. "You throwing a baby over the side of a building." Another pause with no response. "You drowning–"

"STOP. Please." She took a breath. "Those were only nightmares."

"And what you saw tonight wasn't?"

"That's correct." And how dare he with that tone?

"How do you know that for sure?"

"I just *know.*"

"Is it possible that you have only been dreaming that your daughter is alive?"

Alice looked at Dr. Rufus, her eyes narrowing. "You think I can't tell the difference between a dream and reality?"

"Sometimes the mind is powerful enough to blur those lines, especially under emotional stress."

Alice clenched her fists. "I held Ellie in my arms. I heard her cries. I felt her warmth. You're telling me that was a figment of my imagination?"

"Have you ever experienced dreams so vivid you swore they were real? Sleep disorders, lucid dreaming, or night terrors?"

She shook her head, feeling cornered. "No. But–"

"You've been under a great deal of stress recently. You've also been prescribed medications that can alter perception."

"That was for the postpartum."

"How can you be sure that your emotional state, potentially coupled with medication, isn't creating a scenario where you're starting to believe your nightmares — or dreams — are a reality?"

Alice felt the ground shift beneath her as a seed of doubt was planted, nurtured by the doctor's clinical reasoning, growing rapidly in the fertile soil of her fractured emotional state. She had never taken antidepressants before, she had no idea what effect they might have, especially on someone who was chronically sleep-deprived.

And the sleepwalking. She'd woken up in the kitchen, terrified that she'd been the one about to throw Ellie down the trash chute.

"Is it possible," he persisted gently, "that what you experienced tonight might have been a vivid, emotionally charged nightmare?"

Maybe, she didn't want to say.

"Why would I do that? Why would I want to make something like that up?"

Rufus softly sighed. "I don't think you're making anything up intentionally, Alice. The human mind is a complex mechanism, and it has its ways of coping. When you're stressed, especially when you're sleep-deprived, it starts to behave in unpredictable ways. It can make the implausible seem plausible, the unreal seem real. The best prescription I could possibly give you is to get some rest."

"I don't want to sleep." Alice shook her head. "I *can't* sleep."

"Because of the nightmares?"

Alice swallowed as she nodded, feeling uncomfortably vulnerable. "Yes."

Rufus scribbled something on a prescription pad then handed her the slip after tearing it off. "I'm prescribing you Sertraline. It's an SSRI — Selective Serotonin Reuptake Inhibitor. It should help balance the neurotransmitters in your brain, which can improve your mood and potentially help with sleep."

"And if it doesn't?" There was a tremor of desperation in her voice.

"Then we revisit and evaluate. We can adjust the treatment as needed. Psychological conditions aren't straightforward; they require fine-tuning and ongoing assessment."

Alice stared at the piece of paper he held out to her. She'd never taken anything more than an antibiotic or an ibuprofen before, and this was the second antidepressant she'd been offered in a week. But this wasn't Flora — a woman she'd just met and who apparently was willing to lie about Ellie, for some reason. This was a doctor at a prestigious medical institution, who regularly treated people for mental health issues. And he hadn't told her she was delusional or tried to convince her that her daughter was dead.

In fact, he seemed to think she might be fine once she'd gotten some sleep.

Reluctantly, she took the prescription, folding the small paper and tucking it into her pocket. "When can I go home?"

"The nurse will bring you a dose in a little while, and you'll be released tomorrow. Just being in a different environment might be exactly what you need to get a good night's sleep."

Alice thanked the doctor then went back to her bed, laying down and staring at the ceiling tiles as if they might unveil an answer, wishing she could stop craving oblivion as she waged a war on sleep, knowing that once it finally came to claim her, she would be dragged back into the past and ripped to shreds by the haunting.

But when the nurse came by with the little yellow pill, she took it.

Chapter Fourteen

A*LICE* *STANDS* on the edge of the balcony, her heels precariously aligned with the drop into the void below, her frame starkly outlined against the diminishing dusk.

She is the very silhouette of vulnerability and desolation.

Max approaches, his every step heavy with apprehension. The busy city below — a blend of construction equipment, honking horns, and screeching tires — nearly drowns him out.

"What are you doing?" His words are tinged with a fear he cannot fully cloak.

Alice ignores him, clutching a tiny blue onesie to her chest, the fabric embroidered with miniature sailboats. She had chosen it with such care, envisioning the day she would wrap her newborn son in it, taking him home from the hospital to start their new life together.

But now, that onesie serves as a painful reminder of a future that will never be—Samuel is never coming home.

Guilt metastasizes through her conscience, like a relentless tumor.

This is her fault; it must be.

She should have prioritized the life inside her instead of booking more clients.

She should have eaten more leafy greens, consumed more prenatal vitamins, had more protein-rich meals.

She should have never had that sip of champagne at Arial's wedding.

She should have done more prenatal yoga; three classes was not enough.

She should not have failed to interpret the significance of a fleeting abdominal pain.

She should not have been trivializing stress.

"Alice, for God's sake, come down!" His pleas intensify into near-begging.

But Alice doesn't want to come down.

Not when the thought of tipping forward is so appealing, crossing that boundary into free fall and promising to relieve her of her crushing emotional burden.

Her eyes lift toward the twilight sky, seeking answers or, perhaps, oblivion.

A great horned owl glides overhead, its wings expansive against the dusky heavens.

For a suspended moment, their eyes lock.

Max seizes the moment of her distraction to grab Alice, pulling her forcefully back across the railing and away from the waiting abyss.

An insidious crack has now chinked into the edifice of their marriage. An imperceptible fissure at first, it had since spread, webbing across the fragile facade of their union with the inexorable spread of ice on glass.

And it had stayed there ever since.

WHEN ALICE WOKE, she didn't feel better so much as blurrier. It was hard to think through the fog in her head, and everything seemed to be moving faster than normal around her, as if she were stuck in slow motion. She would've given anything for an espresso and a hot shower, but instead, she was offered weak coffee and a cold bagel. She sat in a corner of the dining room, staring out the window at the hospital parking lot in a daze, contemplating her options.

Dr. Rufus had said she'd be released today, but she had no doubt that there would be hoops to jump through. Would it be better to stay rational but insist that Ellie hadn't died, even though she couldn't explain why Max and Flora would lie? Probably not, even though it would make her feel better to have someone on her side. Max's story was much more believable to someone who hadn't held Ellie in their arms just yesterday and fed her to stop her screams.

The idea that she could've hallucinated that was laughable — except that she might have hallucinated Max trying to throw Ellie down the garbage chute. She might have been the one throwing Ellie away, sleepwalking through a nightmare. And if it was possible she'd hallucinated that… maybe it was possible that she'd also hallucinated the past three months of being awakened by her daughter's screams.

Maybe that was why Ellie wouldn't latch no matter what Alice tried, because she was really a doll and Alice had been sleepwalking then too. The doll she'd been carrying around — the doll she thought Max had replaced Ellie with — could be bottle-fed, it had been designed for that. But where would the milk go? Was she also hallucinating the bottles becoming empty? And what had happened to all of the breast milk that she'd been expressing and storing in the fridge — had Max been throwing it away all this time?

She shook her head, struggling to think through the antidepressant haze. She remembered washing out bottles and changing diapers and rocking Ellie for hours while she howled. She would've had to be sleepwalking during the day too, wouldn't she? Or was she confusing nightmares and memories?

When a nurse summoned her to speak with a new doctor — Dr. Rufus' shift had ended at some point while she was sleeping — Alice still wasn't sure what was real and what wasn't.

"I'm Dr. Kynard," he said crisply, gesturing for her to take a seat, "and I'll be evaluating you for release, assuming that you feel ready to go home today."

"I'm ready," Alice said as she sat, even though she wasn't sure she felt ready at all. Because even if the doctor believed her, what was she going to do about Max? And how was she going to stand being in that apartment without Ellie?

"It seems you had an eventful night before you were admitted. Want to tell me what happened?"

I saw my husband murder a strange woman, then he replaced my baby with a doll, removed all evidence that she existed, and repainted the nursery while I waited for the police to show up and do nothing.

It sounded crazy to her, and she couldn't explain how Max could've done any of it in the time she'd been in Flora's apartment. If she told this doctor her version of events, would he refuse to release her? Or would he decide she'd had a psychotic break and give her drugs that made it even harder to think?

Maybe it would be better to focus his evaluation on physical symptoms and see if he could help her figure out how to clear her head. If she could just think straight, she could figure this out, she was sure of it.

"I've been having a lot of nightmares, and I'm not sure, but I might have sleepwalked once or twice," she admitted. "Sleep deprivation can do that to you, right?"

But instead of answering her question, he asked, "Why do you think you haven't been sleeping?"

Was that a trap? If she claimed it was Ellie keeping her up, would that confirm she was crazy?

"I'm not sure, it might just be the nightmares."

"Your husband said you were taking antidepressants, given to you by a neighbor?"

"She's a psychiatrist," Alice said quickly, less to defend Flora and more annoyed that Max had given the impression that she'd just taken a random pill from a stranger. "I'd just started seeing her yesterday. She thought my nightmares might be a symptom of postpartum depression."

"Hmmm." Dr. Kynard stared down at her file for a long moment, and she wondered what it said, if he was reading or just avoiding eye contact. "Have you ever hurt yourself or someone else while sleepwalking?"

"No," she lied, but she flushed a little as she thought about slashing at Max with a knife. She wondered if Max had mentioned that. And if he hadn't, did it mean that she'd dreamed that too?

She wished she could snatch the file off his desk and see what lies her husband might have told about her after she'd been admitted.

Then she wondered if Max had been telling the truth and she was losing her mind.

No, she refused to accept that, because it would mean Ellie was dead.

How could both of her babies be dead?

"Do you have any thoughts of harming yourself?" Dr. Kynard asked.

"No." That was true.

"How about thoughts of harming others?"

She thought again of Max's bleeding forearms and the

look of fury on his face when she had (maybe) attacked him with the knife. What if she did it again, or something worse, the next time she had a nightmare?

"No, I don't want to hurt anyone else," Alice lied, because how else was she going to get out of here and find the truth? "I'm just tired. I want to go home and sleep in my own bed. And if… is there anything you can give me to stop the sleepwalking?"

"Benzodiazepenes like Klonopin and Valium can reduce sleepwalking episodes. But they're potentially addictive and have more serious side effects than the antidepressant that you were given last night. How long have you been sleepwalking?"

"I'm not sure, maybe just once or twice." Or maybe nightly for the last three months, if what Max was saying was true. Which, she had to admit, was the more believable explanation.

"Why don't we see if antidepressants help, and if you're still sleepwalking in a month, or if the incidents become dangerous, talk to your regular therapist." He glanced down at her file again, then added: "Dr. Williams, right?"

She gritted her teeth and nodded. Of course Max had told them Dr. Williams was her therapist; he'd been pressuring her to go back to him for months. No point in arguing, because she wasn't going to say that Flora was her therapist — not after the woman had betrayed her — and she was afraid that if she said she didn't have a therapist, he might not be comfortable letting her go.

And she had to get out of here if she wanted to find the truth about her daughter.

. . .

ALICE WAS RELEASED from the hospital as the sun descended toward the horizon.

Max was waiting for her in the antiseptic smelling lobby, alone, with his face a mask of restrained emotion. Was this concerned, supportive Max, who did everything he could to help her when she was struggling? Or was it the psychopath Max of her nightmares who wanted to throw her baby down the trash chute?

Was it more believable that the man she'd married had become nightmare Max, or that she'd lost her mind after her second baby had died?

She wanted to shy away from the obvious answer.

"Where's Ellie?" Her eyes searched his for a clue to the answer she dreaded.

He hesitated, averting his eyes before replying. "She's at home."

So this was nightmare Max, who wanted Alice to believe that she'd been trying to breastfeed a doll for the last three months. Or was he supportive Max, who was trying to help her through a psychotic break?

A hollow feeling overcame Alice; words failed her. What if she really was crazy?

"I know you're on edge. It's been an incredibly difficult time for you." Max reached out to pull Alice into the comfort of his hug.

But she shrank from his touch, an involuntary recoil from the man whose motives had become increasingly unclear to her.

Max seemed to understand, or at least he didn't press her, instead pulling out his phone to book them an Uber.

Georgina, a woman with a receding hairline and a soft paunch, greeted them with a courteous nod but little fanfare. They climbed into the backseat and were greeted by the reek of a dangling air freshener blending in with the faint odor of fast food.

Georgina tried to initiate some light conversation, but got the silent mood fast.

Alice stared out at the trees whizzing by her window. What would she find when she got home — the nursery she remembered decorating, with the rocking chair and the white crib, or the partially-repainted room littered with boxes?

Back inside their apartment, her disquiet only deepened as she gazed into the living room at the spot where she had a waking nightmare with her husband dragging a dead body across her floor. She could see the dead woman so clearly in her mind's eye. How could he have removed all traces of the murder so quickly and so completely?

The simplest answer was that he hadn't, she'd hallucinated the whole thing.

The memories swirled in a fog, edges blurring, details smudging.

It had felt *so real*. But wasn't that the point if her own disordered emotions or a side effect of the antidepressant Flora gave her had put a hallucination in front of her? Alice had never suffered from them before, so maybe hallucinations felt a lot more real than dreams.

She supposed that made sense, even as unsettling as the thought felt while it clawed at her. Because the difference between her recent life and a nightmare was like the difference between her penthouse on fire and a burning candle added to the existing inferno.

She ventured into the nursery and was instantly confronted by the room's unfinished state, walls half-painted in a blue that was now grotesquely inappropriate. The absence of her crib and rocking chair was a gaping wound. Each missing piece was a stolen memory, the hollowed out space a mausoleum for maternal hopes and whispered lullabies.

"Where's Ellie?" she asked, not even realizing that Max had entered the room until she heard him make a noise behind her.

She turned around and saw his eyes clouded with reluctance.

"Where is she?" Alice repeated.

Max moved to the closet with a nod, then reached for a bag on the highest shelf. He unzipped the bag, took out the lifeless doll, and handed it over to Alice.

"Isn't it time you gave this up?"

She cradled the doll in her arms and stared into its unchanging face. It wasn't warm like Ellie had been, and it didn't squirm in her arms like Ellie had. Alice wished she could will the inanimate thing into life, but this wasn't a fairytale.

"I'm going to bed," he said. "You should try to get some sleep too."

Max left the nursery.

But sleep was the furthest thing from Alice's mind. Her breasts ached, swollen with milk meant for a child she couldn't feed. Why was she still making milk if Ellie had died months ago? Maybe the breast pump was tricking her body into thinking that she was nursing?

If that was true, she should stop using it.

Except, what if she found out that Ellie was still alive, and she could no longer feed her? Was using the pump an act of insanity or an act of hope?

She sat on her beautiful sofa alone in the living room and proceeded to express the milk. The mechanical act felt alien to her, a mockery of the maternal act.

She was stuck on the precipice of an abyss she couldn't fathom, let alone cross.

Even though she had been here before.

ALICE OCCUPIES *the cushioned seat next to Max, feeling the heavy atmosphere in Dr. Williams's therapy office close in around her.*

Williams, an older white man with a silver beard, peers over his wireframe glasses as if scrutinizing a perplexing case study rather than a grieving human being.

"It's been nine months since the incident, Alice," he begins, shuffling papers on his desk as if they had insight into her soul. "And it seems you haven't made much headway in coping with your grief. Have you considered applying more effort?"

Effort? Alice feels like she's been shattered into infinite pieces, each shard straining for reassembly. She can't help but break down, tears cascading down her cheeks as she mutters, "I'm trying. I'm trying as hard as I can."

"But you're lacking family support, aren't you?" Williams presses, seemingly oblivious to the invisible weight compressing her chest, tighter by the breath.

She bites her lip, unwilling to divulge the fractured relationship with her parents.

Her eyes drift to Max, silently pleading for him to steer the conversation away.

"Her parents cut her off when we got married. Not just emotionally — they've withheld the family trust too. It will only go to any child we might have, bypassing Alice completely. So we've been struggling a bit financially. But that's the easy part. Alice hoped that having Samuel might somehow mend the fragmented relationship with her family. Now with him gone, even that slender thread of hope has been snipped."

"I see." Williams says.

· · ·

ALICE STOOD in front of the fridge with the bottle in her hand, caught in a momentary indecision. The thought of preserving this milk for a non-existent child struck her as self-inflicted cruelty. So with grim resolve, she walked to the sink and upended the bottle.

Milk swirled down the drain, its whiteness vanishing into the dark void of her sink.

She glanced at the trash chute, its utilitarian facade seeming almost sinister in the dim light, its maw a silent witness to her unspeakable contemplation.

An idea slowly bloomed like a dark flower in her mind.

Alice left the kitchen, her steps measured but unsteady, and returned minutes later after a trip to the room that wasn't a nursery anymore, now holding the Ellie doll, its plastic eyes devoid of the life she had so fervently wished into it. She examined it for a moment, unsure how she ever could have confused it with a real baby. Yet the hallucinations seemed so real.

She lifted the lid of the trash chute, its darkness beckoning like a gateway to some final form of release. She held the doll over the cavity, hands trembling.

Each tick of the clock was a pendulum swinging over the chasm of her decision.

Just as her fingers began to loosen their grip, ready to consign Ellie to oblivion, a cry pierced the silence. *Ellie's*.

Her heart galvanized into action and she yanked the doll back.

But the room fell oppressively quiet again.

She looked down at the doll, its lifeless visage of course unchanged.

Dolls couldn't cry.

But she had heard it, as sure as she was standing there.

Or was her mind bending reality around her emotional fragility? Again.

Alice clutched the doll to her chest.

Chapter Fifteen

Alice awoke to what sounded like flies buzzing in the ominous stillness of her apartment. *Buzz, buzz, buzz* — an incessant drone that nagged at her frayed nerves.

Buzz, buzz, buzz.

Her eyes flicked open, narrowing in concentration as she identified the sound. Not flies, but the intercom.

Max was fast asleep beside her, his breathing deep and even. Unless he was faking.

She pushed the covers aside and quietly made her way to the phone, feeling more unsettled by the step. The night watchman was an unfamiliar face; not even a blur of uniform, seeing as she barely ever made it outside, and never at night these days.

What could warrant a late-night interruption?

She lifted the intercom phone off its cradle and pressed it to her ear. *Silence.*

Annoyed, she slammed the phone back into its place and turned back toward the bedroom, cursing herself for no longer being able to parse her waking life from her dreams. She must have imagined both the buzzing flies and the intercom while sleeping, and in that order. In the claustrophobic silence that followed, each imagined buzz became a mocking chorus, resonating with the frequency of her frayed nerves.

Alice had just settled back into the sanctuary of her bed when the intercom buzzed again. This time she saw the green light mocking her as it flashed.

She rushed to the phone, irritation replacing her initial confusion.

She picked up the handset, ready to unload a verbal barrage on whoever was responsible for this annoyance, but before she could unleash her ire, the words were sliced away from her by a sound that struck her like a bolt of lightning: *Ellie's cries.*

Her heart pounded in disbelief as she pressed the phone to her ear. "ELLIE? ELLIE!"

How was it possible? Alice flew out of her apartment in a frenzy of motion, still clutching the phone like a lifeline as she tore through the living room and burst into the hallway, barefoot.

She ran to the elevator and slapped her hand against the call button.

The machinery wheezed and creaked to life, climbing to her floor in mechanical agony as Ellie's unsettling cries kept coming through the phone.

Each wail further unraveled her frayed composure.

Max came out of the apartment looking bewildered.

"Alice? Where are you going?" His concern and confusion echoed down the hall.

"*Ellie!*" she managed to gasp, her voice jagged with desperation as the elevator doors open and she darted inside.

Max strode down the hall, his eyes widening as the

elevator doors slammed shut like a final verdict before he could get there.

The car protested in a dissonant symphony of squeaks and squeals.

Like audible echoes of her confusion and dread.

The elevator doors creaked open to an immaculate yet lifeless lobby. The night doorman was sitting behind that walnut paneled desk, engrossed in watching something until he looked up and saw Alice storming out of the elevator.

His eyebrows vaulted upward in surprise and disbelief.

"Where's Ellie?" Alice demanded as she marched up to the desk. "Where is my baby?" Her voice quivered with desperate accusation and her tone alone could be counted as assault.

The doorman blinked, clearly taken aback. "Ma'am, I have no idea what you're talking about. Ellie?"

"Don't lie to me! You have her, don't you?" The acrid note of hysteria in her voice was climbing. "You took my baby!"

"Ma'am, I'm going to need you to calm down." The doorman stood and raised his hands in pacification. "I have no idea what you're talking about." He shook his head. "I've been sitting right there behind that desk all night, and I can assure you that I don't know anything about your baby. Maybe if you want to explain—"

"You know something!"

"What makes you think that, ma'am?"

"My baby called me on the intercom!"

"Your baby called you on the intercom?" the doorman repeated.

"CAN YOU NOT HEAR ME RIGHT NOW?"

"I hear you, ma'am." He nodded to prove it. "But can you tell me *how* a baby uses an intercom?"

"I heard my daughter crying!" But the sound of her daughter's wailing through the handset had gone silent. "Who else has been down here tonight?"

"No one." The doorman shook his head. "Just the usual night deliveries."

Alice glared at him, her lip trembling as she reached for the next best thing to say.

The doorman's face warred with fear and confusion, his eyes going saucer-sized as if suddenly realizing that this situation was far above his pay grade and would under no circumstances be going back down.

The air was charged, as if a single misplaced word could light another fuse.

The elevator doors dinged open again.

Alice didn't turn around to see him, but knew that Max was walking into the lobby.As his footsteps grew closer, he asked, "Alice, what's going on?"

Relief washed over the doorman's face at the sight of her husband.

"I heard Ellie on the intercom."

Max glanced at the doorman before addressing her and the *I'm sorry that my wife is totally fucking nuts* look on his face made Alice want to strangle him.

"It must have been another one of your nightmares." His voice, attempting to cloak concern with reason, was a threadbare blanket failing to warm the cold dread that had settled in her bones. Another look at the doorman, this one seemed to say, *Do you see what I have to deal with?* "She has nightmares."

"This wasn't a nightmare!"

"Then what was it?"

The doorman leaned forward, curious as any of them.

"She's down here somewhere," Alice said.

The doorman looked to Max and shook his head.

"That's not possible." Max shook his head too. "Ellie is back upstairs in our apartment."

Her entire body felt like it could exhale. Was it possible that she was finally waking up from the nightmare and that she'd heard Ellie's real cries, but been confused about where they were coming from?

Maybe she'd been sleepwalking again, and her mind had been trying to incorporate Ellie's cries into her nightmare?

"Oh …" That was all she could say.

"Apologies for the disturbance," Max said to the doorman. "I hope you have an excellent rest of your night."

There were no words exchanged on the way back up to their penthouse, but Max's mood felt like a scolding in itself, more grating than the grinding elevator as it climbed.

She followed him into the apartment, feeling a boiling anger that was probably unreasonable. Alice kept reminding herself of that as she walked through the living room — where she had probably hallucinated her husband dragging a dead body, maybe because of the antidepressant that Flora had given her — then into the nursery, where he handed her a doll.

"What are you doing?" Alice asked.

"I'm handing you Ellie."

"That's not Ellie." She was chewing on her bottom lip, feeling a surge of mounting emotions that would grind her down to powder if she let them.

"That's—"

"IT'S A DOLL!" Alice hurled the stupid thing at him.

The doll hit his body and fell to the floor with a THUD.

Alice imagined she heard Ellie crying, and she had a horrible flashback to the nightmare of waking up in the kitchen thinking that she'd almost thrown Ellie down the trash chute.

She knew damn well that the cry was her imagination this time.

But that didn't stop her from rushing over to where her Ellie had landed and scooping the baby up into her arms, rocking back and forth and clutching her close as if she were a real baby. That she could throw the doll terrified her — what if she accidentally did something like that to the real Ellie?

"I'm exhausted, and I have another long day tomorrow working on the Laurentian files." Max turned his back on her as she wept on the floor, cradling the doll. "I'm going back to bed."

Moments later she heard their bedroom close with a muted thud.

Chapter Sixteen

TENSION BETWEEN ALICE and Max was like a fog in their kitchen the next morning. The space between them crackled with the static of unsaid words, each look and movement heavy with the burden of unshared thoughts.

Max stood awkwardly in the kitchen, eyeing her like a wounded and unpredictable animal.

"I can stay home today … if you need it." He shifted his weight from one foot to the other, nervously running his fingers through coiffed morning hair.

"We both know you can't do that," Alice replied without looking up at him.

He said something else but she chose to ignore him, focusing instead on the rhythm of dripping coffee as it filled the carafe, waiting for Max to leave so she could make her phone call.

He finally walked out of the kitchen. Maybe he said goodbye.

Once she heard the definitive sound of her front door being shut, she got her phone and dialed Mt. Sinai with trembling fingers.

Three rings, then a clinical voice plunged her into a labyrinth of hold menus and extensions. Five long minutes later, she finally had another human on the line.

"Hi there. I would like to request a copy of my most recent hospital records. Am I talking to the right person?"

"Yes, ma'am. The cost for your records will be $75. And you'll need to fill out an online form."

"I can't handle this right now while I'm already on the phone with you?" Her frustration was a living thing, writhing and clawing at the bureaucratic tape that bound her to this cyclical hell.

"No, ma'am, it's all done online."

"How long will that take?"

"It's a one-week minimum for us to process your request."

"But I'm already on the phone with you. Can't I just pay right now and have you email them to me? This is urgent."

"Matters of record usually are," the woman replied without sympathy.

"There must be some way to—"

"Data protection laws requires that we follow a specific process. You'll have to wait, same as everyone else."

Alice tapped her screen and ended the call, dropping her expensive phone on the expensive counter with what would probably end up being an expensive clatter.

Irritation bubbled inside her like a cauldron on the verge of boiling over.

She went to her laptop, navigated to the hospital website and located the required forms, then started resentfully inputting her information into all the stupid boxes, feeling further infuriated by every new screen making additional requests.

She pressed submit, paid for her records, then closed the lid of her laptop, standing from the kitchen stool and walking over to the coffee maker.

She took the carafe and dumped it into the sink, because fuck drinking a drop of anything that Max had made for her while she was this (unreasonably) angry with him. Then she made a fresh pot, determined to get nice and caffeinated before she started tearing the apartment apart in search of clues. This time it would be Alice combing through every nook and cranny of the penthouse, instead of two officers who had obviously been searching for reasons to discredit her more than anything else.

The search had a feverish quality, as if she were a miner digging not for gold but for shards of a fractured truth. Each drawer opened, each cushion flipped, was a desperate gasp for air in the suffocating room of her reality.

Alice wasn't merely looking for a body or signs of life; she was scouring for breadcrumbs in a forest of shadows, attacking the kitchen cupboards like a woman possessed. She flung the doors open so forcefully that they rebounded off their hinges. Her hands tore through jars of spices and and cans of food, casting each one onto the counter along with the utensils lying like forgotten soldiers in her desperate quest.

Back in the living room she dropped to her knees and pushed aside bench cushions, patting and probing the spaces beneath. And still, Alice barely even knew what she was looking for. Evidence of the dead woman? Signs of where Ellie could be?

Her search expanded like a storm gathering strength.

Into the bedroom, lifting the bedskirt, half-hoping and half-dreading that something ominous would reveal itself.

But she found nothing. No blood smears. No baby clothes forgotten in a hasty attempt to erase Ellie's existence.

She stepped out onto the balcony. She looked over the edge and her eyes were drawn to a square patch of land beyond the brick balustrade and the planted trees.

At a glance the area appeared empty. But after squinting … Was that?

She hurried out of the apartment to the elevator, shifting back and forth with nervous energy as it creaked slowly down to the bottom floor, where she bolted through the lobby and around the building to find what she'd seen from the balcony.

A partially hidden shoe.

A woman's shoe, and definitely not hers. Size eight. Just lying there, incongruent in its surroundings. A shiny black stiletto still in such excellent shape, it could not have possibly been tucked into the crook of those two jutting bricks framing the square of trees for long. The incongruous elegance of a shoe in the dirt and leaves was a silent scream in the quiet morning.

Alice bent to touch what was either the relic of a tragedy or a misplaced object.

Her mind spiraled into overdrive as she traced its contours, as if trying to read the shoe's history like Braille. Then she felt eyes on her, and looked up to see a neighbor from across the street, peering through curtains parted just wide enough for her to spy through.

Alice hurried back to her apartment, taking the shoe with her.

Back in the kitchen, her gaze lock onto the trash chute.

She opened the hatch and peered into the nest of shadows yawning into an abyss.

Carefully, Alice slid one foot into the chute, followed by the other one.

But she didn't get far. The steel edges were unforgiving, and she felt the pressure around her hips as she tried to sink further. An uncomfortably tight fit for a body, but by no means impossible, especially for someone more slender.

She grabbed her keys, but left her phone on the counter as she left the apartment.

But she must have been even louder than she imagined because Flora's door swung open the second Alice closed hers. Flora poked her head out to ask if everything was okay.

"Fine." Alice felt instantly suspicious of this woman who had (possibly) lied about seeing her with Ellie, insisting that she was a doll when she (probably) wasn't.

"What are you doing out here?"

"Going for a walk."

Flora looked down at Alice's bare feet. "Without shoes?"

"I won't be gone long."

The elevator doors opened and she stepped into the car. She hit the button for the basement and offered Flora an awkward wave as the doors closed and the grating gears got started on the car's descent.

The basement had unsettled Alice even before her life itself had become a waking nightmare. The lights always flickered inconsistently to cast fluctuating shadows on the walls. The basement reminded her of crime dramas and horror films.

She stepped onto the cold concrete floor with a shiver, then walked the dim corridor toward the garbage room. It was even worse than she remembered; a terrible stench emanated from the garbage bin that caught the rain of refuse from the chute above.

She was smaller than Officer Brody, but more determined to find the truth than either of those two lazy cops had been, so after a deep breath, she grabbed onto the grimy edges of the garbage bin and hoisted herself up high enough to peek inside.

But what was she even looking for? A dead body?

Her eyes adjusted to the dim light and settled on a box, with a stain like a smashed cherry on its side. Her mind went into overdrive and she climbed into the bin as—

A cascade of loose garbage rained down from the chute, followed only a beat later by a black trash bag that burst open upon impact, releasing a whirlwind of rotting food, coffee grinds, and crumpled paper to swirl around Alice like revolting confetti.

The sudden noise of a door slamming pulled her from her daze and replaced her thoughts with a high tide of adrenaline.

She hastily climbed out of the bin and peered down the dimly lit hallway. *Empty.*

A shiver rolled down her spine.

She shook it off, steeling herself for the next part of her exploration.

With a sense of trepidation, Alice continued down to the storage rooms.

She unlocked the door to their unit, but before stepping inside she caught a glimpse of someone — or something — at the end of the hall.

Rory?

The man seemed to vanish into the shadows.

Was the doorman really there, or was her mind playing tricks on her? Again?

Alice entered the storage room to a cache of her and Max's shared past, with both haphazardly and neatly-stacked boxes containing objects that had been deemed unnecessary in their present lives but too meaningful to discard. University textbooks with dog-eared pages stood next to stacks of fabric swatches, wallpaper books, and paint samples — all remnants of a business Alice had loved more than life itself, until she was ready to love the new life inside her even more than that.

Her eyes settled on a box labeled *Samuel.*

She opened it with a shaking hand. She pulled out a pair of tiny blue socks, followed by an array of little boy clothes. The lump in her throat thickened as she unearthed the ultrasound photograph — the first one, where everything still seemed so promising, back when it still felt like she was sliding right down that rainbow into a pot of gold, life sparkling with everything she ever wanted and both of her parents be damned.

Her eyes caught sight of the letter she had written to Samuel after his passing.

Tears started to flow, but then the sound of footsteps creeping outside the door sliced right into her solitude. She listened intently, her breathing shallow.

After a moment that felt like an eternity, the steps faded away.

Relieved but unnerved, she returned to the box, wiping her tears as she looked through memories, both those that were made while he was living inside her, and those that would never be after fate took that shared life away from them.

She gingerly touched the tiny, leather-bound journal she had started to keep during her pregnancy. She turned the pages to see her scribbles of daydreams and wishes.

A small stuffed animal sat at the corner of the box, a teddy bear holding a blue heart, its fur still unnaturally soft and untouched by the hands it was meant for. A blanket, absurdly expensive instead of being knitted by Grandma. Because Max didn't have family either. She lifted the baby blanket to to her face, as if hoping to whiff the past. But it only smelled of stale cardboard and stolen time.

Alice closed her eyes and settled into the sanctuary of her grief.

Who knew how long she stood there intermittently sighing before she finally shook herself out of the emotional abyss and carefully returned the items to the box, sealing away memories with both love and a strange sense of shame that she shouldn't be feeling. In the dimly-lit basement, it felt almost as if the air was refusing to circulate, keeping her in a chrysalis of darkness that made it hard to see anything clearly.

She wanted to take the box upstairs, to escape this stifling atmosphere and sift through these aching memories in the light.

But when she turned the doorknob, the door wouldn't budge.

She tried again, putting her full weight behind it, but the door appeared to be jammed. She pounded on the wood and yelled, but her voice merely caromed off the narrow walls. She swallowed hard and tried not to panic, but the fear was already claustrophobic, and closing in on her fast.

The basement was seldom visited. Of course her cries for help would go unheard.

Alice pictured her phone sitting on the kitchen counter, after she had been sure that she wouldn't need it for her quick trip downstairs.

Another ludicrously stupid move.

She deserved to be down here. Maybe she deserved all of this.

She leaned against the jammed door, fighting the nausea clawing up her throat.

Seized by the sense that she wasn't alone, Alice turned

and saw a great horned owl perched atop a pile of boxes, its large and unblinking eyes staring into the center of her.

A bone chilling terror crawled up her spine; the owl seemed less a bird than a harbinger of her quickly decaying sanity. Its unyielding gaze was an accusation, and a mirror to the madness inside her.

Chapter Seventeen

ALICE COULD NO LONGER TELL if the moisture on her face was from perspiration or tears, though surely it was some wretched blending of both. Each drop was a silent testament to her ordeal, a confluence of fear and sorrow leaving a salted trail upon her skin.

She had cocooned herself in a dim corner, far from the scrutinizing gaze of the great horned owl, which had mysteriously vanished as silently as it had appeared.

Her heart lurched when she finally heard footsteps on the other side of the door.

Alice had almost given up hope that anyone would come, at least any time soon, and for a while even convinced herself that people were looking forward to forgetting her. Not just the family that had cast her into their permanent history years ago, and all the friends who had incessantly messaged her at the start but were now too bothered by her lack of response to try reaching out again, but her husband, too.

Because of course Max was sick and tired of her delusions. Surely he was exhausted by the same insanity that had driven Alice out of the apartment and down into the basement where she could have died.

She pounded on the door. "Help! Help!"

"Hello?"

It was Rory, his voice echoing through the hollow chamber of the basement.

Alice was suddenly standing on full alert, her muscles protesting in fatigue and disbelief, grateful to be rescued and yet still instantly suspicious of anyone who might find her down here. She had hoped that Flora might come looking for her, because at least she had seen her leaving the apartment with what Flora surely must have seen as Alice's typical mania, but that didn't mean she had any reason to suspect that the basement was her final destination.

"Alice?" Rory's eyes widened in surprise, "Is this your idea of hide and seek?"

His question sounded like an insult. The innocence of his query clashed with the tumultuous storm of distrust brewing within her.

Alice glanced over into the corner where she had relieved herself, then back to Rory, still not sure of what to think of his presence or whether it was safe to tell him anything.

"You okay?" he asked when she still hadn't said anything.

"I couldn't get the door open." Her voice was hoarse from all the sobbing, but she did her best to sound strong. "What are you doing down here?"

"I heard noises, thought I should check it out. You okay?"

"I don't know." The question seemed laughable.

"What are you doing down here?" Rory asked her,

even though he had yet to answer that same question for himself.

"I was just looking through some old boxes. Reminiscing."

"Why did you shut the door?" he asked.

She hadn't, but if he was responsible, she didn't want him to think she was aware.

"It was an accident. What made you come down to the basement?" Alice made her question more direct, and if Rory didn't answer her this time she planned to thoroughly lose her shit.

He held up a slender piece of wood. "Someone stuck this under the door outside. Why would someone do that? If this is supposed to be a prank, it sure as hell is a terrible one. And not funny at all."

Despite his words, Rory was only making her more suspicious.

"I'm glad you found me, really I am, so I don't mean to sound anything less than grateful, but why did you come down to the basement in the first place?"

"Because I wanted to help."

"But how did you know to help? Did Flora tell you I was down here?" Alice shouldn't have asked, because now that gave Rory a chance to lie.

"I didn't know it was you down here."

"Who did you think it was?"

"No idea." Rory shrugged. "But I heard someone take the elevator down several hours ago, and then I never heard anyone come back up. You spend all day every day down in the lobby and you get to know the sounds of this building like a hunter knows the forest. You also know things like that the main door gets sticky down here. So I came to check. I definitely didn't expect to find you locked in here, but going with my gut has gotta be the best part of the day for both of us."

Alice stared back at Rory, unsure of what to say or whether she even believed him. Right now, everyone felt like an unreliable narrator in this story, including Alice herself.

"Thank you for finding me."

"You don't look so great, and I mean that with all due respect, of course, Alice. You know I think the world of you, but …"

"What is it, Rory? Can you just goddamned say it?"

"Are you okay?"

Another ludicrous question.

"I'm fine." She gave him a tired smile.

"Do you want me to call the police or anything?" The concern seemed real enough in his eyes that she suddenly wanted to believe him. "Can I help you, Alice?"

Was it possible that she could rely on Rory to be an ally? Or would he take Max's side? For all she knew, the next thing he would do is call Max to let him know what had happened.

"No. Thank you." Then she affirmed her wellbeing again. "I'm fine."

She walked back over to pull the Pandora's box of un-lived memories into her arms before locking the room. It was a heavy burden, thanks to a husband who clearly wanted (needed) her to move on. She now had to carry it alone.

Rory escorted her out of the basement and up to the lobby, where the doors parted and he stepped out. He turned around to bid Alice goodbye before sending the elevator back up to the top floor.

"I heard about last night, and I'm really sorry you're going through all of this. If you need someone to talk to, you know where to find me. I'm always happy to lend a good ear to whatever you're going through. Or two ears, if you think it's a two-ear kind of problem. And I never charge by the hour." He shook his head with a smile. "Though I always accept chocolate.

"I appreciate it, Rory. I really do. But I'm fine." Her smile was like a thin layer of paint over an ugly stain.

The elevator doors closed and the elevator began its grinding journey to the top.

Her arms tightened around the box.

She managed to keep her tears from spilling, through the elevator and down the hall past Flora's closed apartment door.

When she was safely back inside her apartment, she went straight to the living room floor and spilled into a human puddle on the spot where she either did or did not see her husband drag a dead body that he may or may not have murdered across it.

She sobbed for an hour.

Then, with her tear ducts finally dry, Alice got to work.

Chapter Eighteen

THE AIR FELT stagnant as she cradled Samuel's box, finally setting it down on the coffee table before giving it a final glare, eyeing the cardboard like a coffin.

She moved toward the bathroom as if guided by a magnetic pull toward purification. Stripping off her clothes, she stepped into the shower, letting scalding hot water spill over her like liquid absolution. Each drop seared her skin, a baptism of heat attempting to scorch away the layers of doubt and the stain of uncertainty.

She toweled off and wrapped herself in a terrycloth robe that felt like an armored embrace, then crossed the bedroom to where her phone lay atop a vintage dresser.

The screen illuminated at her touch to a text from Max.

Got a fraud alert for $75 transaction. Was that you?

Antidepressant prescription. Approve? she texted back.

Done.

Alice fetched the box that Max had dug out the other night, with Ellie's supposed death certificate. She stared at the dates, first with her eyes dry, but then after only a few minutes they were glistening with tears again.

Ellie's birth and death dates were the same, and there was no amount of blinking that could change what Alice was seeing on the page. Time seemed to congeal around those dates, binding them with an irrevocable permanence that scratched blood into the edges of her reality.

Beneath the death certificate lay a myriad of other objects, each one a shard of a past refracted through the prism of grief. A baby dress, delicate and pastel — the garment she remembered dressing Ellie in to bring her home.

But as her fingers traced the soft fabric, a guttural whisper of doubt edged into her consciousness: *Had she ever actually brought Ellie home, in this dress or otherwise?*

Alice worked to coax her memory into clarity, but the edges of her recollection remained defiantly blurred. Grief and time had added a layer of scum atop her memory.

A hospital wristband surfaced from the jumble inside the box, the sterile plastic looking especially hard against the softness of her baby dress — an exhibit of what might have been and what she could not remember.

Her fingers continued their restless journey through the box, now touching upon memories encased in a sepia haze of happier times, even if the colors of their glossy photos were still perfectly vibrant. The beautiful little box that they took home full of homemade granola from 11 Madison Avenue, where they had shared the finest dining experience of her life, shortly before Mom and Dad cut her off for good. That treasured little box was sitting right next to a menu from Café Fleur, a quaint French restaurant where she and Max had shared escargot and intimate glances during their tentative first date, the folds of that menu stained with splashes of spilled red wine.

A pair of play tickets from An Evening with Tennessee Williams. The theater air had been thick with the perfume of culture, but Alice was thrilled to discover that the performance had bored Max just as much as it bored her, and they were both eager to abandon the venue at intermission and go get some ice cream instead.

A newspaper clipping of Max and his legal team captured in a moment of subdued triumph under the bold headline: *Jury Awards $150 Million in Landmark Medical Malpractice Case Against St. Mercy Hospital*, and a sub-head with the chilling specifics: *Botched Spinal Surgeries and Altered Medical Records Lead to Unprecedented Settlement*.

She lingered on one woman in the photograph, her eyes narrowing in recognition. Alice read the caption and pondered the name, *Carly Hunt*. In the photo, her blazer seemed slightly too large, she had a nest of frizzy hair, and an almost self-effacing air that perfectly matched her perfunctory smile.

But on that dreadful night in the living room, Carly had been wearing a tasteful dress that clung to her form. Still, that hauntingly lifeless corpse was undeniably the same woman.

Alice clicked over to Carly Hunt's online profile as a nauseating cocktail of dread and certainty churned in the pit of her stomach, as if her inner compass had found true north in the worst possible direction. She drew shallow breaths to steady herself as she located *Carly Hunt* amid the roster and clicked over to her profile.

The page opened to Carly in another professional photograph, this one accompanied by a biography detailing her educational background and legal expertise.

Alice didn't care that Carly was a Magna Cum Laude graduate of Harvard Law, or that she specialized in medical malpractice cases. Alice only cared that the longer she stared at Carly's photo, the more certain she became that this was the woman Max had murdered in their apartment, because Alice hadn't been imagining the woman she was staring at right now in full color on the computer screen, after seeing her in newsprint black and white. She was positive it was the same woman who Max had dragged across her living room floor.

She called the firm's general number instead of dialing Max directly.

"May I help you?" the receptionist answered.

"I'd like to speak to Carly Hunt, please."

"One moment." The line clicked, filled with a brief yet incongruous interlude of Vivaldi's Four Seasons.

Another click, then the receptionist was back. "She's not in today, can I take a message?"

"Do you know where she is?"

The receptionist hesitated, then repeated: "Can I take a message?"

Alice jabbed the red disconnect icon like it was a self-destruct button.

There was no doubt about it, Carly Hunt worked with Max. But had the receptionist hesitated because she was protecting Carly's privacy from random strangers, or did she not want to admit that Carly was missing?

Almost immediately after ending the call, the phone vibrated, jarring her into a yelp as *Flora* lit up her screen.

Alice hesitated but decided to decline the call.

She had other things to do right now. Practically compelled by a force she could not resist, her fingers navigated to Instagram and typed Carly's name into the search bar.

But Carly Hunt was much too common a name, and there was a lot of garbage to sift through. She scrolled with frustration through an endless sea of Carlys: teenagers posing at proms, moms sharing moments with their children, some into it and others absolutely not, and a fitness guru showing off her workout routine in attire so skimpy that Alice half-expected to see a nip slip. But not a single photo of the Carly Hunt whose neck had already been turning purple.

Switching gears, she went to the firm's official Instagram account.

She thought that if she sifted through the followers of the firm, maybe Carly, as an employee, would be among them. It was a long shot, but at this point, she was willing to try any avenue that could lead her to the real Carly — the one with the frumpy blazer and frizzy hair and, more critically, the one that she was certain had been lying lifeless on her living room floor.

She navigated to the firm's Instagram page and scrolled through its list of followers, scanning the tiny profile pictures and usernames with an embarrassingly-desperate intensity. Not that anyone was here to judge her right now.

She meticulously went down the line, clicking on any potential candidate who remotely resembled Carly, but finding only dead ends and an increasing sense of gnawing futility.

Until her eyes caught a hashtag under a picture of a familiar face under #legalhottie.

Her stomach lurched as she swallowed, knowing in less than a blink that this was exactly what she had been waiting to find. She tapped the image and opened the profile to an array of photos — definitely Carly, but a version remarkably different from the one she had seen in company pics, or that nightmare in her living room.

Each image seemed meticulously curated to depict a life lived out loud, oozing both confidence and sexuality.

That frumpy blazer and frizzy hair were gone, with form-fitting dresses and professionally styled locks in their place, with captions like #ParalegalLife and #LegallyHot gracing the pictures of Carly at upmarket bars, holding cocktails with a poised elegance.

But what really caught Alice's eye and sent a shiver down her spine were the pregnancy photos. Carly's radiant smile filled the frames as her hands lovingly cradled her baby bump. The hashtags changed, seeming to taunt her: #PregnantAndProud, #MommyToBe, and #ExpectingJoy.

Carly had been pregnant. Max had killed both her and her baby.

Alice picked up her phone and dialed the police.

Chapter Nineteen

ALICE WAITED MORE than two hours for the police to get there, trying to check her privilege while waiting. Yes, she felt entitled for a more rapid response than the one she was getting, and not just because it kept getting harder and harder for it to feel like she wasn't going out of her goddamned mind.

She was a lot more worried that Max would come home before the cops got here, and either she wouldn't have the courage to follow through with a necessary conversation, or he would silence her like he had every other time before. Each tick of the clock was a drumbeat against her composure, an audible reminder that he might get away with it — and she would be married to a murderer.

She spent the entire two hours both scrolling through #legalhottie's (Carly's) Instagram, over and over, from the beginning to her last post and back again, and navigating around to see if she could dig up anything else on the woman.

Rory finally buzzed to let Alice know that Officers

Brody and Lemmon were waiting for her down in the lobby.

"Send them up."

Alice hung up the phone, irritated before the cops were even in the elevator. Of course they had sent her the same two officers as before. She should have known when they made her wait for so long.

It's that postpartum woman in that penthouse house again — you know, the one who is obviously batshit.

Alice was going to make them take her seriously.

"I know the name of the dead woman," she declared as the officers stepped off the elevator, Brody in front and Lemmon just one step behind him.

"Maybe we should go inside." Brody nodded toward her open door.

Alice turned around and led the officers into her apartment, then closed the door behind them, wondering how long she had until Max came waltzing in to muzzle her.

"Look." She presented them with the clipping without leaving her entryway.

"What am I looking at?" Brody glanced at the article then back up at Alice. "$150 Million awarded against St. Mercy? Sounds about right."

"The woman." Alice pointed at the clipping while Lemmon followed her finger. "Carly Hunt. That's the woman I saw in here."

"How do you know it was her?" Brody asked.

Lemmon leaned in for the answer.

"Because she looks exactly the same."

"I thought you didn't know who she was?" Lemmon questioned her.

"I didn't. But now I have that article."

"Where did the article come from?" Brody wasn't even

trying to make it sound like there was a chance in hell that he would believe her.

"I found it down in the basement — why does that matter?"

"Everything matters in a case like this," Lemmon didn't explain.

"And what kind of case is this?" Alice asked.

"Is it possible that your mind is making connections it needs to feel some sense of closure on what you think you saw the other night?"

"If I'm right about this picture, then that means I didn't imagine anything."

"That's a big *if*, ma'am," Brody said with a smile that didn't quite work. "If you don't mind my saying."

"I absolutely mind your saying!" Alice snapped. "You're not listening to me!"

"No need to get upset, ma'am." Lemmon tried to step in.

But then the front door opened and everyone in the entryway turned to look at Max as he observed his unexpected guests.

"Officers…" he said.

"Sir." Brody gave him a nod. "Your wife called us out because she had something to share with us. Do you mind if I ask you a couple of questions?"

"Of course not." Max shot her a look: *What did you do now?*

"Do you know a Carly Hunt?" Brody asked.

"Of course I do."

Lemmon: "How do you know her?"

"We work together."

"Your wife believes that it was Carly Hunt she saw here in your apartment the other night."

"That's ridiculous," he scoffed at Brody before turning to Alice. "You just remembered it was Carly today?"

"I've never met Carly. I saw her on the website."

Max laughed.

"Why are you laughing at me?" Alice wanted to shove her thumbs in his eyeballs. "Stop laughing at me!"

"Sorry. Really." That was more for the officers than her. "I don't mean to laugh, it's just that this is such a good example of what I've been going through here. Of course you met Carly. We were invited to her baby shower. You wanted to give her one of Ellie's baby blankets. I asked if you were sure a dozen times because I felt positive that you would regret it, but you said that would be healing."

Alice's heart started beating harder with the memory. She could feel herself flushing with embarrassment as the images slowly returned to her. So much of that time was a tormented haze that the memory was somewhat fuzzy. Carly, sitting on a couch, the coffee table before her piled high with gifts. Max smiling and nodding beside her as everyone had laughed at a joke Alice didn't get. A sudden desire to run as everything grew hot and close and blurry.

"So you *did* know this Carly?" Lemmon tried to confirm.

"I didn't really know her. But yes," Alice admitted with a nod, "I did meet her once."

"You met her more than once," Max disagreed.

She turned to the officers. "I don't remember meeting her more than once, and barely remember that first time."

"That doesn't change the facts, Alice," Max scolded her.

"How did she know Carly?" Lemmon asked Max.

Brody nodded. "Good question."

The officers turned to Alice and looked at her expectantly.

She thought deep, dug hard enough to make it hurt for an answer but her mind was empty. There was something, though, Alice could see it in the way Max's eyes were gleaming with anticipation for him to pull it out of the air for the officers like a magic trick.

"Do you know the answer?" Lemmon asked.

"I'm not sure."

"So that means no." Lemmon proved he was an asshole.

"Carly was here the other day," Max said to the cops instead of her. "She came by to drop off some paperwork." He turned to Alice. "Do you remember when Rory called from downstairs and you let me know that Carly was at the door?"

"Rory never gave me a name. I don't even think he said it was a woman. Just that someone was here with a file for you."

"You said Carly. And you were standing right there next to me when I answered the door." Then again to the officers, "She doesn't mean to, but Alice can be a bit territorial."

"What time of day was this that Carly came up to the apartment — are you saying she was here at night?" Brody asked.

"It was the morning," Alice said.

"So you do remember?" Lemmon looked at her.

"She came by to drop off the files, then I left and we went into the office together. So that's twice she saw Carly."

"Why drop it off if she was just going to see you at work?" Brody asked.

Great goddamned question.

But of course Max had an answer for it. "Carly had to rush to a family emergency and wouldn't be in the office for a few days. She didn't want the project to stall, so she dropped the files off here and we shared a cab to the office, where her car was parked."

"And I'm sure your building has a lot with cameras and security gates that can back all of that up," Lemmon said.

"Of course," Max replied without flinching.

"What is it that you and Carly do together at the firm?" Brody asked.

It almost felt like the officers were on Alice's side.

"We're litigating an insurance fraud case."

"And you spend a lot of time together?" Brody pressed. "Enough that morning visits are normal?"

"Not normal at all. But our latest case hasn't been going as well as anyone at the firm hoped. And the family emergency caused another hiccup we couldn't afford, so Carly felt guilty. She was working as hard as she could up to the last minute to make everything work out. André at the office gave her a ride home when she was too exhausted to drive, then she made sure I had the files in hand and gave me a briefing in the cab on our way."

"So that was after your fight then?" Alice said.

"I'm sorry?" Max turned to her.

"I saw you two arguing."

"When did you see us arguing?"

The officers were interested in her answer.

"I saw you from the balcony. Right after you left. Standing in front of the cab."

"We weren't arguing." Max shook his head. "You don't know what you saw."

"How do you know they were arguing?" Brody asked her.

Alice faced the scrutiny like a witness on the stand, each question a subtle blade paring away at her certainty. "I could just tell."

"But you couldn't hear anything they were saying, right?" Lemmon raised his eyebrows.

"No. Of course not. But their body language was obvious."

"We weren't arguing," said Max to the officers.

"What was the nature of this family emergency?" Brody asked.

"I don't know." Max shook his head, looking genuine. Apparently he was a better actor than he was a husband. "She didn't say, and I didn't want to pry. We're not that close."

Good one, asshole.

"Why don't you give her a call?" Alice turned to Brody. "Can you make him call her?"

"They don't need to 'make me,' Alice. I have her number in my contacts." Max took out his phone.

"I'm sure you won't mind if we do the calling," Brody said.

Because the man was finally on fire.

Max handed his phone to the officer. Brody scrolled through the contacts until his thumb landed on *Carly Hunt.*

He nodded at his audience as it rang. Then, "Yes, hello, who am I speaking with?" Still nodding. "Great … yes, of course … this is Officer Damian Brody with the New York Police Department … yes … absolutely. May I ask where you work?"

After another short pause where the person on the other end of the line confirmed that she worked at the same firm as Max, so was therefore very much alive and making Alice appear even crazier than everyone already thought she was, Brody hung up the phone.

"Sorry for the trouble," Brody said to Max, nodding at Lemmon to let his partner know that it was time to go without even having the decency to glance at Alice until they were both standing in front of the door.

Then he looked her right in the eyes. "I'm sorry for what you've been going through, ma'am, really I am. My heart goes out to you. But I'm going to have to ask you to please not call us again."

The officers left.

Max looked at her, his eyes shadowed with a blend of irritation and disappointment, before announcing, "I'm going to take a shower."

Alice stood there, her face flushed, grappling with a shame that coiled itself around her heart. Everyone thought she was crazy, but she'd been so sure that Carly was the woman that Max had murdered. She'd been sure that Max had murdered someone. Had she so blurred the lines between reality and the landscape of her nightmares that she accused her husband of the unimaginable? Or was he really the monster the claws of her instincts kept insisting he truly might be?

The silence left by his departure was a void, and in it echoed the whispers of her intuition, a chorus both accusatory and haunting.

Chapter Twenty

ALICE STEPPED out into the hallway, allowing her apartment door to close behind her with a soft click, but it might as well have been the sound of a prison cell slamming shut.

She couldn't trust the police to help her, even if she found new evidence.

She couldn't trust Max.

She wasn't even sure she could trust herself.

But what were her other choices? Return to Mt. Sinai for a longer stay and trust that the likes of Dr. Rufus and Dr. Kynard could tell her which parts were real and which she'd hallucinated?

After another sleepless night, she'd decided that Flora was her last resort. The woman had betrayed her in front of Max and the police officers by saying that Ellie was only a doll. But she had also said it kindly, and she'd been nothing but supportive, even when Alice had woken her in hysterics in the middle of the night.

So maybe Flora could help her sift through the chaos in her mind and find some sort of relative calm.

She drew a deep breath, having no idea how this might go and feeling mildly frightened of what she imagined to be Flora's judgmental eyes upon answering her door, but Alice kept telling herself that her neighbor could very well be a lifeline, and without it she might tumble into a bottomless abyss from which she could never emerge.

She crossed the hall to Flora's apartment and hesitated in front of the door before raising her knuckles to softly knock.

"Flora, I — I hope I'm not intruding," Alice stammered when the door swung open just seconds later. "You probably have an appointment or something ... I can come back later."

"Nonsense. I just moved here, my calendar is hardly full. And besides, I've been worried about you. Please, come in. I'll make us some coffee."

Flora opened her door with a smile and gestured for her to come inside.

Alice followed Flora into the kitchen, where she sat on a stool and slowly collected herself while watching her neighbor lovingly make their coffee, expertly grinding the beans before transferring them into a French press, her graceful movements lending an artisanal touch to an otherwise mundane task.

"You want anything fancy, or just black?" Flora asked as she lowered the plunger.

"Just black, please."

Flora poured their coffees, then sat on the stool next to Alice. "How are you doing, honey? And don't tell me 'fine.' I'm sorry to say this out loud instead of just thinking it, but I owe you honesty if we're doing this, and you look even worse than you did the last time. Even more like you saw a ghost."

"Funny you should say that."

"It wasn't a punchline." Flora took a sip of her coffee. "But pray tell, why is that funny?"

"I know who the woman I saw in the living room is."

"The one you also saw your husband murder?" Flora's expression was neutral, but it was clear that she didn't believe Alice now.

"Yes, Flora." Alice sipped to hide her irritation. "She works at Max's firm."

"How do you know it was her?"

"I found an old clipping from the news with her in it, and I'm also pretty sure that she came over a few mornings ago."

"The plot thickens…" Flora was getting more interested. "What makes you pretty sure instead of totally sure, or barely sure at all?"

"I only saw her from the balcony. But it definitely looked like she and Max were arguing."

"No shit."

"No shit," Alice repeated with a nod. "I'm glad you think that's a big deal, because the cops sure didn't."

"You called the cops again?"

Alice nodded. "The same assholes as last time showed up."

"What else did they say?"

"That older cop, Brody, supposedly called Carly from Max's phone, but that doesn't prove anything. He could have talked to anyone named Carly, or maybe the number wasn't even hers and Max was playing them."

"So now he has an accessory?"

"You don't believe me," Alice said.

Because Flora's tone had made that clear.

"It's not that I don't believe you, honey. But couldn't this just be Occam's razor — the simplest explanation is the real one, and Brody spoke to this Carly?"

Alice hated that answer because it made her feel even crazier than she already did, but of course Flora was right. Brody could absolutely have spoken to the real Carly Hunt.

But it was also confusing — because everything inside Alice right now kept insistently screaming that Max was a liar.

"Ellie isn't dead." Alice shook her head. "*I know it.* Max has taken our daughter away from me and hidden her somewhere."

Flora's smile, laden with pity, felt like an albatross around Alice's neck, a silent indictment of her spiraling grip on reality.

"Is Max really capable of that?"

"Yes." Alice vehemently nodded.

"Okay, let's agree that he is. *Why* would he do that?"

But Alice was stumped. She had no idea how to answer that, though at least now she had someone to bounce a few theories with, instead of hearing only the echoes of her own thoughts in the corridors of her own mind.

Flora leaned forward, her hands clutching her coffee cup, eyes searching Alice's face. "Has Max ever been cruel to you before this?"

Only in my nightmares.

Alice shook her head. "No, never. Not before this."

"Abusive? Manipulative?"

"He's not like that. Or he wasn't." But if she wasn't crazy and he had done everything she believed he had, that meant he *was* cruel and manipulative. Because stealing her daughter and making her believe that she'd been trying to nurse a doll for months was the cruelest lie she could possibly imagine.

"Did he ever give you any indication that he didn't want Ellie? That he might want to get rid of her?"

Alice hesitated as memories, once vivid, now flickered

at the edges of her mind, like old film reels worn thin by the constant replay of doubt and fear. Except for the night he'd tried to put her in the trash chute. But that might've been Alice, acting out her nightmare as she sleepwalked.

"Max wanted to throw a giant party when we found out I was pregnant. Both times."

"Then why would he possibly want to fake his own daughter's death?"

"I don't know. It doesn't make sense."

"*Think*. Is there anyone else who might benefit from Ellie being 'gone'?"

"No one I can think of."

"Did he ever act oddly during the pregnancy? Any weird behavior, strange phone calls, late-night trips?"

"Not that I noticed."

"Did you have reason to *not* pay attention?" Flora asked.

"I feel like I always paid attention ..." Alice didn't know what else to say, and the heat of Flora's incredulous gaze was starting to make her squirm. "Isn't there something to be said for intuition?"

Flora leaned back, her face taking on an expression of gentle yet hard-won wisdom. "Yes, of course there is, honey. But intuition is a fickle creature. It's fed by your fears, your hopes, and everything you've ever experienced. Sometimes what feels like a gut feeling is really just a blend of anxieties and worst-case scenarios playing some really mean tricks on you."

She paused for a sip of coffee, prompting Alice to do the same. "The mind is an incredible storyteller, and it can weave plots more intricate than any thriller on Netflix. It can make you believe things you'd swear on your life are true, even when they're not. That's why it's critical that we question our own narratives, just as we would any story with holes in it."

Alice didn't want that to be the answer, that she was hallucinating all of this, even though it would mean that Max was actually the loving husband she'd wanted him to be, because it would also mean that she was losing her mind.

But wanting something to be true — or not be true — didn't make it so. And what did it say about her that she *wanted* to believe that her husband was a baby-stealing murderer who wanted to drive her crazy?

She kept sipping her coffee, because she was afraid that anything she said would give that terrible thought away.

Flora asked her a more pointed question. "If Max did kill someone, then where did he put the body?"

"I don't know," Alice admitted with a shake of her head.

"It wouldn't fit down the garbage chute, and no one found it in the basement. So assuming that he did kill her, and that he got the body into small enough pieces that he could dispose of it in the garbage chute—"

Alice felt a bone deep shudder as Flora painted the scenario.

"—how did he get down to the basement, move the body and get back upstairs? It was the middle of the night — wouldn't you have heard the elevator?"

"Yes," Alice replied, forced to come to another conclusion she didn't like.

Because not only would he have had to do all that, he also would have had to dispose of the baby bottles in the fridge, and get rid of her rocker and the crib, and repaint the nursery at the same time.

The more she really thought about it, the harder it was to see how he could have accomplished it all in the short time she'd been hiding in Flora's apartment, waiting for the police to arrive. He would've had to plan it all in advance and have everything ready to go the second she fled the apartment.

Flora had another one coming. "If you truly believe that your husband would be capable of something so terrible, then why are you still staying in the same apartment with him?"

Alice not only didn't want to answer that, she physically couldn't. The words were trapped in her throat like stones lodged in a narrow stream. She sipped the coffee to buy herself time.

"You can drain your mug and drink the refill, I'll still be waiting for an answer to this one. Why are you staying in the apartment if you truly believe that Max is dangerous?"

"I've asked myself the same question."

"Not good enough." Flora shook his head. "This isn't an answer you should be vague about. This is a big inconsistency between your actions and—"

"It's because I doubt myself, okay? There are some things that feel like nightmares, and, yes, it has been difficult for me to tell exactly which sequence of events might be a figment of my imagination. But Ellie was real. I know that as much as I've ever known anything. I carried her, I felt her as she lived in my body for nine months, Flora. And I would bet my life that she's alive somewhere."

"Of course Ellie was real." Flora gave her another smile that Alice couldn't stand, on account of it so clearly broadcasting the psychiatrist's thoughts before she said them out loud. "She just didn't come home from the hospital."

Alice started to cry. Then sob.

Flora rubbed her back. "It's time to let yourself grieve, honey. All this holding on is just making it worse."

Alice wanted to scream that it wasn't true, that her daughter was alive, but even though grief was an infuriating explanation for everything she'd been experiencing, it was the one that made the most sense. It didn't require Max to murder anyone or swap Ellie with a doll or redecorate a room at light speed. It only required Alice to be a broken human being who couldn't move on after a terrible thing happened to her.

"Would you like me to write you a prescription for more antidepressants?" she asked once Alice's tears were all gone.

"They gave me Sertraline at the hospital," Alice rasped, her voice hoarse.

"That's fine for normal depression, but I can give you something a little stronger. I think you need it right now."

Was stronger better? She hadn't noticed any side effects from the pill Flora had given her earlier, but Dr. Rufus' pills had made her feel foggy and tired. "Yes, please."

Flora went to the small cabinet at the far end of the room and returned with a few sample pill packets plus a prescription pad, which she scribbled something on before tearing off the top sheet and handing it to Alice. Then she walked Alice to the door.

"Get some sleep, honey. You'll feel a lot more clear-headed by tomorrow morning."

Alice said goodbye without words, then crossed the hallway to her apartment with a prescription in her pocket and a writhing sea of anguish in her heart.

Chapter Twenty-One

ALICE UNLOCKED her apartment and stepped back inside, feeling the weight of her key turn into the weight of the world. The air was suffocating. She was surprised to see Max sitting on the sofa, glaring at his iPad, but it didn't look like he was actually reading anything.

"You're home early," she said.

He didn't look at her, but Alice could feel anger and disappointment in her radiating off of his body. The silence between them was dense, charged with an undercurrent of reproach that seemed to seep from his every pore, enveloping the room in a chill.

And still Alice felt overheated as the apology left her. "I'm sorry, Max."

He kept looking down at his tablet.

Max?" she tried again.

"What?" He refused to look up.

"I'm sorry."

"What are you sorry for?" Max finally met her eyes. "Accusing me of murder or tearing this family apart?"

She bit her lip. "Both."

Max set his tablet down on the coffee table with deliberate care, as if even that simple act was now weighted with measured disappointment. He rose from the couch, his eyes searching hers as he spoke.

"Could you please promise not to throw wildly harmful accusations my way in the future? Especially while I'm juggling the most difficult case of my career?"

Alice nodded, but her gaze skittered away. It was hard to look at him — not just because shame flooded her veins like hot lava, but also because her body was at war with her mind, one willing to believe in Occam's razor and the other feeling cut by its dirty, lying blade.

"I said sorry, Max. Can we please just start over?"

"Sure," he replied, his gaze momentarily detouring to the dining room before returning to meet hers.

Alice's eyes followed the invisible line he'd drawn across the room.

They landed on a nondescript cardboard box resting on the dining table. Despite its unremarkable appearance, a shiver of foreboding slithered down her spine, like a dark whisper urging her to flinch away and do it fast.

"What is that?" Alice asked.

"We can talk about it later."

"I'm asking you right now. What's in the box?"

His face tightened, draining of color as his jaw hardened. "Why don't you take a shower first?"

"I don't need a shower, Max — what's in the box?"

He sighed, seeming to steel himself before saying, "The funeral home has been calling."

"So?" But she knew, and hearing him say it might shred her down to confetti.

"So, they asked if I could please come and pick them up."

"Pick what up, Max? I need you to say it: *tell me what's in the box.*"

Why am I doing this to myself?

Another deep sigh. "It's Ellie, Alice. Those are her ashes."

The words fell with the weight of finality, each syllable a shovel of earth on the coffin of her hopes. She froze, her eyes riveted to that nondescript box. "That's Ellie?"

A broken whisper, disbelief coating all three syllables.

He nodded, and even though her body wanted to flee the scene and escape the man who could stare right into her eyes while lying, but thanks to Alice's brain, her heart was breaking at the sight of sorrow and exhaustion turning him into a shadow of the man she had fallen in love with.

And that was *her* fault.

Alice went into the living room and stood in front of the box.

Her fingers quivered as she carefully pried open the lid.

And inside she saw a sealed bag with what remained of her daughter: a heap of fine, gray ashes. Her baby Ellie, reduced to this a baggie filled with dust.

A strange buzzing filled the room, a faint hum at first, but in seconds the light drone was suddenly loud enough to drown her thoughts, escalating into an insectile chorus of murmuring buzzes that seemed to resonate from the walls as they closed in around her.

She closed her eyes to get away from it all.

"Alice?"

The buzzing began to recede.

"Alice? Say something. Can you hear me?"

Alice opened her eyes but looked away from the box, over to a bookshelf in the corner. But moving her gaze was a mistake, because that was where the great horned owl was sitting, perched atop the bookshelf like a sentinel of sorrow, its predatory eyes fixed on her, yellow and unblinking.

"ALICE!"

She turned to Max and narrowed her eyes.

He flinched back before instantly regaining his composure. "What is it?"

Alice didn't answer him, instead scooping the box into her hand and cradling it like a bulky Baby Ellie. She carried it toward the balcony door.

"Where are you going?" Max called after her.

But she still didn't answer, opening the door as he ran out onto the terrace.

"Alice! Whatever you're thinking about doing right now, please don't do it!"

She climbed up onto the bench, then up onto the balustrade. Alice had done this dangerous dance before, but never like this, never with a reason, never with a before and after like the one she was staring into right now.

She took out the bag and let the box fall to the ground below. With the city sprawling beneath her, the bag was not just a vessel of ashes but a symbol of all she had lost and could never reclaim.

She ripped it open, at first struggling to tear it, but then the bag suddenly burst open.

As she leaned forward into a sudden gust of wind rushing by her, it took with it the fine particles that were once her daughter, even though that could not possibly be true, and scattered them into the air over Manhattan.

The irreversible act felt like releasing a scream into the void and—

Max snatched the empty box from her hands, his eyes widening at what she had done.

"That was our daughter's ashes," he croaked, his voice cracking, face contorted in an ugly grimace of raw emotion, venting a guttural sound — half-sob and half-something worse as he stormed back into the apartment, leaving Alice alone on the balcony.

Their front door violently slammed just moments later.

Alice went back up to the balustrade and leaned over the side, waiting to see Max burst out of their building and frantically attempt to grab whatever bit of Ellie he could get, though of course that was fruitless, and not just because he was waving his hands through the air to conduct a symphony of loss. That wasn't Ellie.

She was surer than ever. So what if her mind and body didn't agree? If Alice could only side with one of them right now, then she had decided that her body was right. She felt it in every molecule: Ellie was alive and Max was a bad actor in all of this, even if his acting was good enough to fool her most of the time.

But not anymore. Because Alice was sure that if there had been any of her Ellie in those ashes, she would have felt it in her mother's soul the second they were scattered like dandelion seeds in the wind.

A few minutes later she heard the front door slam again, followed by angry stomping before Max was standing on the balcony a few feet in front of her, his eyes red and sweaty face flushed, as if trying to prove he had run a marathon of sorrow, clutching the empty box.

Until he threw it at her, the box gliding through the air like a dud missile, fluttering onto the ground beside her. She didn't flinch, still as a statue, her face chiseled from a slab of contempt.

"You don't have anything to say?" Max barked at her.

She didn't.

Max turned on his heel and strode into their bedroom.

He was frantically stuffing clothes into a duffel bag by the time Alice got there just moments later, following him into the bedroom because she needed to get this over with.

"I'm in court all day tomorrow," he spat. "I need rest and I won't be getting it here, so I'm spending the night at a hotel—"

"GIVE ME MY BABY BACK!" Alice roared.

Of all the possible things she could say, and that one hadn't even been on the list. Certainly not in the tone of a lion. But it just came tearing through her like a freight train breaking through years of rusted tracks.

Max stopped, looking at Alice as if he had never seen her before. "You need help."

Then he left and slammed the door behind him.

She was glad to be alone.

A minute later she was gripping the doorknob to the nursery, drawing another deep breath before she opened it, half-expecting the great horned owl or some other monstrosity lying in wait to torment her.

But the half-painted room was empty. No crib, no rocking chair, no pretty walls.

Only the Ellie doll.

Poison inside her for sure, but right now she needed to drink it.

So Alice hugged the doll tight to her chest, laying with her back to the wall as she petted the back of its plastic head and wondered if she was crazy.

Chapter Twenty-Two

ALICE COULDN'T SLEEP, though that was nothing new; insomnia had been swallowing her for a while, transforming the bedroom that was once her sanctuary into a battleground where she lay sandwiched between the oppressively-still air above her and the mattress below as she waged war with her thoughts.

Tonight was especially painful. More than the sleep that Alice so desperately needed, she longed for proof of her sanity. After several miserable hours alone in bed spent wrestling between the side of her that was glad Max was gone, because he was a rotten, murdering liar, and the shame-filled rest of her that feared she was going insane and trying to drag Max down with her. She'd accused her husband of murder and worse — taking Ellie from her was worse, even though the police probably wouldn't agree. Whether she was right or she was crazy, there was no way their relationship recovered from this.

Her marriage was over.

Alice finally got out of bed and ambled into the nursery, knowing what she was going to do it before she started surveying the room, returning ten minutes later armed with a bucket of pale yellow paint from the entryway closet, along with a brush, now equipped to lose herself in the rhythmic strokes, like silent incantations to whitewash the sorrow saturating these walls.

She worked in a fugue, painting one wall all the way from one side to the other when the atmosphere in the room suddenly changed.

A buzzing shattered the silence, echoing through the apartment like a blitzkrieg of flies and filling her with chills. At least this time she was able to identify the sound of her intercom without hallucinating the flies.

Alice put down the paintbrush, walked into the living room, and answered the call.

For a moment she heard only silence.

Followed by a sound that threatened to destroy her: Ellie crying again.

Adrenaline surged through her veins as she dropped the intercom phone, dashing out of the apartment, then down the hallway to the elevator.

Her finger stabbed the call button.

She waited as the gears ground, listening to the car descending at a torturous pace.

It felt like she was crawling out of her skin all the way to the ground floor, where she burst out of the elevator doors before they were even opening, into the lobby where the night doorman looked up at her from behind the walnut paneled desk in alarm.

"Ma'am?" He looked nervous to see her, but that made sense whether she was crazy or not.

She glanced at the intercom phone and noted that the handset was resting in its cradle. She darted over to the desk and the doorman flinched back as she snatched the receiver into her trembling hand and held it to her ear.

But Alice heard only the dead silence of a disconnected call.

She dropped the phone back onto his desk without a word and ran back to the elevator, ascending back to the top floor as a volley of now-familiar thoughts were blasting through her mind.

Was she losing her grip on reality? Had her desire to hear Ellie's voice manifested yet another cruel illusion? Or was something darker happening here, something even more insidious than she had dared to think?

A surge of dread washed through her body, once Alice was back in her apartment and saw that the intercom phone was still dangling off the hook. She could still hear Ellie's far off wails echoing from the other end.

She picked up the phone with a trembling hand and the haunting cries got louder.

Her heart felt crushed in a vice.

Alice collapsed onto the floor with the phone pressed to her ear, trying to soothe Ellie even though she knew it didn't make sense. There was a better than excellent chance that she was acting nice and crazy right now.

But that couldn't stop her from doing what felt right and soothing Ellie's crying. "Mommy's here for you, sweetie. Just tell me where you are and I'll come get you."

Of course that was ridiculous. Even if she were real, Alice's infant couldn't tell her anything. Each cry sent her deeper into an emotional abyss.

Her rationality had dissolved into a murk of confusion, forever adrift in this ever-darkening abyss of the inconceivable—

Alice woke up in the entryway, clutching the phone.

She pressed the receiver to her ear and heard only an accusatory silence.

Disoriented, she stood and made her way to the nursery. The walls were still half-painted blue. The can of yellow paint and other supplies she'd gotten out earlier were nowhere to be seen.

"What's happening to me?" Alice whispered to herself.

She should talk to Flora.

Alice went to get her phone and saw a notification, a voicemail from an unfamiliar number. She pressed play with a sense of foreboding.

"Hello, Alice. My name is Carly Hunt. We need to talk. Can you please call me back at this number?" And then, just in case Alice couldn't see it on the caller ID, Carly made sure. "It's 212-555-2097."

But she didn't hang up. Instead Carly stayed on the line, breathing into the receiver for several long and haunting seconds before her call finally went dead.

Alice froze, unsure of what to do next, certain that she was somehow playing into a trap. Like there were invisible strings at her back, and a puppeteer playing with her like she was their personal marionette.

But of course she had no choice. Alice had to call Carly back.

Or whoever was pretending to be Carly, to force her hand into this next most obvious move. Alice dialed her back, but after four rings the call went to voicemail.

She tried again and again after that. One more time just in case, and Alice realized that she had listened twenty rings before she finally said, "Hi there, Carly. This is Alice returning your call. If you could get back to me as soon as you possibly can, I would really appreciate it."

Alice hung up and pondered what surely had to have been the strangest voicemail she had ever left in her life, past, present, or future. When else would she ever have occasion to call a woman who might have been murdered by the husband who might or might not *actually* have their baby hidden somewhere?

She stood there frozen, pondering her next best move.

Alice had been petrified to leave the penthouse, but that was probably part, if not all, of the problem, and she would only be making the situation worse by staying here. The answers she was so desperate to find weren't here — she'd already looked everywhere. They were out there somewhere.

If she wanted Ellie back, she would have to find them.

With a small but tenacious spark ignited within her, Alice headed for the shower, sure that some scalding hot water massaging her scalp would help to wash away at least some of her unease.

Then she got dressed, feeling incrementally better as she donned a simple blouse and blue jeans. But for some reason, she couldn't leave the apartment; she found herself paralyzed yet again, this time in front of her door.

She couldn't leave without Ellie, despite knowing that was perfectly insane.

Alice went back to the nursery and gathered the doll into her arms, then returned to the entryway and nestled her into the stroller, making sure to pull the cover over Ellie to shield her from the prying, judging eyes of the world.

The door seemed heavier than usual as Alice left her apartment. Her hand shook as she locked it behind her.

The elevator dinged open and Alice wheeled the stroller inside.

"Everything is going to be okay, Ellie," she promised, because soon she would have her real baby back in her arms. "You just wait. Mommy's got this."

Chapter Twenty-Three

Alice moved the stroller into the elevator.

"Everything will be okay," she assured Ellie again as it jolted to a stop.

The doors opened and she wheeled her way into the lobby.

"Hey there, Alice!" Rory seemed happy to see her, jumping up from his desk and walking over to the stroller as she wheeled it toward the exit. "Let me get that for you."

Rory opened the door, then helped her to guide the stroller down the front stairs.

"And how is Ellie today?" Rory cast a glance at the covered stroller.

Time stood still. Her mouth opened but no words came out. She sensed no mockery in his voice. Was it possible she'd been wrong to mistrust him?

"She's happy." Alice finally found her smile. "Thank you for asking."

She pushed forward into the street before Rory could say anything else. The crisp autumn air felt like a slap of reality, a reminder of the life pulsing beyond her cocoon of distress.

The Brownstones stood like timeless sentinels, their facades a canvas of light and shadow, indifferent to her turmoil. Every whisper of wind through the leaves became a conspiratorial murmur, and the mundane crackle of twigs underfoot echoed like distant gunfire in her heightened state of dread.

"Mommy's got this," she told Ellie again.

But did she? Because the world for Alice right now was a symphony of contradictions: old world architecture flanked the streets like the set of some nostalgic movie, and yet each step on the cobblestones felt like treading on shards of glass. Wind swept through the street like a spectral chorus. Her eyes darted nervously about, as if she expected to uncover some lurking menace hidden among the comforting scenes of domestic life playing out behind warmly-lit windows.

A buzzing erupted from her pocket.

She stopped walking to grab her phone and look at the screen: *Flora*.

She hesitated before answering. The ringtone felt like an intrusive alarm, shattering the fragile bubble of her intent, compelling her to confront a reality she wished to evade.

"Hello?"

"Hey there, Alice," Flora's voice was its usual cocktail of empathy and professional detachment. "Are we still on for today?"

"What's today?"

"We have an appointment for a session."

What session? Had they scheduled one and she forgot? She didn't think so. But if she argued, would Flora take that as another sign that she was losing it?

"I'm so sorry, Flora, but I completely forgot."

"Are you still home? Maybe—"

"We'll have to reschedule. I won't be able to make it today." Alice hung up the phone and started walking toward the subway again, still feeling a riot of danger that wasn't really there. A smiling couple strolled past her while holding hands, and their laughter felt like an accusation. *You're insane.*

She reached the subway entrance and carefully guided her stroller down the steps without any help from Rory this time.

Alice stood on the subway platform, trying to ignore the paranoia insisting that everyone was looking at her right now. And that Ellie was in danger, even though she was only a doll. She started when the overhead lights flickered twice, her eyes darting to each corner of the platform, half-expecting to see some lurking figure emerging from the darkness.

The subway train roared into the station, loud enough to drown out her thoughts as she boarded the car. On the other side of the window she glimpsed Flora descending the stairs and scanning the crowd as if searching for a familiar face. Surely Alice's.

Another surge of adrenaline shot through her veins. Why would Flora follow her? The simplest explanation — that she was worried about Alice — felt wrong to the core. The sinister explanation seemed much less plausible, but Alice couldn't help wonder if she was trying to stop Alice from discovering the truth and finding her daughter.

Which would suggest that Ellie was alive and Flora knew it.

The wheels screeched against the tracks as the subway pulled away to leave the platform behind. A young man caught her eye and gestured to his seat.

She shook her head softly. "I'm fine standing, thank you." The compartment was filled with the usual hodge-podge of New Yorkers. A middle-aged woman with a heavy overcoat and tired eyes sat reading a paperback. A teenage boy wearing headphones bobbed his head to some unseen beat. An elderly lady in a lavender hat and matching shawl clutched a rosary in her wrinkled hands. A young mom juggled a toddler on her lap and an infant in her arms. She hurt the most to look at.

"Your baby is so quiet," a different voice chimed in, breaking her train of thought. It was the elderly lady with the lavender hat.

Alice nodded, but didn't meet the woman's eyes. She would have given anything to hear Ellie cry right then.

She took out her phone and opened the contacts, fingers moving until she had changed Carly's anonymous number from her last call into the contact *Carly Hunt.*

The subway jostled and swayed as it tunneled through the city's underworld, each stop and start pulling Alice's frayed nerves even tauter, until Times Square unfurled before her in a relentless assault of neon and noise.

Alice started walking the three blocks to Max's office building, though she could already see it piercing the sky like a crystalline dagger. Her heart pounded harder as she approached the glass-doored entrance, wondering what she possibly expected to see, or why she had really come down here.

The lobby buzzed with activity — lawyers in sleek suits barking into their phones, receptionists flashing perfunctory smiles, and interns rushing about with an air of calculated urgency. Marble floors gleamed beneath a chandelier that poured buckets of light onto potted plants that seemed greener than Alice thought looked natural, though the designers really had done a wonderful job with this space considering its utility.

She parked herself on a modernist bench. Its angular design was at odds with her need for comfort, but it was still the perfect spot to people watch for a while.

But soon a security guard approached her, his face folded into a mixture of concern and professional detachment.

"Is there anything you need, ma'am?"

Alice rose, straightening her back as if lifting some invisible weight. "No, thank you. I know where I'm going."

She crossed the lobby to the elevator and pressed the call button, ignoring the thousand stares that either were or were not boring into the back of her skull.

The elevator doors finally parted and she wheeled the stroller inside. Smashed her finger on the floor for Max's firm. Unlike the claustrophobic car at home, this elevator was roomy and moved in a whisper. Her twenty-second ascent might have been the most peaceful part of her day.

But then the doors opened to a frenzy, with phones ringing in shrill cascades.

The receptionist caught her eye. Alice recognized her from previous visits to the office when she still enjoyed walking downtown and corporate parties when she still knew how to be social. Alice couldn't remember the receptionist's name, but that mane of fiery red hair was easy to recognize, along with a personality that seemed a bit too vibrant for this clinical environment. It was evident even in the way she waved at Alice.

Alice smiled at the receptionist and started walking over to her.

She steadied her voice when she got there, stealing a glance at the nameplate that read *Eileen*. "Is Max in? I have some paperwork for him."

"Sorry, hon." Eileen gave her a frown. "Max is in court all day. But you can leave the paperwork with me if you'd like."

"Thanks!" Alice kneeled to pull some paperwork that didn't exist from her stroller in a performative gesture, but then paused halfway there and turned back to Eileen with a smile. "Actually, if you don't mind, I'd love to leave it on his desk so I could write a little note." She leaned closer to the desk. "The naughty kind."

"Got it." Eileen winked. "Extra important these days I'm sure."

Alice gave her parting smile, then pushed the stroller toward his office, feeling that specter still clawing at the fringes of her mind.

Outside Max's office sat a desk bearing no laptop or personal touches. Manila folders were intermingled with seeming random office supplies. And the nameplate *Carly Hunt.*

Alice called reception, disguising her voice as she mumbled into the phone. "Carly Hunt, please?"

"One moment."

A woman jumped up from another desk and strode over to the desk. She had a mane of inky black hair and tortoiseshell glasses.

"Carly Hunt's desk," she answered.

A current of déjà vu washed through Alice. That was the same voice that had answered Carly's line — she might even have pretended to be Carly when the police had called.

The real Carly could be dead after all.

Alice ended the call.

She approached the woman's desk. In contrast to Carly's workspace, this one arranged with meticulous efficiency: a slimline Sony laptop, stacks of manila folders in precise alignment, and a tasteful smattering of personal photos framed in silver. Her nameplate read *Marcy Edwards*.

"Excuse me, do you happen to know where Carly Hunt is?" Alice asked.

"Carly? She quit. Overnight." Marcy adjusted her glasses. "I'm covering her desk until they find a replacement."

"She quit? Max never mentioned anything."

"That's where I've seen you." Marcy nodded. "It was all very last minute. Carly apparently got engaged and is moving to Europe with her fiancé."

The nonchalance of the revelation belied the storm of questions it unleashed within Alice, each one a dark petal blooming in the garden of her misgivings.

"I was supposed to pick up some files, I *thought* from Carly. Max needed them for court."

"She did occasionally work on briefs at home. Maybe she has them there."

"Would you happen to have her address?"

"Yeah, sure thing, just don't send me to do it. I'm already sick of picking up the pieces since she decided to disappear."

"Thanks," Alice said after Marcy handed her a slip of paper with the address and a smiley face.

As Alice pushed the stroller back toward the elevator, she felt a wave of icy dread wash over her, leaving in its wake the unsettling certainty that Carly's disappearance was a puzzle piece in a much darker picture.

A picture that was getting more plausible by the second.

Chapter Twenty-Four

ALICE SANK into the hard plastic contours of her seat.

The chaotic lullaby of the subway resonated with the tumult of her thoughts, an urban requiem for her fractured peace, vibrating through her bones as she tried to ignore the screaming contradictions inside her, same as she tried to ignore all the dangers in this car.

She took out her phone to see if Carly had called her back. Of course she hadn't. Not then, or any of the next six times Alice compulsively checked.

She tried calling again, listening to four lingering rings before her attempt rolled into voicemail. She hung up without leaving a message.

The screaming inside her got louder.

Alice leaned forward, peeling back the baby blanket to peer in at her artificial daughter lying in the stroller. Glassy eyes reflecting her fractured psyche in a macabre mockery of motherhood resting in the stroller. That thing wasn't Ellie and it never had been. But still it had borne silent witness to her unraveling, easing some of the soul-wrenching suffering that her own husband had been so indifferent to.

Alice caught her haggard reflection in the window, a ghostly apparition bearing the marks of countless vigils superimposed upon the darkness rushing by.

There was no hiding the absurdity of this situation: she was carting a doll around downtown New York in that fancy stroller and calling it her daughter, when everyone who knew Alice also knew that her daughter was dead.

She was sick, and she should have stayed home. Or, it was probably a good thing that she finally got out of the house, but should have had the good sense to at least leave the stupid doll at home where it belonged.

Or maybe the trash chute, if Alice knew what was good for her.

But leaving the dumb doll behind, or tossing it into the trash, would have been like abandoning Ellie, even though that was ridiculous and Alice knew it in her brain, but her body still felt like rebelling against the idea of letting the doll go until she could replace it with the real Ellie.

Synthetic perfection and an unblinking stare made a poor substitute for the real thing, but clinging to the doll felt like a lifeline to her sanity, when in truth it could reflect her slow descent into madness.

The train trundled to a halt and the screech of metal on metal pierced her thoughts.

Then a woman was suddenly leaning forward, cooing: "What a sweet little baby!"

The womans' kind eyes were crinkled at the edges, with a soft halo of graying curls framing her face. But her words, infused with unintended cruelty, stung like salt in a fresh wound, unraveling the fragile mask of Alice's composure.

Alice couldn't stand to look at her. Or at the doll,

which suddenly felt like something she'd been saddled with, a painful reminder of the daughter she'd lost. It was a grotesque parody of Ellie. A symbol of her failure as a mother. And a symptom of her possible insanity.

"Thank you." She stood as the doors opened with a pneumatic hiss. "You can have her."

Alice made for the door, stepping off the subway and abandoning the stroller with a forced detachment. She could hear the car erupting into chaos behind her. Murmuring passengers were getting loud fast. An orchestra of concern and confusion.

She made the mistake of turning back to see the crowd clustering around the stroller, still inside the subway car, as a man lunged forward and tried to grab her and prevent her escape, managing only to grab her sleeve as she made her escape.

"Wait!" He yelled, reaching out to grab her again. "You can't leave your—"

She shed his grasp with a sudden, frantic twitch of her arm — a jerking motion fueled by raw, instinctive panic — as she bolted away in a blur of desperation.

Alice made it halfway to the stairs before a shrill whistle cut through the tunnel. She kept running for daylight, ignoring the sound of someone in pursuit. But the officer caught her just as she emerged into the daylight, his firm grip pulling her back downstairs and toward the subway car, still idling, now with a crowd around it.

"How could you abandon your baby?" demanded the gray-haloed woman, and Alice felt the same shame she would have felt if she'd abandoned Ellie, irrational as that was.

A younger woman, her sharp features softened by bewilderment, gingerly lifted the blanket. Her fingers were tentative as if defusing a bomb.

"It's a doll," she announced with a sterile dispassion.

In the echo chamber of the subway car, those three words descended like a sword on a neck to sever the pretense of normalcy.

Murmurs swelled into exclamations as bystanders craned their necks, some standing on tiptoes, others pushing forward for a glimpse of the artificial child. The collective gasping of onlookers crescendoed into a chorus of confusion.

"A doll?" echoed several people in disbelief.

"Are you kidding me? Someone check on her, she needs help!" shouted a young man in a baseball cap, his voice tinged with concern rather than judgment.

"What the hell is wrong with people these days?" muttered an older woman, clutching her purse and shaking her head.

"Yo, someone's gotta call this in, that's not right."

The gray haired woman was now crying as she pointed at Alice. "Why? Why would you do something like this? *It's sick!*"

The police officer turned his stern gaze on Alice. "Ma'am, this kind of stunt constitutes public mischief—"

"It wasn't a stunt."

"Then do you care to explain?"

The words were stuck in her throat, it was like she had an entire sandbar down there.

"People were scared, thinking that your child was in danger—"

Alice lurched forward, yanked Ellie out of the stroller and clutched her tight, then yelled, "SORRY!" and bolted back toward the stairs.

This time no one followed her.

Chapter Twenty-Five

ALICE ARRIVED with her heart still beating much too fast as she stopped in front of Carly's apartment building. Her finger, still trembling with remnants of adrenaline, hovered in front of the buzzer.

Then she pressed the button to ring her, prepared to send a shock of sound to grate against her fraying nerves. But no sound came. Her anticipation hung suspended in a moment of silence, her heart thumping a counter-rhythm to the absent buzz.

And while Alice was glad to be spared the sound of all those flies, her pressing of the button had been entirely mute.

She kept pressing it for five minutes, not expecting her situation to change but also not knowing what to do, until a man bustled out of the entrance. His gaze, a fleeting and inscrutable dance of curiosity and disregard, brushed past Alice, leaving a residue of unease as he crossed the street.

Alice slipped inside before the door could close, considering the stairs before picturing elderly Mrs. Cohen, her former neighbor, tumbling down the stairwell to her death. She opted for the elevator, despite a guarantee of claustrophobia she could already feel.

Her ascent to the fourth floor was slow, almost contemplative, but at least it was silent compared to the elevator at home. Mirrored walls threw back the distorted image of a woman clutching her doll with haunted eyes and a face carved from grief.

The doors slid open with an indifferent chime and Alice stepped onto burgundy carpet that muffled her footfalls, as if even this hallway felt a need to silence her despair.

Another deep breath did little to steady her as she rapped sharply on 4C.

Still no answer, same as the silence she had faced while still outside, so Alice hadn't been expecting anything different so much as hoping for it. But she knocked again, pounding as hard as she could just in case there was someone in there.

She clutched Ellie tighter to her chest as the door abruptly swung open and Alice found herself face to face with a man she didn't recognize.

"Took you long enough." He looked her up and down, narrowing in on whatever she was hugging to her chest. "That ain't a pizza."

"I'm sorry?" Alice looked behind the man to see a mountain of boxes behind him. "I'm looking for Carly Hunt. Does she live here? I tried calling from downstairs but the buzzer is broken and—"

"She don't live here anymore."

"Where does she live?" Alice asked.

"No idea." He shrugged.

"I'm sorry." She tried to smile. "My name is Alice, I was hoping that—"

"My name's Eric." He extended a hand in offering.

Unsure of what else to do, she shook it. "Nice to meet you Eric." That one came easier. "I'm sorry for disturbing you, but I was hoping you could help me find Carly."

"Why are you looking for her?" Eric asked, sounding more curious than suspicious as he offered her an awkward smile. "I'm not sure I can help you, but I am sure that I can try."

"My husband is a lawyer. He works with Carly and asked me if I could pick up some files. This is the address that Max gave me."

"And Max is your husband?" Eric raised his eyebrows.

"Yes." Alice smiled and nodded, like the answer hadn't been perfectly obvious. She swallowed her impatience as he leaned against the doorframe.

"I knew that Carly was a paralegal, but not much more than that. She never really talked much about her work. We liked to watch movies on Wednesday nights, because that's always my night off, but our jobs were the last thing either one of us ever wanted to talk about. I used to live with my roommate across the way." Eric nodded vaguely down the hall. "But Richie has IBS, so our place was constantly marinated in eau de intestinal discontent, if you know what I mean."

"And you live here now?" Alice asked, trying to understand where Eric was trying to go with his story.

"Good apartments are like gold dust in this city, so when Carly mentioned she was moving out, I offered her $500 bucks to take over the lease."

"Do you know where she might have gone? Or how I can reach her?"

Eric scratched the back of his neck. "I'm not exactly sure where she moved to. Last thing she mentioned was something about getting hitched and packing up for a life overseas with her fiancé. France or Fiji … something with an F. Maybe Fresno?" He laughed. "I can for sure say it wasn't Funkytown."

"You must have some forwarding information for her, right? What if you got some of her mail or–"

"No idea, Alice." He shrugged. "She seemed in an awful hurry to get on with her life. I asked her if we would ever have another Wednesday night and she couldn't even answer me. I think she wanted to say sayonara to all of this." Eric twirled a finger.

"Did you ever see a picture of Carly's fiancé? Or did she mention his name?"

"Not that I remember," Eric said, shrugging again.

"I really need to get those files, or my husband is going to lose his case."

She must have look crestfallen, because he looked suddenly determined to make her feel better.

"You should talk to her mother!" Eric opened his door wide and she could see even more boxes. "Carly said they were close, and I know for a fact that they always talked on Monday night, because I usually got the Readers Digest version of whatever they talked about on Wednesday. I have her number from the time Carly asked me if I could play tech support and fix her mom's Wi-Fi over the phone. Never underestimate the bonding power of a router reset."

Eric took out his phone and pulled up the contact for *Carly's Mom*, then turned around, grabbed a small notepad from atop a nearby box, and scribbled something onto the paper. He tore that page from the top of the pad and handed it to Carly.

"I think her name is Roberta, but it might have been Rachel or Roxy. Something with an R for sure. Maybe I should'a put that into my phone instead of 'Carly's Mom.'"

"Thanks." Alice smiled and meant it. "You've been very helpful."

"No problem." Eric gave her a lopsided grin. "I hope you find her. Tell Carly I said *hey*, and that I hope she's doing well."

"Of course." Alice turned to leave just as the pizza was being delivered.

"Your buzzer's broken," the delivery boy announced.

"Sorry about that!" Eric didn't look sorry at all, his face was lit like a neon marquee. "But I sure am glad to see you."

Alice turned to go again, but this time Eric stopped her.

"That sure is a sweet baby you've got there! Quiet as a little mousey tiptoeing on cotton."

"Yes," Alice agreed with a tightening knot in her stomach. "Barely a peep out of her most days."

"Yeah," agreed the delivery guy, working for his tip while clearly wanting to get the hell out of there. "Cute kid."

But Ellie was a baby doll wrapped in a blanket. She wondered how they would react if she lifted the blanket and showed them the doll's face.

"Thank you." Alice's whisper was hoarse, her half-smile pained.

She made her way back towards the elevator as Eric's voice rose in volume, ready to hold the pizza man hostage with one of his stories.

The elevator dinged softly and the doors parted with a sigh.

Alice stepped in, her hand instinctively tightening around Ellie as she hit the button for the ground floor. The doors closed, killing the sound of Eric blathering to the delivery guy.

Two seconds after she stepped into the lobby, Alice pulled out her phone to give Carly's mother a call.

Chapter Twenty-Six

THE CHILLY AIR clutched at Alice as she exited the lobby onto the street. Each gust whispered rumors of unseen eyes trailing her every step, the city's heartbeat echoing her own mounting unease.

Alice dialed the number with a pounding heart, wishing she at least knew the name of the woman she was calling.

The ringing was interrupted by a weathered yet warm sounding voice. "Hello?"

"Hi there, my name is Alice, and I was wondering if I could speak with Carly?"

The slight pause had her imagining the woman who belonged to that warmly-weathered voice (Roberta, Rachel, or Roxy) now frowning in thought.

"I'm afraid that Carly is out at the moment." Now she sounded cautious.

Alice shifted her weight, clutching the phone like a lifeline. "Do you know when she'll be back? It's important that I speak with her."

She hummed a note of uncertainty. "Who did you say you were again?"

"Alice. Alice Langford. Carly never mentioned me? This is Carly's mom, right?"

"Gwen," replied the woman who was not named Roberta, Rachel, or Roxy.

There was a rustling, like Gwen migrating to a quieter spot. "Carly left early this morning." The timbre of her voice shifted, now colored by a tint of concern. "Why are you looking for her?"

"She was supposed to meet with me, but she never showed up."

"That doesn't sound like Carly."

"No, it doesn't. That's why I'm calling."

"Might I ask why you have my number?"

"Carly and I met at a networking event for paralegals and legal assistants last month. She mentioned she might need some help with a project, and gave me your number just in case I couldn't reach her."

The lie rolled off Alice's tongue with an ease that frightened her, a fiction spun from the loom of her desperation. Gwen obviously knew that Alice was full of shit.

"What event?"

"We were introduced to each other by Jenna Richardson at the Annual Legal Assistants Symposium." There was no Jenna Richardson, but Alice started lying as fast as she could. "She thought Carly and I would hit it off, and boy was she right. We grabbed coffee at Been There Done that over on 5th and Carly told me she had been feeling overwhelmed with a high profile case at work. She said she was looking for someone to help her draft motions and—"

Alice paused her bullshit at the sound of a crying infant that sounded exactly like her Ellie. The sound that had once tortured her was now music to her ears. "Was that a baby?"

"Yes, and he's been under the weather. So if you'll excuse me–"

"I understand this might not be the best time, but it's really important that I speak with Carly. Could I come by and talk to her in–"

"I will tell her that you called, *Alice*."

Gwen said *Alice* like she didn't believe it was really her name.

The baby continued to scream: a raw, primal sound clawing at the edges of Alice's fraying sanity, sharp and jarring like glass shattering against cold marble. Not because she wanted to escape it, but because she wanted to follow it to its source and comfort the infant making it.

"Please. If–"

The line clicked dead before Alice could finish her final protest, leaving her with the echo of silence and the aftertaste of failure.

Frustration knitted her brow as she redialed. But the phone was now just a slab in her hand ringing fruitlessly into the void.

But then it dinged and the pulse quickened in her throat as she swiped the screen: Instagram heralding an update from Carly.

Finally, Alice had something new to go on.

But was it something she wanted to see? Her finger hovered over the screen, the anticipation a tightrope walk between the urge for knowledge and the fear of its weight. How would this new information complicate what she already did and didn't know?

A glinting diamond was perched on Carly's finger like a crown jewel, with the hashtag #lawfullyeverafter accompanied by #engaged beneath the photo.

Exactly the kind of post Carly should be posting, if she was alive and preparing to move to Europe with her fiancé.

But also, exactly the kind of post a murderer might make to give the impression that Carly was still alive. That finger could belong to Carly's corpse.

She stared at the screen, unsure of her next best move.

So far, all of her accusations had been directed at Max, who was unlikely to file charges against her, at least as long as they were married. But now she was considering involving strangers in her suspicions — or delusions — and the subway incident had reminded her that there could be serious repercussions if she was wrong. If she accused the wrong person, she could end up in jail, or worse, back in the psych ward, involuntarily.

And yet, despite the evidence used against her, Alice was certain that even though her mind playing tricks on her, she also felt positive that something she didn't understand was triggering those surrealities, and that a handful of her experiences were real, despite the lies being forced down her throat.

She didn't want to believe that she was batshit crazy.

But she would never which was true by doing nothing.

So she typed out the words, *Carly, are you alive?*

Her comment sat on the screen, stupidly laden with the weight of her frantic worry. Of course she deleted it. Why leave evidence of her insanity there for a court to use against her later? Alice second-guessed herself for another couple of moments then decided to put her phone away.

But it buzzed back to life in her hand. *Carly Hunt* flashed across the screen as if she had manifested the call into existence. Alice's heart hit a triphammer pace.

She swiped to answer.

"Is this Alice?"

"Yes. Is this—"

"I was hoping that we could meet."

"I'm free right now. Where do you want to meet?"

"I'll need a couple of hours." Carly's weariness was threaded through her words. "I have to get the baby down for a nap."

Just hearing the words felt like a stab in the gut. She would give anything to be putting Ellie down for a nap right now.

"How about two hours from now," Alice suggested, "wherever you want to meet?"

"Do you know the Beanstalk Café'?

"That's near Central Park?" Alice confirmed.

"It is."

"Then I know it."

"See you then," Carly said.

The call went dead. The silence was a void, the cessation of sound magnifying the clamor of thoughts that Alice struggled to quiet.

Alice thought again of Flora searching the subway station, possibly worried that she'd gone off the deep end and was about to get herself deeper into trouble. Or possibly, trying to stop her from searching for Ellie?

Either way, maybe it made sense to reassure the woman, just so she wouldn't be waiting on Alice's doorstep to make a big fuss when she returned.

No, that wasn't it. The real reason was that she didn't want Flora to tell Max that she was getting worse. And possibly recommend a stronger antidepressant or a trip back to Mt. Sinai.

Her adrenaline settled as she texted Flora: *Just spoke to Carly. Meeting her shortly.*

Alice watched the three dots until they disappeared in place of Flora's words: *You must be very relieved.*

Relief still eluded her, but Alice could agree on a simpler truth. *It'll be good to finally get some answers.*

And Flora texted back, *I'm sure this will put your mind at ease.*

Now Alice had to kill the next two hours without going out of her mind.

Time stretched like an endless corridor before her, with each tick of the clock yet another mocking echo in the chamber of her restlessness.

Chapter Twenty-Seven

ALICE WANDERED AIMLESSLY through the crowded streets for two interminable hours in a furious effort to distract her spiraling thoughts, but failed miserably.

She started off in a quaint bookstore, thumbing through pages she couldn't focus on, inhaling the musk of old paper as if it could calm her nerves. Each book harbored a potential escape, yet her mind was a prisoner to its own chaos, the words blending into a blur of ink and helplessness. And while trying to lose herself among those musty tomes, she felt an unexpected pang after picking up a brightly-illustrated children's book that she would never ever read to Ellie.

She fled the bookstore as she blinked back tears, taking refuge in a nearby café, where she sipped on a too-sweet latte in a dimly-lit corner, the sugar failing to soften the bitter taste of anxiety. The liquid warmth was a hollow comfort compared to the feel of Ellie's small body nestled against her in a way that she would never feel again, if she had ever actually felt it at all.

When her cup was empty, she wandered down one

street after another, perusing an array of window displays, the mannequins staring back at her with blank placid faces. Immobile yet dressed for a life of vibrant autumns. Like her doll.

She finally succumbed to the pull of Central Park, where she chose an outdoor table to sit and wait for Carly to arrive.

Seated on a park bench, the world seemed to carry on with an energy that she couldn't match. Alice envied the effortless orbits of the lives around her, while hers spun wildly off-axis, a rogue planet ejected from the solar system of normalcy.

A father jogged past, pushing a stroller with a giggling child, the sound both sweet and jarring to Alice as she thought of the laughter she would never share with Ellie.

A group of tourists, their accents sounding like music as they took pictures; they were free to enjoy the city's charm, untethered by the gravity of loss.

A woman draped in a red scarf that fluttered like a flame against the breeze sat down to read adjacent to an old man tossing crumbs to pigeons.

It was finally time to meet Carly. Alice walked to the Beanstalk Cafe and asked for a seat outside.

The coffee shop was a cozy warren of mismatched armchairs and rustic wooden tables, and the scent of roasted coffee beans permeated the air in an aromatic welcome. Outside, the cafe spilled onto the sidewalk with a handful of wrought-iron tables shaded by colorful umbrellas, offering a quaint view of the bustling street and the emerald expanse of Central Park beyond.

Alice had Ellie propped up on the chair beside her, staring out at the park's expanse as if she, too, was on the lookout for Carly. A server approached her, smiling bright like the afternoon sun, apron dusted with flour like a badge of her bustling day in the café.

"Would you like a highchair for your baby?" she asked.

Alice hesitated, not really sure of how she should respond before deciding on the truth. "No, thank you … she's just a doll."

That bright smile faded like a sunset slipping into twilight as the server's features shifted from warmth to a coolly-puzzled reserve, making Alice feel like a crazy person.

"What can I get for you?"

She definitely didn't want any more coffee. "A chamomile tea, please."

"Coming right up." The server gave her a half-smile before departing, clearly relieved to be leaving Alice's table.

Her gaze returned to the park, watching a young couple sharing an ice cream, then to a street performer gathering a crowd, and children chasing one another. She felt an acute envy for their unfettered joy, so distant from her own veiled sorrow.

A pair of pigeons landed on an adjacent table, tilting their heads curiously at Ellie.

Alice shooed them away.

Then she turned and her heart skipped erratically as she saw a familiar figure approaching from a block away, undeniably the same woman whose lifeless presence had haunted her living room. And yet here she was in the flesh, Carly Hunt striding confidently toward her, very much alive with a casual wave directed at Alice.

Time seemed to still as Carly navigated the sidewalk, dodging pedestrians with the ease of a seasoned New Yorker. Alice's heart thudded harder, each beat a drum roll leading to this moment of reckoning, a pivot upon which her sanity teetered.

Confusion gnawed at her; this was not the woman she had expected to see, though Alice could not have said what she actually had expected.

She finally waved back.

Carly smiled and started to run across the street.

But then another impossible nightmare unfolded right in front of her, making Alice long to believe that she was still trapped somewhere in her dreams.

Carly's light jog morphed into a sprint, as the sudden, horrific blare of a car horn shattered the scene.

The cab barreled toward her at a merciless velocity, smashing into Carly with a sickening crunch that resonated through the air. Her body crumpled against the hood before being flung aside like a rag doll with a violence that turned grace into chaos.

Time seemed to fracture again, the world now moving frame by slow motion frame.

Onlookers were horrified. Shouts clawed through the air in terror and confusion as the offending vehicle — a smear of metallic yellow — fled without pause, turning a corner and disappearing into a throng of traffic.

Carly's descent had been a sickening ballet. The sound of Carly landing after twisting through the air was a wet snap that spoke of broken bones and stolen breath.

Alice stood rooted to her spot, refusing to accept the sight in front of her.

Her eyes had lied too many times for Alice to believe what she was seeing now.

Pandemonium ensued; people rushed forward, a few fumbling with their phones as they dialed for help. Others stood petrified. Central Park's melody of leisure was now underscored by the shrill pitches of panic and the grim undertone of tragedy.

Her limbs refused to comply with her frantic brain,

locking Alice in place as the aftermath of the accident unfolded right there in the street just a few feet away.

Her mind screamed for her to move, to run toward Carly, to do something. *Anything.*

But her feet were rooted to the concrete, her gaze affixed to Carly's still form, crumpled on the hard pavement — a discarded puppet whose performance had met an untimely end. An invisible force field seemed to encase her, a cruel bubble separating Alice from the carnage that her eyes refused to accept.

The sirens were already screaming.

Her paralysis finally broke with a visceral jolt, propelling Alice from the chair in a rush of adrenaline.

"Miss! You forgot your baby," shouted a stranger sitting at a nearby table.

Mechanically, she reclaimed the doll, holding Ellie against her chest, the plastic body a grotesque mirror to the lifelessness that lay splayed out before her as she bolted from the café, pounding the pavement with reckless urgency as she dashed across the street toward Carly's still crumpled form.

Police cars converged on the scene with a clamor of authority just moments later, parting the sea of onlookers. The wailing ambulance crescendoed to a deafening pitch as it pulled up to the accident and the doors flew open.

Medics rushed out in a choreographed dance of emergency care, but their faces soon settled into grim masks.

She watched a frenzy of attempts to resuscitate Carly dwindle into surrender, until it was clear that the young woman's spirit had clearly vacated her body.

Just as Carly had been about to tell Alice the truth, she had been killed. Maybe murdered.

Alice stood engulfed in a silence that screamed louder than any sirens.

Chapter Twenty-Eight

ALICE RETURNED to her apartment apartment building after a somber walk she barely remembered making, drifting through a world that had lost its axis.

The rise to her floor felt like an ascent through heavy clouds of disquiet, and after stepping off of the elevator and into the hallway, that corridor never felt lonelier.

She entered her home, where every room had been painstakingly designed with her loving touch, but now it felt like the walls and furniture and decor all belonged to someone else.

She was still standing in the entryway, clutching the Ellie doll and feeling unsteady, like she might tip over and fall onto the floor at any moment, when a rhythmic knock at the door dragged her back into a reality she barely recognized.

Alice opened the door to see Flora standing in the hallway, her presence at the threshold somehow both a comfort and an assault.

"Now's not really a good time," she murmured, the words barely escaping her lips.

"I don't mean to intrude," Flora said, her voice softly tentative. "I just wanted to see how you were doing after meeting with Carly."

The name reverberated through her mind like a bell tolling for the dead, summoning the vivid image of the accident itself and the horrific aftermath, from that first screeching siren to the removal of her body.

Flora's concern deepened as she observed Alice's face, surely paling as it contorted with the memory. "Alice, are you alright? You're scaring me."

Her voice broke as she confessed the unfathomable truth. "Carly … was killed. It happened right in front of me. A hit and run."

"Oh my!" Flora gasped, and though her face was awash with the blow of such unexpected news, she still stepped forward, her professional poise surrendering to human instinct. "Oh, Alice … you're in shock. Let me come in; let me take care of you."

After a hesitant pause, Alice opened her door wider.

Flora entered the apartment.

"May I?" Flora nodded at the doll.

Alice gave her a tentative nod, then loosened her grip on Ellie. She watched as Flora carefully placed the doll on the couch, her touch gentle, almost reverent.

Then she returned to Alice and gently took her by the hand, leading her into the bedroom and tucking her in lovingly, more like a mother to a daughter than a therapist to her patient. The sheets were cold and unwelcoming against her skin, but Alice still knew that this was where she should be.

"I'll be right back," Flora said, slipping out of the bedroom and returning several minutes later with a small pill and a glass of water.

Alice swallowed the pill without question. It was a

small act of acquiescence, trust in Flora's judgment anchoring her in the tumultuous sea of her thoughts.

"I'll read one of your magazines in the living room and check on you in a bit." Flora offered her yet another kind smile. "Get some sleep."

"I want Ellie," Alice whispered to Flora before she left.

"Of course." If Flora was judging her, Alice couldn't hear it in her voice.

She left the room and came back with Ellie, tucking the doll into bed beside Alice before leaving. Then the room blurred as the pill pulled Alice into the depths of a restless slumber.

Time became a muddled stream, moments folding into each other, until the sound of a key in the door signaled Max's return. His presence was a shadow through her haze, a disturbance in the still waters of her drug-induced calm. She willed herself to wake up all the way, wanting or perhaps even needing to hear what her husband was saying.

What lies he might be telling Flora that Alice would need to catch him in.

The murmur of voices drifted deeper into her awareness, a distant conversation between Max and Flora that seemed both urgent and distant. She caught only snippets of their exchange as her mind struggled to weave their words into something coherent.

"Alice was meeting Carly? Today?" Max sounded incredulous, his voice tinged with a concern that sounded either genuine or practiced. She couldn't tell which.

"She needed closure, you know, after the other night. Wanted to be sure of what she saw … or thought she saw."

Max sighed after a heavy silence. "That's just like Alice, always needing to see things for herself." His sorrow seemed to gain weight. "Carly was … she was exceptional.

Always hardworking. And she was getting married, ready to start her life over. This is a tragedy for so many reasons."

"I gave Alice something to help her sleep," Flora said.

"And the doll?" His voice was closer now. Perhaps he was peering into their bedroom, looking at his wife cradling the lifeless surrogate for their dead daughter.

"It's helping her cope," Flora replied, a defensive edge creeping into her voice. "For now, at least."

Max made a noncommittal sound, a grunt that could have meant anything.

Alice felt a flicker of irritation at his constant inability to understand. Or his refusal to. How could he be so unaffected by their daughter's death?

But she couldn't even hate him right now, even though she wanted to.

Their voices grew too muffled for her to mine any meaning from them as the pill pulled her back into oblivion.

Days merged into a single, indistinguishable haze, each one bleeding into the next with no clear demarcation. The passage of time smeared into a single, gray smudge, the sun's arc irrelevant behind the drawn curtains of her mind's retreat. She existed in a state of half-consciousness, roused only by the necessities of survival — eating, drinking, sleeping — and even those activities were enveloped in a fog.

Her reality was marked by regular appearances from Flora, who would sit by her bedside with a glass of water and a small white pill. Max occasionally materialized in the bedroom, but never to sleep. His presence hovered at the periphery of her awareness, his voice a distant baritone that sometimes broke through the strangled caterwauling of her medicated dreams.

The pills made time elastic, stretching and compressing

moments into a continuous loop. With each pill swallowed, she sank further into the soft oblivion of her bed, the outside world becoming a distant memory.

Alice remained dimly aware of Flora and Max conversing, their voices blending with other ambient noises that filtered through the thick curtain of her fugue.

Her will to engage with life had evaporated. The thought of rising from the bed, of planting her feet on solid ground and facing the day, felt daunting, like she was being asked to scale a mountain. Food lost its appeal; the act of eating became mechanical, something done to satisfy the concern in Flora's eyes more than any hunger of her own.

The outside world could have been anything while trapped in her state of hibernation — another planet or perhaps a different dimension entirely. The bed became her entire universe, with Ellie nestled beside her, a silent witness to the endless expanse of yawning time.

Max's presence was more tangible the next time he entered the room, his figure solidifying out of the medicinal haze holding her captive. His figure loomed, a paradox of comfort and confusion, his once-familiar touch now a strange pressure against her skin.

She blinked up at him, and for a moment, Max was just her husband again — concerned, his brow creased with the weight of compassion.

He sat on the edge of the bed, his hand reaching out to tenderly brush the hair back from her forehead.

"Alice," he whispered, his voice a mixture of sadness and perhaps admiration. "You're so strong, but you don't have to be strong right now. What you saw ... it must have been so unspeakably awful."

Her eyes, though heavy, locked onto his with an intensity that belied her weakened state. His hand lingered on her cheek before he pulled it away.

"I stopped by the hospital and got your records so you wouldn't have to wait." He pulled an envelope from his coat pocket.

Alice merely nodded, her gaze following the descent of the envelope to her nightstand. But she made no move to reach for it, and he didn't remonstrate her for the lie she'd told. She wondered dully how he had found she'd requested them, but what was the point of asking? He knew, and there was nothing she could do about it.

Days unfurled like the slow turn of pages in a book forgotten on a shelf, each passing with the same gray tint as the one before it. Max's footfalls were a metronome ticking away the moments of her grief-stained stasis.

Alice had no idea how much time had passed when his silhouette filled the bedroom doorway and said, "I'm going to Carly's funeral. You should come. It might give you some closure."

The word *closure* felt like a betrayal, a forced end to a chapter Alice wasn't ready to conclude, a narrative that refused to be neatly tucked away.

"I can't." Alice turned her face into the pillow.

Max answered her with a sigh, then she heard the soft whisper of fabric and a faint click as the door shut behind him, leaving Alice alone once more.

A quarter hour or so later — time had mostly lost its meaning — she picked up the phone from her nightstand and listened to her last voicemail from Carly, ten or twenty times — not that it ever gave her any answers. No secret messages that might explain her senseless death.

Suddenly compelled by a force she couldn't name, Alice pushed herself from the bed and staggered to the bathroom.

The mirror reflected a stranger, vacant-eyed and gaunt, her skin stretched too tight over sharp bones. She was the living embodiment of grief. No one would question whether she belonged at Carly's funeral.

She went to her closet and trailed her fingers across the hanging garments until they settled on the solemn black of mourning, settling on a simple dress, unassuming in its elegance, the fabric light despite its dark hue — a sheath of crepe that once fell in gentle ripples around her knees now hanging loose and straight in a mocking echo of the vibrancy it had held on her livelier frame.

Alice went back into the bathroom, her hands shaking as she tried to apply makeup, and maybe paint some life back onto a canvas that had grown too stark. But the colors were all wrong — too bright and harsh against her pallor.

With a cry of frustration, she scrubbed her face clean, abandoning the artificial pigments in favor of her honest reflection.

Determined, or perhaps desperate, she pulled up Carly's obituary on her phone.

The words blurred through her tears, but she could clearly read the church's address and that was all she needed.

Alice called a cab, then she peeked out her door into the hallway, made sure that the coast was clear without Flora anywhere in sight before scurrying down the corridor into the elevator.

But just before pressing the button, Alice realized that she couldn't stand the thought of making that screeching descent yet again, and didn't want the elevator to alert Flora that she was leaving the building.

With a burst of clarity, she fled into the stairwell, the echo of her steps a staccato rhythm against the deafening silence.

One floor down, Alice realized she had forgotten to bring Ellie.

Chapter Twenty-Nine

The stairwell was a vertical corridor of echoes where her every footstep resounded with a ghostly persistence, filling her mind with unwelcome flashes of the day Mrs. Cohen's lifeless body was found sprawled on the steps.

Her breath hitched with each passed landing, and Alice half-expected to stumble upon some new horror, but the only presence in the stairwell was her own. She clung to the railing, feeling the cold metal under her hand.

"Alice!" Rory called out to her as she crossed the lobby.

She felt bad about not answering him, but Alice seriously had no idea what she could say, so she gave him a quick wave and kept walking. He waved back, but his smile slipped a little.

The cab was already waiting for her when she stepped outside.

She climbed into the back and gave an address to the driver. He was the silent type, but the ride did little to calm her rattled nerves. When the taxi finally pulled to a stop in front of the church, a solemn edifice of weathered stone and stained glass, Alice was seized by a sudden sense of unreality.

Stepping out of the cab, she wondered what the hell she was doing. And more to the point, whether this was a giant mistake.

Though even if it was, Alice knew that she had no other choice. She needed a clue about what Carly had wanted to tell her, and someone here might know. Or know enough to let Alice fill in the rest.

So she drew a deep breath and entered a world of lamentation. And just in time, since it seemed like the funeral was just about to start.

The church was filled to near-capacity, the pews a sea of somber attire and downcast eyes. Whispered condolences in hushed murmurs echoed off the vaulted ceilings, and the atmosphere was thick with the scent of lilies and the stifling weight of grief.

She slipped into the back like a ghost among the throng of Carly's friends, family, and colleagues. Alice scanned the crowd until she saw Max sitting with a contingent from the law firm, their suits sharp and expressions taut with controlled sorrow. He held a veneer of composed sorrow, his customary control betrayed by the slight tremor in his clasped hands. Everyone looked saturated with grief.

Thankfully, Max didn't look her way.

An older woman cradling a baby caught her eye. The lines on her face were deepened by grief, and tears streamed freely down her cheeks. Alice realized with a pang in her chest that the woman must be Carly's mother, Gwen.

And the infant in her arms — so small and oblivious to the sorrow surrounding it — seemed to be around the same age that Ellie would have been.

Her heart pounded as she watched them from the

shadowy recess in back of the church. The baby, with its plump cheeks and innocent eyes, was a living echo of Alice's daughter. A piercing mix of envy and sorrow twisted within her, and she had to grip the pew in front of her to keep from falling over.

ALICE WATCHED THE CEREMONY UNFOLD, a silent observer to the pageantry of grief. Eulogies painted the deceased in a warm light of fond memories, her life recounted in anecdotes that drew soft laughter and fresh tears from the pews.

She was an intruder in this scene, her connection to Carly a tangled web of secrecy and deceit. Yet, as she listened to the stories of Carly's kindness, her ambitions, and her love for life, Alice couldn't help but feel the loss with a hollow ache in the pit of her stomach.

She turned back to look at the baby in Gwen's arms, unable to tear her gaze away. Its occasional coos and gurgles were an incongruent soundtrack to the funeral's somber tone. The baby was a beacon of life amid so much despair, and a cruel mirage to Alice.

Alice ached to rush over and snatch the infant from Gwen.

Her breaths came in shallow gasps as she fought a wave of oncoming tears, her longing for Ellie intermingling with the grief that hung like a shroud over the congregation. She was caught in the gravitational pull of a shared loss and needed to escape.

But then Gwen handed the baby to the person next to her and approached the podium with a tremulous step, the weight of her grief like a tangible shadow in the silent church.

She started to speak in a fractured whisper before she

found a voice loud enough to grieve her daughter's stolen future.

Gwen steadied herself at the podium, gripping its edges as she leaned forward and filled the church with her sorrow.

"My daughter Carly was just at the start of everything. She had dreams larger than the sky — my little girl was going to get married, move to Europe, and live the life she had always loved to meticulously plan."

Her gaze swept over the crowd as her eyes brimmed with tears. "But now, that life ... those dreams, they're just echoes, ghosts of what should have been."

Gwen paused, swallowing hard as she took a breath from the raw and haunting melody, each note a shard of the life Carly would never live, each pause a chasm of the silence she left behind.

Then she continued, her every syllable still steeped in pain. "My grandson Daniel will never feel his mother's arms around him, hear her laughter, or experience the boundless ocean of her love."

Alice couldn't help crying as she thought of Ellie growing up without her, never knowing how much she'd loved her from the moment the nurse had placed Ellie in her arms.

A tear escaped, trailing down Gwen's cheek as she continued. "How do I tell my grandson about the woman who was so full of life, who should have been there for every scraped knee and birthday? For every proud moment? How do I explain that his mother is now just a memory, a photo we speak to instead of the living and loving presence she was meant to be?"

Her voice broke as she finished, "Carly was ready to start a new chapter, but now, we're all left clinging to the pages she's already filled, knowing that her story ended far too soon."

Gwen bowed her head, her grief a silent scream in the still church.

Then she dissolved into sobs, until a kind arm encircled the loudly grieving mother and guided her away from the podium and back to the solace of her pew, where she could mourn behind the shield of her family and friends.

After another several speakers, Max rose from his seat with a somber grace, his shoulders squared as if to bear the weight of his words. Alice was surprised — he never talked about Carly at home, and the few mentions she remembered were focused on work, like Carly's planned departure interfering with his big, important case.

How had he known her well enough to be asked to give a eulogy?

Was she reading too much into it, or was it possible he'd simply been asked because someone at the firm needed to do it?

"Carly was more than a paralegal to us," he began, his voice steady but tinged with the rawness of loss. "She brought light into every case, every long night at the office. And she had dreams. Oh boy, did she have dreams ..." He paused, looking down at his hands before meeting the eyes of everyone gathered. "Carly was going to be a brilliant lawyer. She left a mark on us, on the very fabric of our firm. We are better for having known her, and now, we are lesser without her."

Nothing he'd said about Carly was personal, but Max's restrained grief seemed genuine — and just the right amount for a deceased co-worker who he respected professionally but didn't know personally.

After a respectful pause, Marcy Edwards approached the podium, her hands clasped tightly in front of her.

"I remember when Carly got engaged ..." A small smile flickered through her grief. "I've never seen her so full of joy, or so vibrant. She would come into the office with her eyes sparkling after a another deliriously happy weekend with her fiancé. Her happiness was contagious, and Carly ..."

Her voice trailed off as she fought back tears. "Carly *was* happiness, and it is cruelty incarnate that she was taken away from us so soon."

As the tributes wove a tapestry of Carly's time on Earth, Alice noticed a haunting absence that begged for scrutiny. Throughout the mosaic of praise and remembrance, there was no fiancé to speak on behalf of Carly, despite how in love they supposedly were.

The omission felt ominous to Alice, and as the ceremony drew to a close with a lingering sense of too much unsaid, an uneasy quiet seemed to whisper of secrets still buried.

And after that final amen echoed through the church, her resolve hardened.

Alice would unearth those buried truths, no matter the cost.

Chapter Thirty

THE WAKE WAS HELD in a modestly-decorated hall attached to the church, where the air was thick with the aroma of strong coffee and the undercurrent of whispered conversations. Round tables were draped in white linen, graced with small glass bowls packed with white and blush colored roses for centerpieces. Waitstaff moved like wraiths among the clusters of black-clad individuals, offering trays of delicate finger foods that seemed incongruous with the dark gravity.

Alice navigated through the subdued crowd, her presence almost spectral as she drifted from one conversation to another. She overheard a pair of Carly's former colleagues discussing her dedication to her work, their words painting a picture of a paralegal fiercely committed to justice. One of them recounted a late night at the office, Carly poring over case files long after everyone else had gone home, her desk lamp the sole island of light in a sea of darkened cubicles.

She encountered a group of Carly's college friends, who reminisced about their undergraduate escapades through laughter and tears, sharing stories of Carly's infectious enthusiasm, how she had rallied them during finals with midnight coffee runs.

And at a corner table, Alice paused to eavesdrop on an elderly couple speaking of Carly with the fondness reserved for a surrogate granddaughter. They told a young woman next to them about the time Carly helped organize a charity event, her organizational prowess turning a modest neighborhood gathering into a bustling fundraiser that became an annual tradition.

Alice saw Marcy standing by a window with the posture of someone bracing against an invisible storm, staring out at the gray sky as if searching for a sign. She turned with a start when Alice approached, her surprise registering in a slight raise of her eyebrows.

"Alice! I didn't expect to see you here. I didn't know you were coming."

She mustered a half-hearted smile, the muscles in her face barely accustomed to the gesture after days of numbness. "It was a last-minute decision."

"You could've sat with us at the service," Marcy offered.

"It was last minute," Alice replied, repeating herself as if to reaffirm her own sudden appearance. "I needed to be here, but I wasn't sure until I arrived."

Marcy nodded, her expression softening with understanding. "We're all still trying to make sense of it all. No one can believe she's gone. Just like that." She sighed. "It really makes you think."

"Would it be possible for you to introduce me to Carly's fiancé? There's something I would love to ask him."

Marcy not only didn't answer Alice right away, it seemed like her question might have been out of bounds.

The request hung in the air, an unwelcome intrusion into the carefully-curated atmosphere of muted grief.

Her eyes darted away momentarily before meeting Alice's gaze again, her mouth tightening.

"I'm sorry, I can't introduce you." Marcy's voice was tinged with a mix of embarrassment and confusion. "No one really knew who her fiancé was. Carly kept her relationship extremely private. Secret, really. We've all been speculating, but…"

She trailed off, shrugging helplessly.

Alice felt a jolt of surprise, her mind racing. "Nobody has met him? At all?"

"No." Marcy shook her head. "Most of us figured that maybe it was a client because, you know, the firm has such a strict policy against fraternization."

The revelation added yet another layer of mystery to Carly's already-enigmatic personal life. Her curiosity deepened, eyes narrowing as she processed the new information.

"And she quit so suddenly," Marcy continued, her tone a blend of reflection and disbelief. "One day she's part of everything, and then she's leaving to start this whole new chapter with her secret fiancé."

"Did everyone think he would show up today, to mourn?"

"Maybe he did?" Marcy shrugged. "But if so, then he wasn't a client. The only one of our clients here today is over there." She gestured subtly across the room to a man conversing quietly with a group, with a statuesque woman standing next to him. "That's Mr. Dennison, and his wife came with him. So it obviously can't be him."

Alice didn't know what to think. She excused herself from Marcy with a polite nod and a murmur of thanks, slipping away into the flow of mourners like a shadow among shades. Then she drifted through the crowd, her eyes scanning faces and listening to snatches of conversation that ebbed and flowed around her, a symphony of sorrow and remembrance without any of the clues she was hoping to mine. She moved through the crowd like an actor in a play she hadn't rehearsed, unsure of her lines, role, or purpose.

Then, in the throng of black suits and somber dresses, she spied Eric — the man who had taken over Carly's lease. His tall frame and disheveled hair were unmistakable, even in this sea of grief. He stood alone, nursing a water, his expression one of contemplation rather than mourning. She navigated toward him.

Eric looked up from his introspective solitude once Alice was standing in front of him.

"I'm sorry about Carly," she said softly, her voice threading through the hum of the room.

"It was just so sudden ..." Eric sounded too gobsmacked to add anything else.

"Had you spoken with her recently?"

He shook his head, the lines on his face deepening. "No, not since before I saw you a few days ago." Eric narrowed his eyes at her. "Have you lost weight?"

"I'm on a diet." Alice tried to smile, but it had to look like a grimace painted on a marble statue, frozen and unnaturally strained.

Her lie was apparently a nail in the coffin of their conversation.

Eric shuffled on his feet, but Alice needed an exit anyway after catching sight of Carly's mother.

"If you'll excuse me." Her departing smile was surely more convincing as she bowed her head at Eric, then turned around and walked over to Gwen, sans baby.

Maternal grief was carved hard into her features.

"Mrs. Hunt? I'm Alice," she introduced herself. "We spoke on the phone the day that Carly ..." Alice couldn't finish her thought. "I'm so sorry for your loss."

Her red-rimmed and weary eyes focused on Alice. "Yes, I remember. You wanted to talk to Carly. And how did you know my daughter?"

Alice guessed that Gwen was trying to see if she could remember her lie.

Surprisingly, she did, down to the made up woman who introduced them. "Jenna Richardson introduced us when we were both at the Annual Legal Assistants Symposium."

Gwen nodded, apparently willing to believe that no one would be so crass as to lie about how they knew Carly at her funeral.

Alice needed to say something to make the relationship more real. "I was going to help her out with some paperwork that her boss needed from her. I think his name was Max — do you know him?"

"Only from his eulogy." Gwen wiped a tear from her eye. "But she sure did love her job. It broke her heart to leave. But she didn't feel like she had any other choice ..."

"So you knew her fiancé?" It was a shot in the dark that she needed to take.

"I never met him." A shadow crossed her face. "Carly was going to introduce us this weekend ..." Her voice trailed off, choked by a sob.

A family friend, with a gentle touch and sympathetic eyes, brought Carly's baby over to Grandma, nestling the infant into her arms.

Alice's heart hammered in her chest as she glimpsed the baby, its small form swaddled in pale blue, a living echo of the child that Alice held only in her dreams. She watched the way Gwen's tears slowed when she held the baby, how a small, sad smile curved onto her lips despite the sorrow.

She longed for a closer look, to confirm the nagging suspicion that gnawed at her — could it be her missing Ellie? The baby seemed just the right age.

But the infant's face remained obscured, tucked away from view, shielded from the chill of the hall and the intensity of Alice's stare.

Alice felt her forehead beading with sweat as she watched Gwen cradle the baby closer, her tears making way for a momentary peace as she held her grandchild.

"Gwen, would you come over for a moment?" a woman's voice called softly.

Gwen turned, the conflict evident in her eyes as she glanced down at the baby and then back at an older couple waiting to speak with her. "I … Of course, give me just a second."

"I can hold the baby, if you need," Alice offered, her voice surprisingly steady considering all of the wonderful and terrible thoughts that were waging a war inside her mind.

Gwen hesitated, her gaze flickering between Alice and the approaching couple. "Would you mind? I'll only be a moment."

"It's no trouble at all," Alice assured her, her arms already outstretched in anticipation. "Take your time."

The weight of the baby settled into them — a comfortable, familiar burden that she had been longing to feel.

With the baby cradled against her chest, Alice's heart raced with a silent alarm, each beat a drum tolling the approach of an unseen storm.

And what Alice knew she was going to do next.

Now that the certainty of truth was a drumbeat she could not ignore.

Chapter Thirty-One

ALICE CLUTCHED the baby to her chest, his warmth seeping into her like a long-forgotten balm. But standing there looking down at the slumbering infant, and inhaling her smell, the certainty within her grew like the first few drops from an oncoming storm.

This was Ellie. It *had* to be.

In her arms lay the promise of a miracle, the potential to undo the agony of her loss. Alice allowed herself, for just a moment, to be cradled by the sweet delusion that the universe had corrected its cruel mistake.

She slipped into the ladies' room as Ellie woke up, squirming in her arms, her little face scrunching in discomfort or perhaps confusion at the sudden change of arms and scent. Alice searched the infant for the familiar features, for the resemblance that haunted her dreams.

Her heartbeat grew unsteady as she observed the baby under sterile lighting to find subtle differences, in the curve of this baby's cheek and the color of its eyes.

With trembling fingers, she undid the swaddle and peered into the diaper, her soul suffering another round of perforations as she discovered the undeniable evidence.

The realization was a cold wave, a cruel hand that reached into the chest and squeezed. It wasn't just the wrong gender — it was the wrong life, and no amount of wishing could morph this child into her Ellie.

The room spun as Alice reeled from the revelation.

The walls started closing in on her as the air began to thin.

The restroom door swung wide, and a woman burst inside, her face flushed with alarm and eyes wild with the frantic energy of the search. Mid-forties or so, her hair a windblown array of golden-brown locks framing her face in worry.

Footsteps thundered toward her, a crescendo of urgent echoes against the tile. They were coming for her, for the baby — the baby that wasn't hers.

Panic clawed at her throat, a visceral fear that choked Alice as she held the baby boy closer, her arms a trembling shield.

Gwen burst into the bathroom, her expression a tempest of anger and fear. "What do you think you're doing?" Her voice was sharp as broken glass.

Alice replied in a jumbled rush of breathless apologies. "I thought — I was just going to change him—"

"With what? Where are the diapers?"

The crowd at the door grew, their silhouettes a jury of shadows against the hallway light, their murmurs a chorus of condemnation. Alice could feel their eyes on her, their judgment piercing through her already fragile composure.

She clutched the baby to her chest, her mind a whirl-wind of desperate thoughts.

"I just needed to make sure," Alice whispered, more to herself than to the hostile audience, her eyes wide and pleading. But in their minds, there was no excuse for her actions, no rationale that could explain away the scene before them.

Gwen's hands were decisive and firm as she reclaimed her grandson, eclipsing Alice's feeble resistance. The baby erupted into a wail, his face scrunching up in a portrait of distress.

"Who are you really?" Gwen demanded, her voice now laced with a sharp fear as she clutched the crying child, scrutinizing Alice with a newfound wariness.

She could scarcely muster an answer, her own heartbreak mirroring the infant's cries. Words failed her, the weight of mistaken identity crashing down upon her in a suffocating wave. She turned abruptly, her escape as erratic as her thoughts, pushing through the bathroom door and out into the hall.

Alice fled, the faces around her blurring into a meaningless panorama of murmuring sorrow, with one face snapping sharply into sharp focus — Max's eyes met hers across the room, widening in disbelief, his shock a silent echo of her own as their gazes locked for a suspended moment.

Then she broke the connection with a desperate sprint. Her escape was as much from the judgmental stares as it was from the piercing recognition of her own folly.

Her flight from the church hall was a blur of motion and muffled sound, her heart pounding in her ears as she burst through the doors into the cold clarity of the outside world. She didn't pause to catch her breath; she couldn't afford to — not with the coil of panic and the sting of tears threatening to overwhelm her.

The subway station was a haven, a place where she could disappear as just another face among the weary commuters. Here, in the bowels of the city, among the weary faces and stale air, Alice found the anonymity she craved — a chance to vanish from the narrative that had ensnared her as she pressed herself into a corner of the train car, staring blankly at the flickering lights and graffiti-scarred walls as it lurched into motion.

She spent the ride home in a daze, not knowing what to do next. She was crazy. She had nearly kidnapped somebody else's baby, deluding herself into believing it was Ellie because she wanted her daughter back.

But Carly had a baby of her own — Alice had known that, she'd attended Carly's baby shower, as Max had reminded her when she'd called the police officers back to their penthouse.

The suddenness of Carly's resignation. Her shocking death, just as she'd agreed to meet with Alice. The mysterious fiancé who didn't bother to show at her funeral. It had all seemed to point to a sinister conspiracy, with Carly at the center.

But now, in hindsight, Alice couldn't explain how it made sense. Why would Carly quit her job for a fake fiancé just so she could hide Ellie when she already had a son? And what did it have to do with Max's apparent attempt to fake Carly's death? If she was leaving for Europe, there was no point in making Alice think Carly had died, or that Max had killed her. And why would Max really want to kill Carly, who he apparently respected enough to give a eulogy for her?

None of it made sense because it was all based on Alice's grief-stricken hallucinations. And she had nearly kidnapped a baby because of them.

Every time she'd been wrong, she'd been so sure she was right. But that was how delusions worked, wasn't it?

Was she going to sleepwalk through the rest of her life, trapped in one nightmare after another?

By the time the train reached her stop, she was so distraught, she could hardly keep from crying. She practically ran from the station to her building.

"Hi there, Alice!" Rory called out as she hurried into the lobby.

"Hi, Rory," she replied without emotion, and without stopping.

Alice entered the elevator, her every movement mechanical, driven by a force she could no longer comprehend. She leaned against the cool metal wall, her breaths shallow, her thoughts a cyclone of anguish and disbelief.

The elevator groaned until the doors dinged open on the top floor.

She rushed down the hallway and into her penthouse, hoping that Flora wouldn't appear to disturb her.

The nursery door was still half-painted in blue, and Alice couldn't stand the sight of it. Feeling compelled by a need to obliterate the pain, she rode the elevator back down to the basement storage room. The dim light flickered as she stepped in, shadows dancing across the forgotten belongings.

Alice rummaged through the clutter until her fingers found the cold metal of a toolbox. She only needed the hammer.

The nursery walls shook under the fury of her blows, the plaster cracking and crumbling, dust and debris cascading down like tears of the building itself. She swung with a reckless abandon, each strike a release of the rage and grief that had built up within her. The soft thud of hammer on drywall became a thunderous roar in her ears.

When the hammer finally fell from her grasp, her bare hands took over, clawing at the remnants of the wall, tearing away chunks of drywall. Her fingers bled, but she didn't stop. She *couldn't* stop, not until the nursery was as broken as her heart.

The sight of the wire, snaking out of the hole in the wall and across the nursery floor, was like a physical blow, snapping Alice out of her destructive trance. It trailed away, a silver sliver against the carpet, leading her out of the chaos she had created.

Her hands, slick with blood, fumbled as she followed the wire, pulling it, unraveling its path with a growing sense of dread as it weaved its way into the bedroom, ending at a small, innocuous speaker nestled in the light fixture.

The device was so commonplace, so easily overlooked, yet now it screamed of significance. With each step Alice took, the taut string of her sanity unwound, the implications of this latest discovery gnawing at the edges of her mind.

She knelt beside the radio she found hidden beneath the bed.

Her bloodied hand hesitated before depressing the button, a half-prayer whispered from her lips for silence.

Instead, the room erupted with the sound of Ellie's cries. A ghostly chorus that seemed to emanate from every corner, binding her to the spot with the chains of a harrowing realization.

Chapter Thirty-Two

ALICE SAT with her back against the cold, unyielding wall, feeling the texture of the paint pressing into the fabric of her shirt, granules like tiny accusations against her skin.

The room echoed with a profound silence, so deep that it almost felt like its own kind of noise. For a while, she was too rattled to do anything else, but after the stillness finally became too much for her, Alice restarted her nightmare again and replayed the cries from that speaker.

Yes, those terrible wails still sounded like the innocent sobs of her daughter. With each replay, the cries burrowed deeper into her psyche, a relentless assault that refused to let her bury the rising tide of maternal instinct screaming for her to act.

Alice pressed the button again and a cry tore through the silence, raw and piercing. A sound that clawed at the insides of her chest, a wail that spoke of an anguish too profound for words. Did those screams really belong to Ellie? The sounds were so visceral, so violently present that they seemed to echo in the room long after the speaker stopped broadcasting that wailing dirge.

And yet, was that even her daughter's voice? The timbre, the pitch — it all seemed right, but how would Alice actually know? She didn't know what happened to Ellie, or how long ago it had happened, so perhaps that caterwauling could belong to anyone.

But she did know one thing: Max had been using the recording to torture her, making sure she was so sleep-deprived, driving her to the point of sleepwalking in a nightmarish fugue state where nothing seemed real.

But why? What did he gain from any of this?

Did he want to live with a crazy woman who woke him up in the middle of the night and accused him of murder?

And what about her hallucination of Carly's murder — had Carly been a willing participant in that illusion, or had Max forced her to play dead on their living room floor?

What did Carly have against Alice? Why would she agree to fake her own death when she was already planning to get married and move to Europe?

None of it made any sense. And until she could explain how it all fit together, she couldn't tell anyone else what she knew, because they would think she was crazy. She kept replaying the cries, trying to understand exactly how her life had turned into this horror show, until a knock at the door fractured the misery.

Alice froze, silencing the speaker and perking her ears.

The knock came again and she scrambled to hide the speaker, tucking it away in the closet, then quickly hiding the wire before she rushed into the entryway.

She looked out the peephole to see Flora standing outside her door with a look of concern that made Alice feel unreasonably guilty. She smoothed her hair, wiped the traces of fear from her face, and opened the door, surely looking frazzled and yet still more composed than she actually was. Her attempt at normalcy was a crudely-fashioned mask, fragile and ready to slip at the slightest touch of truth.

Flora's gaze seemed to hit her with a blend of concern and something else — was it suspicion? "Are you okay?"

"Of course. Why?"

"I heard banging."

"Oh that." Alice managed a brittle smile. "I just decided to do a bit of remodeling in the nursery. You know, since it isn't going to be a nursery."

Flora's expression fell from suspicion to pity. "I stopped by earlier, wanted to see if you'd like to have coffee, but you didn't answer."

She tried to steal a glance over Alice's shoulder.

"I went out. To Carly's funeral." Not that she should have to explain.

"Oh ..." Flora's eyebrows knitted together. "I didn't realize that you'd gone out at all."

An odd thing to say, made even odder by the way she had said it.

"Was I supposed to let you know before leaving my apartment?" Alice asked, sounding more defensive than she wanted to.

"No — of course not!" Flora waved a hand. "I just mean that I didn't hear the elevator, and you know how loud that thing is."

"I took the stairs."

"You took the stairs?" Flora repeated in a voice that suggested Alice had just delivered the most surprising bit of news so far. "Why would you take the stairs?"

"Like you said, the elevator is loud. It's been giving me a headache."

"I can understand that!" She laughed, but for some

reason Alice didn't believe her. "Did you want to come over for some coffee–"

"No thanks." Alice shook her head. "I just want to rest."

"I have cookies," Flora teased in a voice that was clearly meant to entice her. "From Butter Me Up, of course."

"Maybe later." Alice offered her a tired smile. "Right now, I just really want to rest."

"Of course." Flora nodded. "I understand. But it's a standing offer. Sometimes when we want to be alone is when we need company the most."

"I'll keep that in mind." Her smile was getting harder to hold. "Thank you for stopping by."

Alice closed the door before Flora could say anything else.

Her hand trembled as she turned the lock, the click of the deadbolt sounding unusually loud in her ears. She leaned against the door, her mind again a maelstrom filled with too many thoughts. The baby's crying continued to echo in her head, haunting her every step as she moved back toward the nursery.

This time she went straight to the doll that had become a surrogate for her daughter during the times when reality became too unbearable, according to Max.

Alice stared at the eerily-realistic face for a while before she finally began to undress her, searching for any sign of a receiver that might help to explain the nightmarish screams that she had heard on the speaker.

But even after a thorough search she found nothing.

Alice removed the doll's diaper next. That time she found an AirTag. Her search was frantic, driven by a need to comprehend the incomprehensible, to find reason within the unreasonable — a quest that only spiraled further into confusion.

It was a stunningly uncomfortable discovery. Because who else could have possibly put it there other than Max?

Less than an hour ago, she'd been sure that she was crazy and that Max had been trying to save her from her grief. Did this AirTag prove that the man who had promised to love and protect Alice forever was instead playing some seriously dangerous games with her mental state?

And if so, then *why*?

It had to be him, because no one else would have ever had access to the Ellie doll. But even if Alice finally knew who was doing this terrible thing to her, his motives were still unclear.

She had also been paranoid lately, and maybe that was happening right now. Disregarding all of the things that *couldn't* be true — like seeing a dead Carly getting dragged across her living room floor before seeing that same woman getting run over in the street — what did Alice actually know?

There wasn't much about this situation that she could be totally sure of right now. Maybe Max had put the AirTag in Ellie's diaper to keep tabs on her. Maybe he was worried about her and needed to know where she was. Maybe she was wrong and he was right about all of this, regardless of what her heart and soul kept insisting.

The fabric of her reality seemed to fray at the edges as she held the cold, metallic disc between her fingers, wrestling with truths and lies that collapsed into each other. Alice needed answers, and she knew of one place in the penthouse where she might be able to find them, even though the thought of looking filled her body and soul with the worst sort of chills.

Her steps were leaden as she left the nursery and headed for the bedroom with the ghost of Ellie's cries still clawing at the edges of her psyche.

She walked straight to the nightstand where Max had left the envelope, but picked it up with trepidation, drawing a deep breath as if about to dive into the depths of a black ocean.

The hospital report was cold and clinical, delivering truth with unforgiving clarity. Her eyes traced the lines, each word a step down a path she could never retreat from.

According to the report, Ellie died from lack of oxygen.

The words should have served her a final verdict, a guillotine blade severing the last threads of hope. And yet, even as the room spun around her it still felt like a lie.

Even after seeing the supposed truth in black and white something bone deep inside Alice insisted that her Ellie was alive.

But if so, then where was she?

Max had brought the document to her, but what if he had altered it? Or fabricated it altogether? It could be fake, just like Ellie's birth certificate could be fake. She didn't know how one counterfeited things like that, but she also didn't know what either of these documents were supposed to look like, so how would she know if what she was looking at was real?

Her fingers were agents of raw desperation, suddenly clawing at the hospital report without even knowing what she was doing, shredding the paper, as if dismantling the document could simultaneously destroy the reality it proclaimed.

She snatched up the pieces, her actions frenetic, each rip a tiny echo of the scream building inside her chest.

Compelled by a manic impulse, Alice shoved a wad of the torn report into her mouth, the paper dry against her tongue, sticking to the roof of her mouth, a bitter communion of ink and fiber.

The paper turned to pulp as she chewed.

And Alice kept thinking, *Where the hell is my daughter?*

Chapter Thirty-Three

MAX BURST through the apartment door with a force that sent it crashing against the wall, the sound reverberating through the penthouse like a gunshot that Alice could feel with her back against the wall in the nursery.

Seconds later he was standing on the threshold, his chest heaving and body tensing as if preparing to ward off an assault.

The nursery was unrecognizable. Chunks of drywall littered the floor where Alice had struck with wild abandon to reveal jagged edges and exposed beams. His eyes swept across the devastation inspired by the chaos that had exploded within Alice. She took some satisfaction from the glimmer of fear in his eyes, among the anger and the disbelief.

"What have you done, Alice?" His words were heavy in the air, a plea for some semblance of reason that she could not give him.

She refused to answer, or even look at him. Her silence was a monolith, impenetrable and resolute.

"ALICE!" Max yelled at her.

But still the fury burning her blood to a boil forbid her to meet his eyes or so much as mutter a word. Alice was afraid that starting to say anything might only lead to her gouging his eyes from their sockets.

Max marched over to her. "You're really not going to answer me?"

His question hung in the air as Alice stayed silent, the tumultuous storm within her threatening to break free. Clenched fists rested on her knees, the only sign of her effort to contain the rage.

She sat amid the nursery ruins, her gaze fixed on a point far beyond the confines of those four walls, replaying scenes that no one else could see, her silence a fortress she refused to leave.

But Max's presence was like a storm of its own, his energy restless and agitated as he paced the length of the shattered room. A tempest in a teapot, his movements constrained by the physical limits of the space. He seemed to be fighting an invisible adversary, clenching and unclenching his fists in impotent fury.

He spoke again, calmer this time, his voice tinged with a desperation that bordered on hysteria. "Do you have any idea what I went through today?"

Of course she didn't answer him.

And that brought the anger back into his voice. "You're goddamned lucky that the cops aren't here right now, Alice! I had to spend an hour defending you! Carly's mom threatened to call the police on me, Alice. On us. She wanted to press charges, and would have, if not for all the lawyers at the wake convincing her not to."

His words filled the room in a bitter tide lapping upon her shores. She felt a sharp stab in her gut, the threat of legal consequences piercing the fog of her rage.

"And this?" Max gestured angrily around at the obliterated nursery. "Are you really not going to own any of this—"

Alice leapt to her feet in a sudden burst of unexpected movement, her mind a whirlwind of fear and confusion, fragments of thought colliding with the force of her tumultuous emotions.

Max staggered back several steps toward the door as her hand moved almost of its own accord, fingers uncurling from her clenched to reveal the AirTag that had been pressed into her palm. Then she flung it at Max.

The AirTag sliced through the air in a blur of silver to strike him on the chest like a missile of accusation.

Max recoiled, more from the implication than the impact, his face registering shock, confusion, and a dawning realization. He'd been caught and he knew it.

His eyes locked with hers, and for the first time since he had entered the room, Alice met his gaze, hers ablaze with a dangerous intensity.

"You put this in the doll?" Her voice was a low growl, every word edged with a venom that made him fall yet another step back. "To track me? To keep tabs on me as if I'm what … some criminal?"

His initial surprise morphed into defensiveness, posture stiffening as he sought to justify his actions. "Yes, Alice! Of course, I did. Because I can't trust you not to do something like what happened today. Or worse …"

"Worse like what, Max?"

"Like something irreversible."

"Like killing myself?" she taunted. She didn't believe for a second that he'd tracked her to keep her from committing suicide.

His hands balled into fists."I don't know, Alice!" His jaw clenched hard as he spat. "Anything stupid!"

Her breathing was erratic, her chest rising and falling

with the tempest raging within her. "You were tracking me the day I went to the coffee shop," she accused, her voice slicing through the thick air between them like a blade.

His scoff was a harsh sound in the wrecked nursery. "That's what you think? That I have nothing better to do than track—"

"You could have killed Carly. You had the means, the opportunity." Her words were a gamble, cards played from a hand of desperation, a wild toss of the dice in a game where the stakes were her sanity and the truth.

"Killed Carly?" He threw his head back and laughed, a sound devoid of any humor. "Really, Alice? *That's* where you're going with this? First you accuse me of murdering her in our living room, and when that theory didn't pan out, now I killed her in the street? With what car, Alice?"

"She wanted to talk to me, Max. Why did she want to talk to me?"

"How the hell am I supposed to know?" He took a breath. "I understand that you're upset, and under a lot of stress right now. But regardless of what you believe, I'm not the one who's been living in a fantasy world."

There it was again. He always went right to that, accusing her of not being able to tell what was real and what was not. And she'd let him plant that seed of doubt in her. She'd stopped trusting her own intentions.

She wasn't going to let him keep getting away with that.

"I know you had something to do with this," Alice insisted with a snarl, bitter sarcasm rolling off her tongue. "I'm sure she just wanted to meet me so we could discuss the weather, and a random hit and run just—"

"I was in court, Alice. *All day.*" Max enunciated each word with precision, a visible pulse ticking in his jaw.

Her laugh, devoid of amusement, filled the room.

"Court? Really, Max? Why should I believe you're not lying about that, same as you've been lying about everything else?" Her tone was acidic, dripping with doubt.

"You want proof? Fine. I'll give you proof!" Max growled as he pulled out his phone. "Anyone at the office could prove my whereabouts on the day Carly had her unfortunate accident."

"Anyone in your office will just say whatever you want them to say. It's a law firm, so the place is filled with lawyers, and according to you, lawyers are all professional liars."

"I said that lawyers have to frame the truth for a living, Alice. That isn't the same as lying. I'm calling Marcy Edwards."

Max put his phone on speaker as the number rang through.

Alice crossed her arms, furious yet unable to quell her curiosity at seeing where this call to Marcy might go.

Ringing cut through the tension until the line connected, then Marcy's voice came through the speakerphone, sounding tinny and distant.

"Hi, Max. Is everything okay? How is Alice?"

"Not good, Marcy." He drew an overly performative breath. "You're on speaker right now. I need you to tell Alice where I was on the day that Carly died."

"I could double check the calendar if you need me to, but I'm sure that was a court day. The third one that week. For the Laurentian deposition."

Max held the phone out toward Alice, his eyes searching hers. There was no triumph in his expression, only a weary hope that she would finally believe him. Like he simply needed her to see the truth, to understand that despite everything, he wasn't her enemy.

But Alice still refused to believe him.

"Is that all?" Marcy asked.

Max turned away from Alice with a bitter shake of his head. "For now. Thank you, Marcy."

Despite Marcy's words, Alice remained unmoved. The affirmation of Max's alibi might as well have been the distant murmur of a foreign language, for all the conviction it inspired in her.

Who cared if he'd been in court? He could have had an accomplice. Arranged it all in advance. Maybe he'd hired a hitman. People did that, didn't they?

But it didn't matter how he'd done it. Carly was dead, and there was nothing she could do about that.

Her thoughts circled back to a single, relentless track. "Where is Ellie?" she demanded, her voice steady but her eyes wild, the untamed part of her that refused to be placated by lawyers' reassurances.

His expression crumpled, the facade of calm control giving way to the storm of frustration and helplessness that had been gathering force behind his stern demeanor.

"You need help, Alice. Real help." His voice was a mixture of warning and weariness. "Dr. Williams will hear about this tomorrow. You can't go on like this. We can't go on like this. *I* can't go on like this."

Her response was visceral, a guttural cry that seemed to come from the depths of her very soul. It was more than words could express, more than tears could communicate. It was the sound of a heart breaking, a spirit raging against an unbearable reality. With a scream, Alice lunged at Max, her hands outstretched, not to harm but to reach for him, to make him understand the depth of her pain, and the urgency of her need for answers.

He retreated several steps back again, this time all the way to the door. For a moment, she'd made that glimmer of fear come back, and she was glad. It was his turn to be afraid.

She watched him open his mouth, probably readying another attack, claiming that her outburst was evidence that she was crazy. But she had found the radio under the bed. Proof that he'd been manipulating her, pushing her to the brink of exhaustion, eroded her ability to tell what was real so that she doubted her own mind.

Go ahead, explain again how this is all my fault, and see what happens.

She would tear through him, just liked she'd torn through the wall.

But he just shook his head.

"I can't do this," he muttered, more to himself than to her. "I'm staying at a hotel."

Max turned and strode out of the nursery, through the wreckage of their once peaceful apartment. The door slammed shut behind him and reverberated through the empty apartment.

Then Alice stood alone amid the chaos, her scream still hanging in the air, a raw and ragged banner of her grief. Max was gone, the silence oppressive, and the question that had torn everything apart remained unanswered, a gaping wound in the fabric of her life: *Where is Ellie?*

The door, now closed, was like the full stop at the end of a sentence that had been too agonizing to endure.

Chapter Thirty-Four

Despite Max's aggressive departure from the apartment, Alice never heard the expected sound of the elevator's arrival. She found herself straining to hear the familiar whir of its gears, but even after a long moment she still heard a nothing that filled her with an unexplainable dread. Her heart pounded a staccato rhythm that seemed to fill the space where the elevator noise should have been.

There was no way that Max would have taken the stairs.

So with a mixture of trepidation and defiance, she slipped out of the penthouse.

Once in the hallway, Alice could barely make out the soft cadence of voices. Max's deep baritone mingled with Flora's softer timbre. The combination made the hairs on her neck stand at full attention.

The low and secretive tones of their exchange wafted through the still air, curling around the corners of the hallway like whispers of suspicion, wrapping around Alice like a chilling fog.

She was suddenly paralyzed, her feet cemented to the carpet.

The murmur of voices faded into Flora's penthouse, leaving Alice alone to wrestle with what had clearly been a clandestine conversation. She hadn't been able to catch any of the words, but the tone had definitely been conspiratorial.

She crept down the hallway toward the closed door, as if there was a chance in hell she could hear anything through it, and despite the danger of getting caught. But what if she couldn't hear the shuffling of feet ahead of Flora's door swinging open? What would they do to her if they thought she'd heard?

Time seemed to stretch indefinitely. But Alice couldn't leave without any answers when they were obviously right on the other side of that door.

Yes, there was a chance that the two of them were discussing ways to help her. But a gnawing in her gut that Alice had been suffering for too long said that they were plotting against her.

That last thought was enough to shatter her paralysis and get Alice back inside her apartment where she belonged. For now. Let them think she didn't know they were working together.

Back in the penthouse, Alice found herself enveloped by an oppressive silence. It was as if the walls themselves had absorbed the echoes of her earlier breakdown and now exhaled a heavy, stifling air that settled around her.

She began to pace, each step an echo in the cavernous quiet, her mind like tide pools of suspicion and half-formed theories as she continued to fiercely wonder about the whispered exchange between her husband and Flora.

A sudden grinding of the elevator so long after Max's departure from the apartment snapped her back to the present. She ran back to the entryway and peered through the peephole to see Max standing in front of the elevator.

The sight was jolting, not for his presence, but for the utter lack of anger in his movements and expression. It was a dissonance that clawed at her, the calmness of his demeanor belying the storm she knew raged beneath. Or did it? What if her reaction to his accusations — and to the discovery of the AirTag — was exactly what he wanted?

She ducked back inside to make sure he didn't see her, trying to make heads or tails of the incongruity between the Max she had confronted and the man who bore what almost seemed like an air of tranquility. It was as if there were two versions of her husband: one consumed by fury and threats, the other a stranger with unfathomable motives and unreadable expressions.

A cold shiver running down her spine. The disparity between what she expected and what she witnessed amplified her inner disarray.

Drawn to the bathroom by a sudden impulse, Alice retrieved the bottle of pills that Flora had given her from the medicine cabinet. They rattled like dry bones as she held them, knowing what she needed to do.

Moments later Alice was standing over the toilet, bottle poised in her hand.

Flora had promised that the pills would keep her calm, but now Alice couldn't help but seeing them as chains. She had too easily trusted her new neighbor, but now recognized her folly. The pills weren't helping at all; although they weren't as bad as the others that she'd received at the hospital, they could be making her more volatile or making it harder for her to think. Who knew if they were even what Flora said they were?

With a surge of resolve, she twisted the cap off, then

one by one she spilled the pills out from the bottle and watched them cascade into the bowl with little plinks.

She flushed her toilet and the pills swirled away in a vortex. Alice wasn't just rejecting Flora's supposed help, she was shattering the chains of perceived benevolence, a phoenix rising from the ashes of her compliance, reaffirming her commitment to seek the truth, no matter how jagged or painful that reality might be. From this point forward, she would assume that everyone she knew could be the enemy. Max. Flora. Anyone from the law firm.

Everyone but Rory, who'd treated her with kindness and respect even when she'd seemed to be genuinely crazy.

Then she was staring down into the empty toilet bowl, her reflection in the water a distorted version of the woman who had once believed her life to be as orderly and serene as the penthouse where she now found herself a prisoner.

No, she wasn't a prisoner. Not now that she knew her suspicions weren't delusions.

If anything, Alice was more empowered than she had been for a long time now. She still didn't know exactly what was going on here, or who else was complicit in this dark campaign against her sanity, but at least she could finally grip at the edges of a theory.

She left the apartment again, closing the front door as quietly as she could, then rushing toward the stairwell to avoid the grinding elevator. She wondered if Flora would be watching out the peephole of her front door, now that she knew Alice might take the stairs.

The stairwell was dimly lit, the bulbs casting long and angular shadows that seemed to stretch out like fingers reaching for her as she descended. Each step was a quiet thud in the otherwise silent passage, a rhythmic beat that matched the still-quickened tempo of her heart.

Alice entered the lobby to soft, ambient music, the same kind that was always playing in the background, but it seemed louder now, same as the rest of her severely distorted world.

Rory smiled like always, warm and unassuming as he waved. "How're you holding up, Alice?"

"I'm good, Rory. Thanks."

"And the little one?" His voice was rich with genuine concern.

"We're … managing. Thank you." She managed to keep her mask of composure, necessary before she asked the question that she had run down all of those flights of stairs to pose, hoping her query sounded casual, despite being laced with hidden urgency. "Can residents call each other directly through the intercom?"

"You mean without going through the desk?" Rory clarified.

"Yes." Alice nodded. "Is something like that even possible?"

"Sure is." Rory didn't seem suspicious at all. "Straightforward even."

"How would I do that?"

"You just dial the three-digit code for whatever apartment you're trying to reach."

"You mean the apartment number? Or is there a different code?"

"Just the apartment number. Like I said, it's cake."

"So if I someone wanted to call up to our place from anywhere else in the building, they would just dial 901?"

"Bingo." Rory nodded.

"Thank you. That's great to know." She turned away from the desk, the pieces of her plan slotting together with a clarity that was both exhilarating and terrifying.

Alice knew what she had to do, the seeds sown by

Rory's innocuous instructions now sprouting into a strategy.

Her ascent to the top floor was much more strenuous than her flight down, but she made the trip with even more urgency, racing down the hallway after bursting through the door and rushing back into her apartment.

Alice went straight to the intercom once inside.

Her fingers hovered over the buttons with a hesitancy that belied the adrenaline coursing through her veins. After a steadying breath, she pressed the digits 9-0-2, initiating a connection that would either confirm her suspicions or cast them into a well of even deeper doubt.

The line clicked, a hollow sound that seemed to fill the room, then Flora's voice came through, tinged with an expectancy that didn't belong. "Max?"

The single word, a question and a name, was the confirmation Alice needed.

Her throat tightened, a mix of vindication and a sharp pang of betrayal tightening around her heart. She disconnected the call, severing the line as cleanly as she had been cut by the revelation.

She stepped back, leaning against the cool wall as she gathered her thoughts. Seconds ticked into a minute or so before Alice heard a knock on her door.

She went to the entryway and peeked through the peephole at Flora, but refused to answer her call or open the door.

"Alice? It's Flora. Please, we need to talk." Her voice was flavored with a concern that now sounded false to Alice's ears.

She didn't move, or respond. Her eyes were fixed on the door, but her vision was turned inward, replaying the events of the last few weeks, every interaction with Flora now cast in a new and much more sinister light.

Her knocking continued, a staccato accompaniment to Flora's pleading words, but Alice was still as a statue, her resolve as hard as the marble underfoot.

This was her line in the sand, her stand against the encroaching tide of deceit that kept threatening to sweep her away. Alice would not yield, and she would not give voice to the inferno of questions and accusations that burned on her tongue. Not until it was time to play her hand.

"ALICE!" Flora was now louder than ever, and yet her bellow carried the sound of defeat.

And still Alice refused to open the door.

Because it was better to be alone with the truth than in company with lies.

Chapter Thirty-Five

THE ABRASIVE GRIND of the elevator jolted Alice out of her troubled thoughts.

Flora was on the move, which meant that the same needed to be true for Alice.

Panic surged through her like wildfire; each beat of her heart was a drum of war, rallying her to action against the unseen forces marshaling against her. Flora's departure was surely another piece in the intricate puzzle of deceit that had become her life. Those whispered words exchanged with Max surely weren't idle chatter — they were threads in a web that ensnared her, each one a potential clue to the monstrous plot unfolding around her.

Alice grabbed the Ellie doll and bolted out of her penthouse, barreling straight for the elevator. She stabbed at the call button with her thumb. The luminescent numbers above the doors seemed to mock her urgency with their sluggish progression until the doors lurched open and Alice slipped inside.

The descent was torturously slow, the machinery

groaning in protest as if burdened by the weight of her fears.

A sudden stop midway jerked her from her anxious reverie.

The doors opened, and a middle-aged man entered the elevator, his presence an unwelcome intrusion into her crisis. He cast a sideways glance at Alice, taking in her disheveled appearance — the wild eyes, the hair escaping its confines, the breaths that sawed in and out of her chest, heaving against the doll that was not a baby.

He edged to the corner, stealing furtive glances at Alice while pretending to be absorbed in the scrolling news on his phone until the doors dinged open again. She felt the weight of his gaze like a judge's gavel, each stealthy look a verdict on her frantic state.

Alice spilled into the lobby, running past the night doorman now on duty as her eyes immediately locked onto the figure of Flora outside, poised at the curb, her hand raised to signal a yellow cab pulling up to the sidewalk.

Alice's heart skipped, then doubled its beat, every alarm in her head screaming for her to follow Flora to wherever she was going.

Flora's cab pulled away from the curb just as Alice spotted Rory outside in his own vehicle, presumably heading for home. She darted toward him and he paused, his expression shifting from surprise to concern as he lowered his window.

"You okay, Alice?"

She got into his car without answering, pointing at the taxi now a half block in front of them. "Rory, please, you have to follow that cab!"

"I can't — you need a car seat for the baby. It's not safe."

"It's a doll, Rory. Ellie is at the sitter's. Please, we need to go now!"

An expression of confusion and incredulity lingered on the doll, but Alice needed him to step on the gas.

"Max bought it for Ellie, but I got used to carrying it around with me. I'm not even sure why I grabbed it just now before leaving the apartment. But *please*, I need you to follow that cab before it gets away with us."

"Okay, Alice. You got it." Rory pulled into traffic. "Just like in the movies, right?"

"Just like in the movies," she repeated.

Mercifully, Flora's taxi was still in view, and Rory seemed intent on not letting her down. A few blocks later, she asked, "What do you know about Flora?"

"Not much." He shrugged. "Just that she rented the place a couple of months ago."

"Rented? I thought she bought her apartment?"

"Definitely not." Rory's response came with a furrow of his brow. "I figured you would know that Max bought the apartment. He sorted things out with Mrs. Cohen's estate — avoided a lot of legal hassle."

A cold fury settled in the pit of Alice's stomach, pulsing in time to her heartbeat. Max had deceived her from the start, hiding his purchase of Mrs. Cohen's penthouse, pretending he didn't know Flora after he'd rented it to her, then nudging Alice to be friends with the woman, who happened to be a psychiatrist, at exactly the time when he'd started insisting that Alice needed to go back to therapy.

She'd been set up.

Was Flora even a psychiatrist, or had that been part of the ruse?

Rory didn't try to talk to her as he drive, seeming to realize that she was strung too tightly to keep up her end of a convercation, which she was grateful for. She couldn't help holding her breath each time the taxi pulled farther ahead or another car managed to slip between them. If they lost Flora, they might never find where she and Max were hiding Ellie.

The city's vibrant cacophony gradually gave way to the muted hum of the outskirts. The jagged skyline softened into rolling hills and tidy homes nestled between lush swathes of green. Tight, angular streets bloomed into wide, meandering roads, and dense clusters of buildings thinned out to reveal the tranquil spaces of suburban life.

Alice sat tense and vigilant in the passenger seat, her gaze never leaving the taillights of Flora's cab that bobbed ahead of them like a beacon. They wound through neighborhoods where the night draped everything in stillness and shadow, save for the occasional porch light or street lamp to puncture the darkness.

After what felt like an eternity cradled in the night's embrace, the taxi turned into the driveway of a quaint two-story house, its windows dark and unwelcoming. Rory parked a block away, partially-hidden behind a van, but still close enough that they could see the front door of the house.

Flora got out of the cab and disappeared inside the house without so much as a backward glance.

Alice turned to Rory, her voice a mixture of gratitude and urgency. "You can go now. I'll be okay."

He hesitated, his protective instinct warring with the determination on her face. "You sure? It's late, and this doesn't feel right."

"I insist. And please … don't tell Max about this."

Rory agreed with a reluctant nod.

A minute later, his car was retreating into the night.

Alice crept closer to the house, heart pounding in her

ears, every sense straining to pick up any sign of what might be transpiring within.

The muffled timbre of an argument reached her, words indistinct but emotions clear — tension, frustration, and an undertone of desperation in Flora's voice that spoke volumes.

"Just a few more days, then I promise to come and get her."

Flora's words were a cold hand squeezing Alice's heart, every syllable a countdown to an outcome she anticipated as much as she feared.

She waited, concealed by the night, until Flora reemerged and left as abruptly as she had arrived. The taxi pulled away, and silence settled back onto the street.

Time seemed to stretch into an endless thread as Alice waited, a shadow melded with the darkness, her breath a ghostly whisper in the cool night air, each second a heavy heartbeat echoing the turmoil within, until she finally felt like enough time had passed for her to execute this next part of her impromptu plan.

Alice approached the door, her knuckles rapping against the wood with a mixture of fear and fortitude.

A woman answered. An expression of anticipation swiftly shifted to bewilderment at the sight of a stranger standing on her porch.

Without missing a beat, Alice took the plunge, her voice carrying a confidence she didn't feel. "Flora sent me to get the baby."

The woman's relief was obvious in her sigh. "Thank Christ she's come to her senses. I can't be her babysitter. I have three kids with my second husband and sure as hell don't have time to play nursemaid to my daughter's child. Just give me a minute."

The door remained ajar while Alice stood there, waiting for the woman to return.

Her heart stopped when she did.

The woman was cradling a baby that Alice would recognize anywhere.

She put Ellie into Alice's arms, and for a heartbeat, the chaos of the universe stilled, a hushed breath between mother and child that whispered of storms weathered and battles won.

Mother and daughter, separated for too long by a web of lies and machinations, were finally — and mercifully — reunited.

Chapter Thirty-Six

ALICE LINGERED at the doorstep for a moment longer, the weight of Ellie finally in her arms like an anchor grounding her to the spot. The world seemed to pivot on its axis, the surreal becoming real as she clutched her daughter tighter in affirmation of their reunion.

The night air, which just moments ago had carried the chill of uncertainty, now seemed to embrace her. Once menacing shadows now danced playfully at her feet, the rhythm of her footsteps a soft drumbeat marking her journey from despair to hope as Alice scanned Ellie from head to toe, each tiny feature, each breath the baby took was a mantra repeated in her mind: *She's real. She's real. She's real.*

As Alice walked down the path to the street, the echo of an approaching vehicle sent her heart leaping up into her throat. Fear clouded her mind with visions of Flora returning to try and steal her daughter. Or worse, to run her over, the same way that someone had killed Carly. Except that this time, two people would die.

She hugged Ellie tighter.

But the headlights revealed Rory's familiar car, and her pulse steadied, the night's embrace shedding its cloak of fear to reveal the comfort of an unexpected ally.

He leaned back and opened the rear door for her.

She climbed inside, holding Ellie close.

"This was the babysitter's?" Rory asked.

"Yes." Alice felt sure that he knew she was lying.

"You have a beautiful daughter," was all he said while pulling out into the street.

Ellie's cry pierced the quiet cabin. A small and needy sound that tugged at her soul.

Rory handed her his coat without a word. "If you need to feed her, don't mind me. Just use this for privacy."

Though hesitant, Alice felt the natural pull of motherhood as she arranged the coat around herself and Ellie, then pulled up her shirt and undid the quick-access clip on the strap of her nursing bra, baring one breast. She guided Ellie to her nipple, half-expecting the attempt to fail, but Ellie latched on immediately, and a connection as old as time itself bridged between mother and child.

Nourished by love and the physical bond that had been denied for too long, Ellie suckled, her tiny fingers gripping with an instinctive trust that wove a silent promise of unwavering love between them. Rory quietly drove on, giving them the peace and quiet, as the steady rhythm of Ellie's feeding became a lullaby that soothed her mother's turbulent heart.

Alice adjusted the coat tighter around Ellie, who had now settled into a contented silence. Rory's voice, gentle and unobtrusive, broke the comfortable quiet.

"Do you want to go home now? It's probably way past this little one's bedtime."

She hesitated, her gaze lingering on Ellie's serene face. He'd already done so much for her without a single question. She felt bad asking for more help, but she had no one else to turn to. "Could you … could we go somewhere else first?"

Rory glanced at her through the rearview mirror, concern etching his features. "Sure, Alice. Anywhere you need."

She directed him to a quiet street corner a few blocks away from her destination. Stepping out of the car, she dialed Gwen's number, her heart like a bass drum in her chest. Rory watched her with concern as the phone rang.

"I'm sorry for calling so late," Alice began hurriedly when Gwen answered, her voice a mixture of apology and urgency. "I have information about Carly. Can we talk?"

A sharp click and Gwen was gone.

Undeterred, Alice called again, her resolve hardening.

"Stop calling," Gwen said when she answered. "Or I'll call the police."

Alice's next words were a gamble, spoken into the dark void between hope and desperation. "I know who killed Carly."

A long pause was gnarled in tension before Gwen finally replied, icy and cautious. "Come over. But if this is a trick, the police will be involved."

"The trick has been played on me." Alice hung up and got back into Rory's car.

She relayed the address and he eyed her with silent questions.

Alice settled back into the seat, cradling Ellie.

Rory drove to Gwen's building, but left the car running when he got there. "I'll wait out here for you, Alice."

"You don't have to do that."

"We both know that I'm not going anywhere." Rory gave her a smile.

And Alice felt a wash of solace from his loyalty. "Thank you, Rory."

Still holding Ellie tightly to her chest, she approached Gwen's front door, the porch light a beacon in the overwhelming darkness that had been her life for too long now.

She rang the bell, her heart pounding a rapid timpani against the stillness of night.

The door creaked open, revealing Gwen's silhouette framed by the soft interior light. Caution was etched on her face, but it melted into a look of concern as she took in her visitor's weary yet hopeful expression.

"I'm sorry for scaring you at Carly's funeral," Alice's said, her words salted with the honesty of her ordeal. "I've been dealing with severe postpartum depression."

Gwen stepped aside, allowing her entry into the house.

"I understand," she replied, after closing the door, her voice softened by the shared knowledge of a mother's struggle. "Carly had a really tough time with PPD too."

The warmth of the house closed around Alice as she moved further inside, Ellie a comforting weight in her arms.

"I think there's more to it," Alice continued, her eyes searching Gwen's. "Our babies, they look alike, don't you think?"

Gwen considered this, her brow furrowing in thought. "Carly mentioned something like that once, in passing."

"I believe Carly was on her way to tell me something important about Max," Alice pushed on, her theory gaining strength. "I think he might be Daniel's father."

Gwen's face hardened, the color draining from her cheeks. "You think Max killed Carly? Because of the baby?"

Alice reached out, her hand seeking Gwen's in a gesture of solidarity. "I can't shake the feeling that Max is involved with all of this somehow. Of course I don't want to believe it, he's my husband, but we need to know the truth."

Gwen's hand was cold, and her grip tight. "I can't … If that's true …"

Alice pulled back, nodding. "I know. It's a lot. But we owe it to Carly and to ourselves to find out what's really happening here. For the sake of our children."

"How sure are you?"

"I'm not *sure* at all." Alice chose her words carefully, wanting Gwen to trust her, but not wanting to upset the woman to the point where she did something rash. "But he knew exactly where I would be when I was meeting Carly and–"

"We need to call the police."

"We don't have any evidence. But I'm going to get some." Alice took a deep breath and kissed her daughter on the forehead. "I just need for you to do me a favor first."

"Anything," Gwen replied.

Chapter Thirty-Seven

RORY'S CAR idled in the shadows near the back entrance of Alice's building, his engine's soft purr the only sound to break the stillness of an unsettling night. The shadows seemed to whisper secrets, dark tendrils of the night air brushing against her skin like omens of the confrontation to come.

Even in the dim light, it was easy to see the questioning look in his eyes. "You sure you want to go through with this?" His voice was low, his concern evident.

"Yes." Alice nodded, her grip on Ellie tightening a fraction. "I have to know."

She saw the reluctance in his gaze, the unspoken offer to accompany her. But she shook her head before he could voice it.

"I need to do this alone. But would you wait for my call? Just stay by the phone. I might need you to … to do something for me."

Rory nodded, then they stepped out of the car, the cool night air enveloping them as they made their way to the rear entrance.

She ignored the flutter of nerves in her stomach, quelling them with thoughts of what was at stake here.

He held the door open for her, his presence reassuring despite the anxiety clinging to her ribs. "And if you need me to come up …"

Alice cut him off with a gentle *no*, as she entered the building, the weight of Ellie in her arms working as a grounding force, even if she was only holding the doll.

"Thank you, Rory. For everything. But I really need to do this part on my own. And really, taking Ellie for me is more than enough."

Rory gave a final nod, then his silhouette receded as he made his way to the reception area and she made her way to the elevator. The doorman had become her unexpected ally, and she couldn't be more grateful.

Alice pressed the call button with a resolve that belied the tremor in her fingertips. She stood there, feeling seconds elongate into hours. The elevator arrived with its usual ding, but the sound was like a starting gun, propelling Alice into action.

Her ride up was a capsule of solitude, mercifully uninterrupted as that terrible grinding provided the regular soundtrack to her ascent.

She exited onto the top floor and moved decisively toward Flora's door.

Her knock was firm, echoing down the empty hallway.

But there was no wait — the door swung open almost instantly, revealing Flora's figure framed by the soft light of her apartment.

Judging by her hair, makeup, and posture, she had been expecting this unexpected encounter. A tightness around her eyes and a rigidity to her stance betrayed her tension. Flora's energy was a coiled spring, a veneer of composure stretched over a core of readiness — or was it apprehension?

The standoff at the doorway was electric, as if charged by a storm. Alice's voice, when she spoke, was steely and unyielding, her words delivered with the precision of a blade.

"I know about you and Max," she declared, her eyes never leaving Flora's. "I know that you're sleeping together."

Flora's face remained impassive, a mask that didn't quite reach her eyes. They flickered, not with denial, but with the calculation of what to say next. There was no shock or rush to protest. Only an unsettling calm.

"I've been to see your mother," Alice continued. "And now I have Ellie. She's safe and sound, so whatever you two were planning, it's already finished."

"You've been busy." Flora's lips pressed into a thin line, the only tell in an otherwise-composed demeanor. Her voice was smoother than her silk blouse, but Flora's eyes were hard.

"You killed Carly for Max, didn't you?" Alice didn't wait for an answer, because she already knew the truth before knocking on Flora's door, and now it was even clearer in the woman's lying eyes. "You're not even a psychiatrist are you?"

Flora's facade finally cracked, a subtle shift in her stance, "You think you've figured it all out, don't you?" Her tone was sharp, like the edge of an unsheathed knife. "You're in over your head."

Alice felt a surge of power. It coursed through her veins, a tidal wave crashing against the shore of her former helplessness, now standing strong as a cliff against the sea. "I know enough."

Flora leaned against the doorframe, her posture casual

despite the tension simmering between them. "You're delusional. You've proved that repeatedly."

"No, Flora. I'm finally seeing things clearly."

"Do you think you're the only one he's lied to?"

"What are you saying?" Alice asked as a cold realization settled into her bones.

"I was a lawyer at the firm, too, before I quit. Max likes to play games. Carly was just another piece on his board. He promised her a future. He let her believe they would get married."

"And the baby?"

Flora's face was confusion swallowed by dawning horror. "What baby?"

"Daniel." Then Alice made it clearer. "Carly's baby."

Flora's facade was now crumbling fast.

Alice felt unbridled glee in kicking it down. "Daniel is Max's son."

The news hit Flora like a physical blow, right hand flying to her mouth, her eyes brimming with tears as she tried to deny it.

"*No*," she whispered. "It can't be."

Alice's conviction was ironclad, her voice rising like a clarion call. "They look too similar, Flora. So similar I thought Daniel was Ellie at Carly's funeral. It's more than coincidence — it's genetics."

Flora leaned back, her eyes cold and calculating. "You can ask Max himself. He followed you and Rory."

A chill ran down her spine, and Alice instinctively clutched the doll tighter to her chest as the semblance of control she had felt only moments ago slipped like sand through her fingers.

Flora gave her a scornful laugh. "You really think I don't know that's just the doll? We know that you left Ellie with Carly's mother."

The room spun, her heart pounding against her ribcage. "What have you done?"

"Oh, Alice ..." Flora's voice dripped with feigned sympathy. "By now, Gwen is probably dead, and Max will have Ellie. Everyone will think you went back there to take Daniel." She leaned forward and whispered, "Just like you did at the funeral."

The breath hitched in Alice's throat.

Panic and fear mingled with a mother's fierce protectiveness.

Alice stepped back from the door, her mind racing for a way out of the tangled web that her husband and his mistress had woven around her.

"No," she whispered fiercely with a violent shaking of her head. "I won't let that happen."

Flora smiled like a predator baring its teeth before the kill. "It's too late, Alice. The story is already set. The troubled mother, unhinged by grief, takes a life in a desperate attempt to claim a child that isn't hers."

"The truth will come out," Alice declared even though the words clawed at her throat before leaving her lips. "Lies have a way of unraveling."

"And who will unravel them, Alice?" Flora's gaze was triumphant. "You?"

Another triumphant laugh.

"This isn't—"

But that's all Alice got before Flora delivered her next punchline, her voice seasoned by a venomous satisfaction as she delivered each word, "And when you kill yourself tonight, it will all be over. Everyone will assume that you committed suicide because you're nothing more than a postpartum mess."

Alice recoiled in horror and disbelief.

But Flora kept going, her eyes gleaming with malice.

"Max has been following you. We've known where you were every step of the way. We *let* you take Ellie — as if my mother would just hand her off to some stranger."

A cold dread settled over Alice, the implications wrapping around her like chains.

"Max will be here any minute," Flora said.

Then Alice lunged at her and—

Chapter Thirty-Eight

THE STRUGGLE ERUPTED LIKE A STORM, Alice and Flora grappling in the doorway, two silhouettes in one chaotic dance of fury, punctuated by sharp, jagged movements as they spilled into the apartment.

The living room became a blur of swinging limbs and contorted expressions of desperation and rage.

Alice's breaths were ragged screams, each exhale a battle cry as she pushed against Flora with all the strength that terror and adrenaline could muster, retaliating with a feral intensity, her fingers clawing, seeking to grip, to immobilize, to control.

They crashed into furniture, knocking over a lamp that shattered with a sound that perfectly matched her fracturing sanity.

A picture frame met the same fate, its glass splinters reflecting their brutal struggle in countless sharp angles.

Alice felt a stinging across her arm, a superficial cut from the debris, but it was nothing compared to the piercing fear for Ellie's safety that fueled her resistance.

Cushions tumbled to the floor, a vase of flowers

became the next casualty, water pooling on the hardwood as if the floor itself was weeping.

Alice's arm hooked around Flora's neck in a choke-hold, her forearm pressing down with a pressure born of raw instinct.

Her gasps were hot against Alice's skin, her breathing erratic as she fought for air. But Alice's grip was an iron band, unyielding and desperate.

Flora grabbed a nearby statuette and brought it down hard against Alice's back.

The pain was a white-hot line of fire that broke her hold, but still she refused to relent. The two women parted, their chests heaving and eyes wild, circling one another like wounded but unyielding predators.

Then Flora charged with a sudden lunge.

Alice sidestepped, using Flora's momentum to drive her into the wall.

A hard THUD seemed to shake the apartment.

Flora slumped, dazed, but only for a moment before she pushed off the wall and dove back into the fray.

As the violent ballet continued to career through the apartment, the tide finally turned against Alice.

Flora gained the upper hand with a sudden vicious twist, and Alice found herself pinned, cheek pressed against the dining table with the enemy's breath like a hot fog on her neck.

Crushed beneath the weight of her adversary, a furnace of resolve ignited within her, transforming fear into a weapon.

"You're going to write a note, Alice," Flora hissed in a serrated whisper. "A goodbye letter to this cruel world that just couldn't understand your pain."

"Never," Alice replied with a sobbing growl.

Flora tried to force her hand around a pen. "Write it, or I swear I'll carve the words into you myself."

The threat was no mere hyperbole; Alice could feel the sharp edge of a knife blade tracing a cold line along her arm, a promise of pain that Flora was all too ready to keep.

Alice jerked her arm away, but not quickly enough to avoid a shallow cut.

Warm blood trickled over her skin, dark red against her pale flesh. The pain was a glaring beacon, a rallying cry that summoned every ounce of her strength to the surface.

"Do what you have to."

The knife, now slick with blood, flashed in Flora's hand.

Alice, her body screaming with pain and defiance, braced for another slice.

Flora, her expression a twisted rictus of rage, obliged, dragging the blade across Alice's forearm, drawing a fresh line of crimson to soak her blouse.

Alice's scream was primal, a roar of all the anguish and terror she had bottled up. The sound of a cornered animal fighting for its life, and for its young.

With a Herculean effort fueled by raw, maternal instinct, Alice lurched into action, her movements not her own, but that of every mother bear, lioness, and wolf that fought against the world to protect their young.

Their hands met in a vicious tangle as Alice fought for control of the knife. Her fingers wrapped around Flora's wrist, squeezing with bone-crushing pressure.

Flora's eyes widened in shock, the tables turned in an instant as Alice wrested the knife away.

With the elevator's grinding gears as her battle drums, Alice drove the knife forward in a terrible arc that found its home in Flora's throat.

A gurgling cry escaped Flora as she collapsed, hands clawing at her neck, the lifeblood pulsing between her fingers.

Alice didn't watch her fall, racing to the phone instead.

She sprinted with a limping gait, adrenaline numbing her pain.

But as she reached the phone, a shadow loomed in the doorway.

Max stood on the threshold, the very picture of the monster she had come to fear, holding a gun, its barrel aimed at Rory, who cradled Ellie in his arms. The sight of her child in the line of fire ignited a fury that burned hotter than any wound Flora had inflicted.

"Sit down on the couch. Both of you." His command was punctuated by the cold, metallic click of the gun's hammer being pulled back.

Rory, with a protective arm around Ellie, complied in silence, moving toward the couch. Alice followed, her body taut with terror as her eyes stayed fixed on Max's gun.

His own gaze then fell upon Flora, her body crumpled on the floor, life ebbing away from the wound in her throat. A hint of a smirk played on his lips as he observed the scene.

"Well, that looks like one less loose end to tie up for me. " He nodded toward Ellie with a tilt of his gun. "Hand her to Alice."

Rory hesitated with a silent plea in his eyes.

Alice shook her head fiercely. "No, Rory, don't–"

"Do it, or I swear I'll shoot you both right now!" Max bellowed.

Reluctantly, Rory handed Ellie over to Alice, who encased her in a protective embrace.

The room was still for a heartbeat before the sound of a gunshot shattered the silence. Rory's body jerked once, then slumped to the floor, a blooming red stain on his shirt.

Max turned back toward Alice, a cruel satisfaction in his eyes.

But Flora, with the last of her strength, grabbed at his ankle.

He stumbled, caught off guard by the sudden grip of his mistress.

Alice seized the moment, snatching Flora's knife from the floor, still smeared with blood. Clutching her daughter close, she bolted for the door, desperate to escape this place and protect the precious life in her arms.

With Ellie's tiny heart beating against her own, Alice dashed past the threshold, the hallway beckoning with a glimmer of hope.

Chapter Thirty-Nine

Alice raced down the hallway.

Max's enraged bellow echoed through the corridor behind her.

She reached the elevator, frantically jabbing at the button, but the doors remained firmly shut, the indicator light mocking her with its unmoving glow as Max's heavy footsteps got heavier, his fury tangible in the air.

If Alice didn't run right now, she would be dead.

She spun on her heel and sprinted back to her apartment, lungs burning from the effort as she slammed the door behind her and threw the deadbolt.

That would only buy her seconds, considering the monster had a key.

She raced to the landline, her hands shaking as she snatched up the phone to dial 911. But Max burst through the door before she could, and his presence filled the room like a thunderhead.

In the narrow space between salvation and doom, her fingers were vice-like around the phone as Max descended upon her with the force of a storm.

Their struggle was silent, except for the sound of labored breaths and the scrape of flesh against plastic. But Alice had to protect Ellie, and Max took advantage of that, feinting toward the baby, then grabbing the phone at the last moment.

With a sudden, brutish yank, he yanked the phone from her desperate grasp and the receiver became a casualty of his wrath, the cord snapping with a violent jerk to skitter across the floor. The space around her shrank, the walls themselves seeming to press inward, complicit in his sinister advance.

Then Max loomed over her, breath heaving, eyes alight with a feral gleam as he gave her a snarl of triumph. She staggered backward.

Ellie's cries pierced the tumult, a tiny siren of innocence amid the jarring din of violence. Alice's heart twisted in her chest at the sound. Her daughter's terror was a sledgehammer pounding against her resolve.

"Did you kill Mrs. Cohen too?" Alice's voice was strained, her accusation sharp as the blade she longed to still be holding. Her question sharpened into an accusation. "You killed her for the apartment!"

His bitter laugh echoed off the walls, his eyes narrowed to slits of malice. "Oh, Alice, missing the bigger picture like always."

They clashed again, two forces colliding in an eddy of desperation. Her attempts to wield the knife were met with his superior strength and hampered by her need to keep Ellie safe, so he couldn't steal her back. The weapon slipped from her fingers as he effortlessly disarmed her and sent the blade spinning out of reach.

"You've been quite the little murderer tonight, haven't you?" His words cut deeper than any knife.

"Why, Max?" Alice recoiled, not from the loss of the

weapon, but from the truth splintering through her. "After all these years, why?"

"Your parents' money, Alice." His face contorted with a sneer and the room spun with the vertigo of her unraveling life. "It was always about the money. After they cut you off, I had to find another way. I thought Samuel would be my in—"

"YOU'RE A MONSTER!" Her throat tightened, bile rising as she absorbed the magnitude of his betrayal.

"Ellie's the rightful heir to your family's fortune. It's all just dollars and good sense."

Her knees nearly buckled beneath the weight of his admission. The daughter that they had brought into this world together was merely a pawn in his twisted game.

"And Carly?" she managed to choke out.

"Carly got sentimental, started having second thoughts about taking Ellie. She wanted to confess, to return to her little fantasy with me." His eyes were cold and remorseless. "I couldn't allow that."

The room spun around Alice as the final piece clicked into place. "You killed her to keep her quiet."

He nodded, still devoid of any human emotion. "She was a loose end. And loose ends get tied up."

Alice backed away, each step heavy with despair.

"You're a monster." The words left her in a whisper that time, her voice barely carrying across the distance between them.

Max only smiled, the expression monstrous in its glee. "Yes, Alice. But I'm the monster who wins." He circled her like a shark scenting blood. "I've laid the groundwork perfectly. You're the deranged wife, teetering on the edge, driven to madness by grief and paranoia. Although you weren't quite disintegrating fast enough at first. I had to nudge you along with a little scopolamine."

"You've been drugging me?"

But of course he had. The nightmares, the sleepwalking, the thick fog that lingered in her head long after she got out of bed. It wasn't postpartum depression — he'd been giving her drugs to make her hallucinate.

To make her think she couldn't tell the difference between a doll and her daughter.

To make her feel like she was going crazy.

Her heart pounded in her ears as she inched backwards, her mind racing for a solution, any solution.

"You won't get away with this," she said, though the conviction in her voice waned beneath the gravity of Max's looming presence.

"But I will." His eyes gleamed with a dark triumph. "Everyone will think that you jumped off of our balcony, Alice. They'll say that you killed Gwen in a fit of insanity, sought out Flora in the heat of desperation, and when she threatened to call the police, you silenced her too."

Terror clawed at Alice's insides, a relentless beast threatening to overwhelm her.

"No one will believe that," she protested weakly, but she knew they would, especially the police, who already believed her to be unhinged. Brody and Lemmon — and everyone else — would feel *sorry* for Max as they unwittingly helped him cover up his crimes by blaming her for everything.

Max laughed, a sound so devoid of humanity it chilled her to the bone. "It's such a perfect story, and you played your role to perfection. Even him." Max gestured at the Rory's body. "Rory, the faithful doorman, tried to stop you from your tragic leap, and you shot him. It's all so … Shakespearean."

Alice had run out of retreat, her back literally against the wall.

"And now," Max said, closing the distance between them with the certainty of a man who believed he had already won, "it's time for the final act."

He reached for her, his fingers grazing her arm, and Alice knew with a visceral certainty that this was the moment — fight or fall.

Of course she was going to fight.

Chapter Forty

Max's hands clamped onto her arms with a death grip, fingers biting into her flesh as he dragged her out toward the balcony, their feet scuffing and stumbling over the penthouse floor in a deadly waltz as she thrashed against the gravity of his malice.

The open air loomed ahead, the cityscape a distant blur of lights and shadows.

Alice fought with every fiber of her being, her nails finding his skin, drawing lines of blood as she thrashed against his hold. Her screams were raw, ripped from a throat tightened by terror, echoing into the night in a frantic plea for life.

His face twisted into a snarl as he brandished the gun, pressing the cold metal against her temple.

"You can either decide to jump yourself, or I'll shove you over the edge."

She replied not just with words, but with the ferocity of her stance; she was the immovable object confronting the unstoppable force of his corruption. "You'll have to throw me off, and they'll see the marks on me. Once the cops see the bruises on my body, everyone will know what really happened here."

A dark chuckle rumbled in his chest.

"Rory gave you those bruises when he tried to save you from your madness. It's tragic, really." His eyes glinted with malice. "When I come home to find you gone and Rory dead, who will ever suspect me?" He leaned forward with a grin. "A man of my standing?"

The cool wind slapped against her skin as fresh wave of dread rolled through her body. Then she heard Ellie start screaming, but for the first time in months, those screams weren't evidence that she was failing at being a mother, but motivation to find a way out of this impossible situation. Because if Max killed her, Ellie would be raised by a monster who would use her for his own selfish purposes. Who would manipulate Ellie without remorse, perhaps even kill her too, if it got him what he wanted.

Alice was not ready to become another one of his victims, or to let Ellie fall prey to this monster either. She would fight, for her daughter, for herself, for the truth to emerge from the darkness of his deceit.

His grip tightened as he dragged her to the balustrade, ready to cast Alice into the void. But her eyes, alight with an indomitable will, met his one final time.

"You'll never win, Max," she breathed, the determination in her voice a violent contrast to the fear that quaked through every inch of her body. "Even if you push me, you won't have won. Because you can never kill the truth."

"That's fine." He shrugged. "I just need to kill you."

A sudden knock at the door was like a thunderclap in their standoff.

They both froze.

"Police! Open up!" The voice was authoritative, clear

through the door. "We received a call from a Rory Martin. He reported a man with a gun threatening his wife."

Alice used all of her strength to scream. "HELP US! HE'S GOING TO KILL ME AND MY DAUGHTER!"

The officers outside were unyielding. "Open the door now!"

Max's hesitation fractured the momentum of his rage, if only for a heartbeat.

He turned, releasing Alice's arm as his snarl faded into a calculated expression of innocence. Striding back into the apartment with the pretense of control, he swung open the door to reveal two officers poised with tension.

Jameson, a tall man with a seasoned look and close-cropped hair, stood with a firm hand near his holster, his posture exuding a calm authority honed by years on the force. Martinez stood beside him, her stature smaller but no less formidable, mirroring his readiness.

Alice scrambled across the floor to Ellie, scooping the infant into her arms and huddling in the corner, the baby's cries mingling with her own sobs of terror and relief. "He tried to kill us! He was going to throw us off the balcony!"

Jameson stepped forward, Martinez drawing her weapon and offering cover as he cuffed Max's wrists with practiced efficiency, no questions asked.

The clicking of the handcuffs was the chime of liberation.

"This is bullshit." Max spit his defense with indignation and venom. "She has an established history of postpartum depression. She was hurting our baby — I was only trying to stop her when she attacked me."

The officers traded a look: this was clearly more than a simple domestic dispute.

"Can you tell me what happened?" asked Martinez.

Alice clutched Ellie closer, her voice trembling as she

recounted the harrowing events. "I suspected my husband … of killing his mistress, Carly. She worked at his law firm before he got her pregnant. I discussed the situation with my therapist, Flora, who lives next door. When Max found out, he … he totally lost it. I think he killed her before coming for me and Ellie. Rory, our doorman, tried to stop him, and he shot Rory."

"Where is Rory now?" Jameson asked.

"She's lying, she killed the doorman," Max said. "If you call Mt. Sinai, you'll find that she's recently been treated for paranoid delusions."

"I'll be back." Martinez glanced at her partner, then left the apartment.

A strained silence permeated the penthouse. Max's glare bored into Alice, and every second that ticked by felt like an hour, yawning into an awkward eternity as they awaited the officer's return.

A static crackle preceding her voice on the radio when she entered the apartment again. Her gaze landed on the knife lying discarded on the floor.

"Whose knife is this?" she demanded, her eyes flicking from the weapon to Max.

"I don't know," he lied, still feigning his innocence with confused desperation. "This is all some misunderstanding."

A figure emerged from the apartment across the hall before he could twist his narrative any further. Rory, bloodied and barely able to stand, crawled into the room with his gaze locked on Max.

"That's the man who shot me," Rory gasped out, his finger trembling as he pointed at Max. Martinez rushed to his side, her voice urgent as she called for medical assistance.

The accusation was a final nail in his coffin of lies. But

still Max was unwilling to surrender. "It's them, they're having an affair. She's trying to frame me!"

Rory, still on the floor but bolstered by the officer's support, shook his head weakly. "No. I'm just the doorman. He's been … he's been threatening Alice for a long time. She called me tonight, terrified, saying that she felt sure her husband was going to kill her. I came up to help, and that's when he shot me."

"Is this true?" the female officer asked Alice.

Alice met her eyes, a profound sense of peace settling over her despite the chaos. For the first time in what felt like an eternity, she wasn't alone. She wasn't fighting against the world. She nodded and kept her voice steady.

"Yes, it's true. He's been threatening me. I was afraid for Ellie's life and mine."

Max's protests grew louder, more frenetic, but now they were the cries of a cornered animal, futile and ignored.

Alice moved closer to Rory, taking a seat next to him on the cold floor, cradling Ellie against her chest as Jameson led Max out of the apartment, and the screaming of approaching sirens filled the night air.

Chapter Forty-One

Alice stood outside the gray, imposing prison walls, holding Ellie as a cold breeze tugged at her coat, but it was the weight of finality settling on her shoulders that truly made her shiver.

Inside, she endured the gauntlet of security checks. Each mechanical beep of the detectors felt like the cold echo of a judgment, the sterile walls standing as silent witnesses to her somber pilgrimage as she walked through a sterile area leading to the visitation room. The place was devoid of all warmth, lined with chairs that seemed to absorb the desperation and sorrow of its visitors.

Max was already seated when she entered, the fluorescent lighting casting an unflattering pallor on his face, accentuating the dark circles under his eyes and the haggard lines of stress that had etched themselves deeply into his cheeks since the last time she had seen him.

Max leaned forward as she sat, his voice was not just a whisper but a serpent's hiss, his words slithering across the space between them with poisonous intent. "I hope you're happy now, Alice. You've destroyed everything."

Her expression stayed stoic, and her gaze unflinching.

"I came to tell you that I've been granted full custody of Ellie." She could have notified him by mail or by phone, but she wanted him to see her determination to protect their daughter, to make sure he understood that she would never back down. "She's safe from you, forever. And no matter what happens, you will *never* see her again."

Max's reaction was visceral, his face contorting with fury. He was no longer interested in pretending he wasn't a monster.

"I should have pushed you over the balcony when I had the chance. The day after we brought Ellie home. I could have found a way around your parents' trust in court."

Alice ignored him.

"Ellie will never even know who you are," she said instead.

Max spat at the glass in between them, his venom leaving a wet trail down its surface. Alice smiled as wide as she could.

Then she stood up and left the prison.

With each step away from the cold confines of the correctional facility, a layer of the haunting past flaked away, leaving her lighter, freer.

Her smile faded as she stepped onto the subway. The steady hum was a lullaby to the misery behind her. As the cityscape blurred past the window, it was as if the grime of her ordeal was being washed away.

Alice let the cool air fill her lungs as she ascended the subway stairs, then walked the few blocks to her building.

Rory was sitting behind the walnut-paneled desk, back at his post, although he was paler than usual and moved more slowly, thanks to his still-healing gunshot wound. His presence was a beacon of normalcy, the sight of him a patch of blue in stormy skies, promising calmer days ahead, and his smile a welcome sight.

He took Ellie in his arms, his playfulness bringing a moment of pure joy amid the lingering shadows of recent events.

"How was it?" Rory asked.

"As good as I could have expected." Alice shrugged. "It would be nice if New York had the death penalty, though."

"Maybe it's better that he suffers forever."

"Maybe." She shrugged again. "How are you doing?"

"I'm holding up," Rory replied, gently bouncing Ellie in his arms. "A little lead in the body is a tough way to learn I'm not as young as I used to be. But the physical therapy is going well."

"You want to come up for dinner tomorrow?"

"Have I ever refused you before?"

"Nope." Alice smiled. "Not even once."

Ellie laughed as Rory handed her back.

"She sure likes her Uncle Rory."

He flashed a warm smile, the corners of his eyes crinkling with genuine affection. "Well, she's got good taste. Plus, I've always been a hit with the little ones. Must be my approachable face."

"Or your expert bouncing technique," Alice replied. "I'm expecting some guests in an hour or so."

"Company, really? Besides just me?" Rory grinned. "I'll send them up when they get here." He slid an envelope across the desk, thick and marked with the instruction not to bend. "That came for you, but it wouldn't fit in the mail slot."

"Thank you, Rory."

Alice took the elevator to the top floor, then once back in her apartment, with Ellie gurgling on a blanket, she opened the envelope.

Her medical records were inside. The real ones, untampered with, confirming the birth of her healthy daughter, Ellie Grace.

Alice scooped Ellie up from the blanket and went out to the terrace.

The twilight sky stretched vast and open above as she stepped onto the balcony with her daughter nestled against her chest. The wind tousled her hair, whispering of new beginnings and the promise of peace.

For a fleeting instant, the city's constant din receded into a hush as her gaze swept over the horizon. And there, perched with a guardian's vigilance on a window ledge across the street, was a great horned owl.

Its amber eyes met hers. Then with a majestic unfurling of wings, the predatory bird took flight and disappeared into the dusky light.

A knock at the door drew Alice back inside.

She crossed the room, Ellie's soft cooing a counterpoint to her racing heart.

Alice wasn't sure she was even ready for this, but opened the door before she could stop herself.

And there stood her parents.

Words lodged in Alice's throat, a dam against a flood of emotions. Yet, no words were needed as her parents enveloped her in their embrace. When she'd called to tell them everything, they hadn't said what she'd expected: *I told you so.* They'd been horrified by Max's maliciousness and worried sick about Alice and Ellie. She hadn't even finished the story before they'd asked her permission to fly out for a visit, to take care of her while she recovered and to get to know their granddaughter.

And to help take care of Ellie while she remodeled every inch of the penthouse, to erase all signs of Max's existence and transform it into the perfect place to raise her daughter.

Now that she was finally reconciled with her family, all of the damage that Max had done to her life was repaired, and everything she'd lost had been restored: her love for her parents, her devotion to her daughter, and most of all, her belief in herself.

Alice would never doubt herself again.

Jessica Clarke had the perfect life. Until someone stole it.

She's married to the man of her dreams, they just bought a new house and adopted a new baby. Everything is as it should be.

Until her keys don't work. A woman who looks like her answers the door holding, Jessica's baby. Her husband insists that he's never met her before.

Pick up your copy of Replaced today!

About The Authors

Nolon King writes fast-paced psychological thrillers set in the glitzy world of entertainment's power players with a bold, insightful voice. He's not afraid to explore the darker side of human nature through stories featuring families torn apart by secrets and lies.

Nolon loves to write about big questions and moral quandaries. How far would you go to cover up an honest mistake? Would you destroy your career to protect your family? How much of your soul would you sell to get the life of your dreams? Would you cheat on your husband to keep your children safe? Would you give in to a stalker's demands to save your marriage?

Lauren Street has always loved a mystery. As a kid growing up in bible belt country she devoured every whodunit book she could get her sticky little hands on and secretly investigated all of her (seemingly) normal boring neighbors. Sometimes their pets and farm animals too. All grown up now and living in the UK with her thoroughly unsuspicious (and often unsuspecting) husband, she writes domestic psychological thrillers about families torn apart by secrets and lies. And she sometimes still peers over garden walls to check up on the neighbors.

Also By Nolon King

Replaced

Replaced

In Her Place

Irreplaceable

Cold Vengeance

Cold Vengeance

Cold Reckoning

Cold Retribution

Hidden Justice

Hidden Justice

Hidden Honor

Hidden Shame

Hidden Virtue

No Justice

No Justice

No Escape

No Hope

No Return

No Stopping

No Fear

Once Upon A Crime

Once Upon A Crime

Twice Upon A Lie

Three Times a Murder

Dead For Good

Dead For Good

Left For Dead

Dead Of Night

Wake The Dead

Dead For Life

Stand Alone Novels

Pretty Killer

12

Blown

Miserable Lies

The Target

Secrets We Keep

Close To Home

Heat To Obsession

A Simple Kill

Tell Me No Lies

Red Carpet Black

Fade To Black

Victim